Also by Sarah Remy

Madison Place Press

The House on the Creek

Winter, The Manhattan Exiles, Volume One

HarperVoyager

Stonehill Downs

Across the Long Sea

Praise for

Winter

Indie Reader calls *WINTER*

"…an intriguing and suspenseful page-turner, with complex characters, political manipulation, magic, and a wry sense of humor…a fine urban fantasy, well worth a read."

Publisher's Weekly says:

"Remy's world-building is substantial and her premise interesting, with memorable characters . . . Her take on the Fae is worth exploring."

The Portland Book Review gives WINTER five stars and says:

"Sarah Remy's Winter is the captivating opening chapter to a new young adult fantasy series called The Manhattan Exiles…Remy's descriptions are as unique as her prickly characters…the startling non-conclusion will leave you checking book stores for the next installment."

For Katherine, who's never afraid to try.

As the birds sang their heavenly song in *Tir na Nog*.

~Van Morrison

Madison Place Press

Summer © 2015 by Sarah Remy

ISBN: 978-0-692-45957-7

Cover Art by Candescent Press

The Manhattan Exiles

- Volume Two -

Summer

Sarah Remy

Dramatis Personæ

The Exiles:
1. Siobahn: by blood right queen of *Tir na Nog*.
2. Malachi: Siobahn's husband (deceased).
3. Gabriel: *aes si* and advisor to the queen. Also Winter's guardian and mentor.
4. Barker: Malachi's right-hand man, now Siobahn's bodyguard and muscle.
5. Morris: ex-warrior, now Siobahn's driver and butler.
6. Carran: Malachi's page who once drugged Gloriana
7. Katherine Grey: royal Mender, banished for her part as Siobahn's reluctant ally.
8. Alice: once Katherine Grey's lady's maid.

The Mortals:
1. Bran Healy: detective, MPDC.
2. Richard Lorimer: Winter's compatriot and best friend. Regularly manages to make the universe forget he exists.
3. Lolo: runaway plagued by an internal clock and too much wit. Idolizes Winter.
4. Bobby Lorimer: drug dealer, veteran, and explosives expert.
5. Brother Daniel: Franciscan friar with an apparent education in fay antiquities.
6. Willa Francis: Aine's grandmother. Raised Hannah as her own.
7. Aine: human changeling raised in Gloriana's Court, all the while believing she was *sidhe*.
8. William: wright banished with the *sluagh*.

The Dread Host:
1. The Prince: leader of the *sluagh* army.
2. Miach One-Eye/Water-Bearer: *aes si*, member of *Tir na Nog*'s Wild Hunt.

The Weapons:
1. *Buairt*: rapier forged for the purpose of driving *sidhe* from Windsor Forest and consecrated by the Catholic Church.
2. Nightingale: human changeling made deadly by royal wrights and *sidhe* magic.
3. Finvarra's Horn: silver horn powerful enough to Summon every *sidhe* within reach of its call.

The Youth:
1. Winter Murray: born in Manhattan to Siobahn and Malachi, he's determined to return the exiles home, but not at humankind's expense.
2. Summer Murray: Winter's younger sister. Manhattan princess to the bone, now she's been handed a cursed sword and sent on a dangerous quest.
3. Hannah Francis: *sidhe* changeling, Gloriana's daughter, raised as human in Aine's place.

Summer

Winter

The moment I stepped into *sluagh*-world my lungs rebelled.

I'd hoped to hold that last, deep breath of fresh air I'd inhaled before stepping through the portal long enough to Gather starlight and get a quick look around, maybe even manage a hasty Cant for warmth.

But the atmosphere was as bleak as the landscape, and it came at me like a punch to the gut, squeezing the good air from my lungs, hissing as it sizzled against my skin and snuck in through my nose.

I collapsed, gagging, curling into a ball in the sand, my arms pressed against my face. The poison air seared the inside of my nostrils, my tongue, my lungs. Even squeezed shut, my eyes overflowed with bitter, caustic tears.

Don't come home until you fix the problem, scolded a voice from the recesses of my subconscious. It sounded exactly like my mother. *Don't* die *until you fix the problem, Geimhreadh.*

My mother's the last true Fay Queen. She's also a supremely cold-hearted bitch. She's nothing if not stubborn. I'm her eldest child, her only son, and I know better than to let her down.

I didn't die, not then, not there on the gray, gritty sand. I shook and groaned and coughed foul-tasting liquid down the front of my coat and onto the ground. Slowly the fire in my lungs eased. I could breathe, if I inhaled and exhaled shallowly.

My tongue felt numb and tasted awful.

I rolled carefully onto my side, then to my knees. I dashed still-flowing tears from my face and realized my nose was

1

bleeding. In the inky light my blood looked black. I tried to stop the flow with the cuff of my sleeve.

Then I remembered the mouse in my pocket.

"Gabby!" It hurt to talk. I dug into the lining of my coat, searching for the warm little body.

My pocket was empty. I checked every other possible place in my coat, in my shirt, in my jeans. Nothing.

My burning eyes made everything blur and waver. I huddled on the ground, shaken. A cold wind blew up off the lake. The wind moaned as it slipped around drab boulders. It scraped across my shoulders. I'll admit I sat for longer than you'd think, butt planted in the strange sand and knees under my chin, before I understood.

I hadn't heard a single sound other than the mostly frantic muddle of voices projected into my skull for ten years. Ten years, three months, and fifteen days, and I don't need marks on a calendar to keep track. The day my mother placed her punishing yellow jewels into the lobes of my ears is a day I'll never forget.

Gaping like an idiot, I put my hands to my ears.

They popped, loudly, and suddenly I could *hear* more than just the angry wind. I could *hear* the thump of my heart in my chest, the scratch of the grains of sand beneath my jeans, and the distant splash of waves on the shore of the lake.

The cold burned my face, but the growl of the wind made me bare my teeth in a disbelieving smile.

I walked my fingers along the curve of my ears. The jewels were still there. I was eight when Siobahn attached them. In ten years I hadn't found a magic that would remove their torment. I'd spent a lot of free time looking. Once, on a particularly bad Christmas Eve, I'd tried to cut the fairy amber out of my skin.

Needless to say, it hadn't worked, and there'd been so much blood Richard had made me swear never to try it again.

Summer

"Pog mo thoin," I muttered. "I can hear." My voice was deeper than I remembered, more alive than the flat timbre I'd grown used to in my head. "I. Can. Hear!"

The last was a howl, as loud as I could get, until my lungs hitched and my throat cramped. I rose on my heels in the sand, laughing. I felt light and bubbly and drunk, just like the time Lolo had snatched a bottle of prime Moët & Chandon from the Capitol Hill Hotel and the three of us had spent an evening sharing it as the stars rose in the Reflecting Pool.

I put two fingers to my mouth and whistled, long and low and sharp. The whistle bounced off the rocks around me, then echoed across the lake. The clear beauty of the sound made me shiver. It also chased some of the fizzy joy from my head. Common sense awoke.

In that strange, empty landscape any sound was loud and I was pretty damn sure I didn't want to draw attention to myself.

I stood up, wincing because the bare skin on my hands and face was already chafing in the harsh cold. My eyes ached and burned. I pulled the collar of my coat up around my throat, then tucked my fists into my armpits. I turned around and looked back the way I'd come.

My portal was still there, undulating about four feet above the sand. The Way between worlds was about the size of a refrigerator, wavy at the edges, like too much heat over an asphalt road. I could see clearly through back into the pit. It would be easy to step right through again, back into the Washington Metro, back home.

Instead I swiveled on my heel, dismissing the rift. I'd come to rescue Aine and Richard. I didn't have time for regrets and second guesses. I'd made my choice. I wouldn't change my mind.

My eyes were watering buckets. I squinted, trying to get a better look around. The moon or sun—I wasn't sure which—hung

3

luminescent in the sky over the lake, but the light it shed seemed to shred away into nothing when it hit the sand. Rocks and low, jagged hills rose out of the ground, one-dimensional in the strange light.

The shadows and planes seemed off. I couldn't tell if the rocks hid *sluagh* or something worse. And my nose, which usually served me well in the mortal world of sweat and stink, was useless in the acrid air.

I started walking toward the lake. The ground slanted gently downhill toward the water. As I walked I scanned the sand around my feet. A small part of me hoped I'd find Gabby, maybe thrown from my pocket as I fell out of the portal. A bigger part hoped I wouldn't, because I was pretty sure the *aes si* had been near death when we crossed over, and I didn't want to find her corpse.

As I got closer to the lake the fine gray grains of sand thickened and became small pebbles. They slipped beneath the soles of my boots, rattling. It took me a few steps to identify the sound, and a few more steps before I could stop obsessing over the scrape of pebble against pebble.

I wondered if every new sound would be the same way: a delicious, all-consuming taste of a feast I'd forgotten.

My stomach growled, reminding me that it had been hours since I'd had anything more than a cup of coffee and a danish, and even that small gurgle almost sent me into a frenzy of celebration. Except every time my heart lifted it fell back again to that place behind my ribs where trepidation lurked.

As I drew nearer to the water, the air worsened. I pulled my knitted cap down over my forehead, almost past my eyes, and pressed my arm over my nose and mouth. Still, every bit of naked skin stung and burned. The atmosphere grew heavier, humid.

Literature's my thing, dead poets—mortal and *sidhe*—are my hobby. I'm no science geek. But I figured out pretty quickly it was the lake poisoning the air, whether through evaporation or osmosis or just the rush of wind over surface water. Waves tossed dingy foam up into the air and onto shore. Where the foam hit, steam rose. The boulders nearest the water line were eroded, melted things etched into strange, ugly shapes.

I stopped walking. The black lake spread left and right, mirroring the horizon. I couldn't see the other side, only the sun/moon reflected on the water. And either that orb was growing less bright, or my eyes were failing in the mist, because it was getting harder to see where I was putting my feet. I kept slipping on pebbles and shale.

"*Damnu air,*" I muttered, one of my mother's favorite Gaelic curses, just to hear my own voice again, and because I was starting to get worried. I'd had no real plan when I stepped through the Way. I'd been thinking only of Aine, and of the monstrous *sluagh*, and how they'd bleed her into a shell then snack on her bones.

I looked over my shoulder, back up the rocky slope the way I'd come. I couldn't see the portal any longer, but I could feel it. The magic thrummed in my bones and in my teeth. It was still open. I could go back, before the tainted air ruined my lungs and skin, before I couldn't see my hand in front of my face.

Instead I continued parallel along the shore, the moon at my left shoulder, in what I thought of as a sort of southern direction. The beach was pretty level. The slope rose up alongside my right shoulder. It looked like the lake had formed at the bottom of a crater, from rain or run-off. I knew I'd probably be wiser to climb my way out of the hole, away from flesh-damaging spray, only I'd noticed something about the shore.

I had to go down on my hands and knees to be sure. The grit was damp, the sand beneath wet. The moisture immediately blistered my palms. I hissed, rocking back up to squat, barely remembering not to stick my fingers in my mouth. I hated to think what the lake water would do to my already numb tongue.

My watering eyes hadn't deceived. What I saw made me forget the pain in my hands. Drag marks in the gravel, and where the sand was brushed free of shale, bare footprints, but not your ordinary pleasant-stroll-on-the-beach picture-book prints. Deep, wicked-looking claw marks scored the ground.

"Found you!" Triumphant, I Gathered starlight for a better study.

Only the starlight didn't come. For the first time in my life the Cant failed. I could feel the magic buzz on the tips of my fingers, but instead of exploding into life it fizzled away, like a Fourth of July rocket with a bad fuse, all anticipation and no explosion.

I tried three more times before I gave up.

"Well, crap."

I'd been born a fay prince in a mortal world. I'd never been without the reassurance of innate power. Maybe I'd felt a little sorry for humans, that lesser race who couldn't summon fire with a word, or turn an especially annoying family member into a frog, if only for a few hours.

The *sidhe* are a prideful folk. What had Aine called humans? *Insects*. And *useless*.

Now it appeared I was no more than a useless bug, and shit-out-of-luck.

"Okay. Okay, right."

Maybe I panicked a little. Maybe it was growing way too dark to see, and it was getting harder and harder to breathe, and if I couldn't have my magic, I really wanted my Glock. But I'd left the both my pistol and my fairy knife on the other side with Lolo, because I hadn't planned ahead.

Rookie mistake. Real rookie mistake, Win.

I always plan ahead. It's how I survive.

Summer

I crouched on the sand, arms wrapped around my chest, maybe shivering a little, maybe trying to convince myself that it wasn't magic or iron bullets that made me fierce. That it was quick thinking and a thick skull that's kept me alive in the D.C. underground for the last decade, the Dread Host on my tail.

Only, I've never been particularly good at pep talks, and I just couldn't get this one to fly. Truth is, I might have shuddered there on the beach until the fog etched my skin from my bones and my lungs bubbled with poison, except as the moon gleamed its last effort, somewhere down the shore someone sounded the Horn.

It felt like my heart jumped into my throat, and not because the sound was clear and lovely and *real*. It rang in my ears, loud as I'd always imagined the carol of church bells, but it was more than music I'd forgotten, it was a family legend, and it was a call no *sidhe* could ignore.

The Fay Queen's Horn. Once Finvarra's, it was herald and threat and summons all at once. Even without my magic it was a trumpet I couldn't resist. My blood pounded in response.

I staggered to my feet and half-shuffled, half-ran toward the repeating blast. In the dark I stumbled, falling several times, scraping my already tender palms. I don't know how long the call lasted, or how many times the Horn sounded. I do know the spell lasted even after I couldn't run anymore and I had to crawl like a worm over the shale, helpless to refuse.

Eventually my strength gave out. I lay curled on the ground. The Horn still pulled, a string to my very center. I had just enough sense to do what I should have done in the first place: I yanked my coat over my head, pressing my fists hard against my ears, stuffing fabric into my ear canals.

It worked, the way biting the inside of your cheek works when you can't reach into your boot and scratch that insane itch on the bottom of your foot. Which is to say, I managed to muffle the sound, but I couldn't block the Horn completely.

I'm not sure how much time passed before the dark landscape grew silent. I know when I came back to my senses I was face down on rock, my fingers still stuffed in my ears. Cramps knotted every muscle in my body. I had sand in my mouth; I could feel the poisonous grains eating into my tongue.

"Winter. Get up."

Something grabbed me under the elbow and hauled me upright. The part of me that had grown up in the Metro chasing ghouls knew it was time for heroics. My adrenaline surged, but I could barely sway on two feet. I couldn't see at all. Simply breathing was an impossible, painful task.

I knew I was dying. Instead of angry, or defeated, or even scared, I just felt stupid. Really stupid.

"Winter! Pay attention, child!"

I'd heard that voice in that tenor in my skull for most of my life. I'd learned better than to ignore it.

"Gabby?"

"This way." The grip on my elbow tightened, supporting my weight. It hurt badly, that pressure against my blistering flesh. I couldn't drum up enough energy to care.

"Hurry, Winter. Walk!"

That made me giggle, because I couldn't even feel my feet. In fact, my entire body seemed a foolish thing, too heavy for use, too much work to tend. A few gentle wriggles and I would float free.

"Geimhreadh!" She slammed me back into my almost-corpse, built an invisible wall around the bit that was me, and filled the rest of my head with Gabbiness. Then she made my body walk, a puppet to her strings.

Summer

She'd never done such a thing before; she'd never had the strength to even Summon a slice of pepperoni from my plate to her tiny paws. And I know she'd tried.

It took a powerful Cant to possess someone so easily. My father might have managed, but I'm pretty sure it's beyond even Siobahn's skill. Before Gabby had forgotten how to be *sidhe*, before she'd become mouse, she'd been *aes si*, a skilled sorcerer, valued beyond gold and jewels in the Fairy Court.

I hated being locked away in my own head. I fought with everything I was to break free, but my magic is nothing compared to an *aes si*. Our roles were reversed; I was the mouse scratching on the prison wall.

"I'm sorry, Winter. It's the only way."

I heard honest regret, but also implacable determination. She knew what she did was loathsome, but she wasn't going to let me free. This was far worse a betrayal than when my mother stole my hearing.

Gabby was taking all of me. And I'd never loved Siobahn as I did the *aes si*.

I howled, all rage and disbelief and insult.

"Oh, child," Gabby sighed, ineffably weary.

Then she snuffed me out.

I inched back to wakefulness under my own power and immediately wished I hadn't. My lungs were on fire; my mouth and tongue swelling toward asphyxiation, my eyes crusted shut. I clutched blindly at my throat.

"Drink this. Quickly."

At least this time she gave me a choice. Obedient in desperation, I opened my mouth. Someone poured sweet, warm liquid onto my tongue. The drink stung like liquor when it swirled around my teeth, then, impossibly, began to soothe.

"Swallow," Gabby ordered.

9

I tried. I choked, gagging the *draiochta* back up and all over my chin. The potion hurt worse than Cold Fire on my suppurating flesh, but it healed even as it stung.

"More," I begged.

A cup touched my lips. This time I was able to swallow a mouthful, then a large gulp. The *draiochta* bubbled as it ran down my throat and into my gut. I kept it down. All at once my throat unlocked. My lungs eased. I could almost take a full breath.

"Good. Now your face."

A wet cloth soothed my fingers. Another pair of hands helped me lift the cloth to my face. Gingerly I rubbed it over my cheeks, and across my eyes. The potion felt unbelievably horrible and indescribably wonderful at the same time. Groaning, I pressed the cloth into the corners of my eyes.

"Bless us." I could hear the rush of relief behind Gabby's sigh. *"Your mother always said you were my punishment, Geimhreadh, but I never thought I'd been so wicked. How many times have I watched you almost die, child?"*

"Three times. Maybe four." My lips still felt floppy. I rubbed the cloth carefully against my mouth. "I'm stubborn. But I thought I'd killed *you*, Mistress." Tears leaked between my sticky lids. I let them fall.

"Child." Hands cupped my trembling fingers. *"It takes more than a jump between worlds to kill this old woman."*

Wary, I opened my eyes. Even though I'd felt her touch, I still expected the mouse. Instead I sat almost nose to nose with an unfamiliar fay elder.

Mistress. Wise-woman. Wizard. *Aes si*. Before she earned exile for conspiring against the Fairy Court, Gabriel had been advisor to kings and queens, valued for her powerful magics, and her treasure trove of old *sidhe* knowledge.

I'd known her always and only as a white mouse with a granny's protective nature and a preference for 'healthy' teas.

I couldn't help myself; I scooted back away from her touch. I don't like or trust strangers, plus I've cultivated a really large bubble when it comes to unfamiliar fay; they're usually half-mad and always dangerous.

Mistress Gabriel pressed her lips together. She huffed slightly. The sound of her disapproval was new, but the wrinkle above her nose belonged to the mouse. I could almost see imaginary whiskers twitch.

I relaxed enough to glance away and look around. Gray rock closed in on either side, behind and in front. A low ceiling almost scraped the top of my head, and I'm not tall, especially when groveling in the dirt.

"Nice hole." I couldn't help but notice the bright ball of Gathered starlight glowing merrily against the ceiling. "Bit of a step down from the Metro. Where are we going to put the fridge?"

Gabby huffed again. She *was* tall, taller than me, taller than Siobahn, maybe even taller than my father, and Malachi was the oldest *sidhe* I'd known. Gabby had to curl in on herself beneath the rock ceiling. She looked uncomfortable.

But alive. Very much alive.

I grinned. It hurt, but it was better than the tears, and I couldn't stop.

"A good rat knows when to hide. Small spaces work best." She shook her head, at herself, I thought. *"And this one is far enough away from the lake that the air is breathable."*

She'd plaited her long white hair into a single braid down her back, and conjured white robes to match. Her right wrist was bound in the same fabric, the makeshift bandage still red and bloody.

"Christ, you're hurt! I thought you were dead." I knew I sounded like an idiot, but I couldn't help it. Maybe I was managing to smile and weep all at the same time, maybe I was falling into a few ragged pieces. I reached for a simple Healing Cant. My magic rose and retreated, useless, there and then not.

"It doesn't work." Baffled, I looked up. "I can't get it to work."

Gabby nodded. *"Gloriana created this prison to keep the Dread Host confined. Most* sidhe *magic is useless here, else they would have freed themselves long before you accidentally ripped a hole between worlds."*

"Most?" I echoed. The Gathered starlight in the ceiling, no larger than a tennis ball but white and clear, pulsed with Gabby's heartbeat. And I knew she hadn't carried that healing *draiochta* through the portal in her mousey cheeks.

"There are other ways," she replied, arch.

Gabby had rescued me from the streets of D.C. when I was eight. She'd taught me how to survive on trash and handouts, in soup kitchens and YMCA bathrooms. She'd taught me how to fight the *sluagh*, and she hadn't laughed when I'd sworn to protect every mortal in the District from the Dread Host's predatory hunt, even though she must have known as I knew now that it was an impossible task.

Siobahn had broken my heart. Gabby had healed it. And although her *sidhe* face was harder to read, I knew when my mentor was talking shit.

"What other ways?" I demanded. She twitched, guilty, and looking across at her bandaged wrist, I understood.

"Blood magic," I hissed.

Gabby lifted her chin, defiant, and just missed cracking her skull on the ceiling.

"You were dying, child. And, aye, so was I. We were all but corpses on the sand, and I won't let your mother say I've failed her."

"My mother hates blood magic more than anyone. More than anyone," I added, "except you."

Summer

My family plus one hundred more *sidhe* were exiled from Court for protesting the Gloriana's casual and careless use of blood magic. I'd been maimed because I'd been too young and too proud to resist its temptation. Blood magic is a perversion of the old, true magic, and like all perversions, it walks hand-in-hand with corruption.

"You should have let us die." I said, bitter. "Mother won't forgive us this, not now. Better we'd stayed corpses on the sand."

Gabby shifted. Gray dust from the rock stained her robes. Blood still ran sluggishly from beneath her bandages.

"Better I'd stayed a mouse in Manhattan," she retorted. *"But you had other plans. There are some stories even Siobahn doesn't need to hear. We'll go home, and we won't speak of this. Ever."*

I stared around the hole, at the walls, at the low ceiling. At the pulsing starlight, at the scars slowly healing on my hands, at the blood and pus crusted on the discarded rag, *my* blood and pus.

My jeans and coat were torn where I'd fallen on sharp rocks trying to answer the Horn's call. Somewhere I'd lost the knit cap Lolo had given me. My Doc Martens were still in one piece, and probably the only shiny thing about the mess that was me.

When I'd fidgeted and wiggled and looked around at everything except my mentor, and finally couldn't dick around anymore, I met Gabby's steely regard.

"I'm not going home," I said.

Summer

1. Lost

Summer watched Barker as he approached the sword. She knew he was afraid by the way he walked, loose and slow, like a lion stalking difficult prey. She'd seen lions at the Central Park Zoo and on Animal Planet, and she thought they were beautiful.

But she thought Barker was more beautiful by far, with his dusky skin and wild red dreads, and those yellow eyes that noticed everything.

When she was ten, Summer decided she'd grow up and marry Barker, and they'd have pretty yellow-eyed children, and live together in a posh penthouse off Central Park. That was before Winter told her Barker had a boyfriend back at Fairy Court.

Winter lied sometimes, but as she grew older, Summer decided her brother probably wasn't lying about that and she mostly forgot her crush.

Mostly.

"It's called *Buairt,"* she said now, about the sword. "It means 'Sorrow.'"

"I remember," Barker replied. He stood over the sword, scrutinizing the blade where it lay on display on Summer's hotel room desk. Summer had spread an old Chanel coat across the desk under the sword, partly because the cheap desk was gross, partly because she thought the ugly sword looked better against houndstooth.

"I don't feel anything," Barker admitted. "Nothing at all."

Summer, sitting cross-legged on the hotel bed, chewed at her lip. Her mother would go into a temper if she knew they were

14

experimenting with the sword that had killed the Prince of Fairies. *Buairt* had almost killed Barker, too. It had taken a human priest to save the yellow-eyed fay.

Luckily, her mother was still stuck on the island of Manhattan and had no idea what they were about.

"I think Brother Daniel gave you a soul," Summer suggested. "That's why you don't feel anything. He gave you a soul, a mortal soul, and now the sword doesn't want to eat you anymore. Pretty messed up, if you ask me. But cool."

Barker shot Summer a disgusted look. She noticed he still wouldn't touch the sword.

"Souls aren't accessories," he said. "And the human gods take no notice of our kind."

"Ask Brother Daniel," Summer challenged. "He'll be back any minute. But first—pick up the stupid sword. Stop sulking, do something useful. Pick up the sword!"

Barker growled. His fingers twitched. Then he bent in a swoop and grabbed *Buairt* by the hilt with both hands. His knuckles clenched when he lifted the rapier off the desk. Summer knew the sword wasn't heavy; she'd carried it herself. She thought maybe Barker was trying to make himself not let go.

She met Barker's yellow stare. He glared back. The cheap analog clock on the wall over the hotel bed ticked three times. Summer released a long breath.

"See," she said, relieved. "Nothing. Soul or no soul, it can't hurt you anymore. Which means you're coming with."

Barker set *Buairt* back onto the desk, next to the ruby-studded scabbard. Summer hated the scabbard almost as much as she hated the sword, because every time she looked at it, she imagined squealing pigs. Pigs who had once been men, before Gloriana turned them into animals and had their skin for tanning. Barker scrubbed his hands on the fresh new Levis Summer had found on sale at Macy's. His old jeans had just bagged, he'd lost so much weight. His favorite Stones shirt hung from his shoulders the way her papa's shirts used to hang on Winter, when Winter was eight, before he'd left home.

"I am not," he said, "'coming with.' I'll get you safely to Yorktown, because I owe it to Himself. After that, my debt is paid."

Summer drew her knees up under her chin and put on her best pout. She wasn't really irritated. She knew Winter would change Barker's mind eventually. She was puzzled. Since she'd been old enough to understand the stories, she'd known every *sidhe* exile wanted nothing more than to cheat Gloriana's *geis* and find a Way between worlds and return home to Fairy Court. Some of her papa's people would have killed for a return ticket home. One or two had tried.

Barker, on the other hand, didn't seem at all jazzed about the Cornwallis Cave, or the possibilities it might hold.

"If Mama knew you'd made it off the island," Summer said through her pout. "I bet she'd make you promise to be my bodyguard, and to help Winter kill Gloriana."

Barker ignored her. He walked away from the desk and the sword, instead positioning himself against the closed door dividing Summer's room from Hannah's. There he crossed his arms over his chest and went back into what Lolo liked to call 'CIA Mode', all watchful and remote.

Summer squelched a pang of jealousy. She wanted to like Hannah. She felt sorry for the other girl. But she was tired of watching everyone treat Gloriana's daughter like she was the queen-of-everything, when really it should be just the opposite.

"You Warded her doors." Summer slid off the bed, crossed the room, and rummaged in the tiny mini-bar. She snagged a bag of peanut butter M&Ms and a tiny bottle of Perrier. "We'll know when she wakes up. Maybe you should catch a nap, too. Because as soon as Winter gets back you know he'll want us on the road right away. Win's always worried about wasting time."

Barker didn't answer. He was doing a pretty good job of pretending she wasn't in the room, but something had him rattled. He might be lounging all panther-like, but Summer could see the jumping pulse in his neck and smell the tang of fear off his lovely mahogany skin.

Even though she sometimes pretended otherwise, Summer didn't really like watching other people suffer. So she decided to give the older *sidhe* space and took her snack out into the hotel hall. The carpet and the wallpaper were the same color—a dirty beige with green paisley—and the repeating pattern was dizzying.

She propped the door open with one of Lolo's discarded shoes, then slid down the doorjamb until she crouched on the threshold. She used her teeth to rip open the bag of M&Ms and dug for the green ones.

She'd eaten fifteen green and started on the blues when the elevator down the hall chimed and Lolo jumped out. He came down the corridor in a flat-out run, only slowing when he saw her.

"You don't need to hurry, Win's not back yet." Summer uncapped her Perrier and took a healthy swig. "Where's Brother Daniel? You didn't lose him, did you? We need him."

Lolo snatched the bag of M&M's from Summer's hand. He leaned against the wall, dumping candy into one palm. Winter had made the younger boy wash his braids in The Plaza's giant shower; his hair had been full of a year's dried *sluagh* goo. Lolo had added red wooden beads and bits of ribbon to his new look, plus a necklace of tiny grinning skulls.

Summer thought he looked a little too Rasta, but at least he smelled better.

"I keep trying to lose him," Lolo admitted around a mouthful of chocolate. "He's scary-impossible to shake and I don't think he's even trying that hard." He shook his head, beads clicking. "We've got a problem, Summer."

Summer slid back up the doorjamb.

"What now?" she asked, just as the elevator dinged again. Brother Dan stepped out into the hall. A plastic grocery bag dangled from each of the friar's large hands. He didn't look in any hurry at all.

"Told you," Lolo muttered. "Win's gone."

"What?"

Summer put her hand against the wall so the world didn't tilt. Ever since Michael Smith had killed her papa, she'd been practicing not feeling. Every morning after she woke she'd stare at herself in the bathroom mirror for a good five minutes, until she was sure she wasn't going to cry, and those cold, scream-your-head-off in the shower feelings were safely buried in the pit of her stomach.

She'd almost managed to convince herself that no more Bad Things would happen, because nothing could be worse than watching her favorite parent bleed out on a Sixth Avenue sidewalk.

"What do you mean, gone?" There were little patches of white sparkling in the air. She shook her head to clear them and discovered she was leaning on Brother Daniel's arm, gripping his sleeve with both hands. "What do you mean?"

Brother Daniel led Summer back into the hotel room. He sat her down in the room's one chair and pushed her head between her knees.

"Breathe," Daniel ordered. "Your brother's fine, as far as we know."

"As far as you know?"

That was Barker; soft, smooth and dangerous. Summer felt a little better hearing his voice. She stared between her Chanel ballet flats at the carpet and reminded her fluttering heart that Barker was almost as good as Winter at fixing things.

"We followed him down into the Metro," said Lolo. "Then he sort of disappeared."

"Disappeared?" Summer lifted her head. "That's just Winter. He disappears all the time. He'll be back."

Lolo was holding her abandoned Perrier. He looked down into the mouth of the bottle instead of at her face. "No. He really disappeared. Like—zap—through his portal."

"Your friend closed the rift," Barker argued. "Blew it to hell, along with half of Federal Triangle."

"Yeah, well." Lolo shrugged. He handed Summer her water, even though she didn't want it. "It, like, moved, or something. Or maybe he called it up again."

"He wouldn't do that!" Summer spat, insulted. "He'd never do that. Win wanted that Way gone more than anything else in the world, because then he could come home to Manhattan."

Lolo turned away, shoulders slumped. Daniel crouched at Summer's side. He took her cold fingers in warm hands.

"We watched Winter step into the portal. Lorenzo shouted, but your brother didn't answer."

"You should have gone after him," Summer accused the backside of Lolo's head. "You should have brought him back!"

"I tried," Lolo said over his shoulder. "Brother Asshole stopped me. It's like arguing with a bear—a bear with a shank."

"It looked dangerous," the friar replied. "And an empty Glock won't do you much good against demons, *hermano.*"

Summer knew Lolo had been carrying Winter's gun. She didn't know he'd been carrying it without Richard's special iron bullets. It occurred to her maybe that was why her brother had gone back into the collapsed Metro: they were out of ammunition.

"He wouldn't leave me," she said. "He knows Mama's counting on him. He wouldn't leave *me.* He's coming back."

Barker straightened. Summer didn't like the pity she saw on his usually impassive face.

"We'll go and see," he said. To Summer's surprise he crossed the room and picked up *Buairt*, scabbard and all. "If the Way is open again, her ladyship will need to know." He passed

19

the sword to Summer. "Wear this. Charm it back. You're safer with it than without, and I'm *not* carrying it."

"Better wait until after dark." Lolo drifted around the room, television remote in hand. "The Triangle is crawling with cops and Feds and Homeland rent-a-guns. It's like they think it'll blow up all over again." He scowled at the TV. "Can't believe this place just gets local. Who watches local?"

For a vivid minute Summer hated Lolo. Couldn't he see her world was falling apart? Didn't he care? She wanted to burst up and pull on his stupid beads until he paid attention.

Then she noticed the way he was chewing a hole in his lip while he played with the remote. She realized he was just as scared as she was and that made her have to put her head between her knees again.

"After dark, then," Barker said. "What about the changeling?"

Summer felt the room practically hold its breath as everyone eyed the closed door between suites.

"I'll stay," Brother Daniel said.

"You're big, but without Win here to scare Hannah, she'll probably set the whole building on fire."

"I've got a few of tricks up my own sleeve," Daniel dismissed Lolo's concerns. "I'll stay."

There wasn't much moon up when Summer, Barker and Lolo left the Capitol Holiday Inn: just a sickly yellow sliver. There wasn't much artificial light, either. The power grid still hadn't recovered from Richard's bomb. As far as Summer could tell the city blocks were lighted in random and unreliable squares.

She expected Barker to Gather enough light so they didn't trip over some collapsed junkie or fall into a hole. Instead he pulled three heavy flashlights from thin air, which was really even more impressive.

When he handed Summer hers, the metal casing was still warm.

Lolo whistled softly. "Can you do that? Pull whatever you want from nowhere?"

"No." She wasn't going to tell Lolo that she'd spent half of her life trying, and never managing to Summon a single thing. "Neither can Winter."

"Let's go." Barker switched on his light. He started through the night, black biker boots soundless on the pavement.

Summer followed, trying to be equally silent. It took a small tug of power, and a lot of concentration. It helped that she'd bypassed fashion and worn a pair of soft-soled sneakers. When they crossed through a gloomy park covered with frozen leaves, Summer didn't even crack a twig. She felt a surge of pride.

Lolo rustled through the drifts like an eager puppy, swinging his flashlight from side to side.

"He's cool and all," he said, aiming his beam at Barker's heels. "But in a creepy creeper sort of way. I get the feels he'd cut me into little pieces if you asked him too, and he'd probably like it."

"He would." Summer was glad she'd remembered her gloves, all the way from Manhattan. It was almost as cold in D.C. as it was up north. She stuck her flashlight in one armpit and zipped her coat up as far as it would go. "He's sworn to protect me. Sort of like another *geis*. I'm not sure he'd actually like dicing you up, but he's good at it." Then she whispered: "Remember, he's terrified of the dark."

"What do you want me to do about it?" Lolo demanded. "Hold his hand?"

"*Children.*" Barker managed to pitch his voice so it slipped around the skeletal trees, a whisper, then rang loud in their skulls. *"Quiet!"*

Summer muffled a snort of laughter when Lolo jumped.

"I can't do that, either," she said, then hurried to catch Barker.

The National Mall blazed with the light the rest of the District was lacking. Herds of generators crouched in groups, linked by masses of thick black cable, polluting the night with their rumbles and groans. The generators powered tall, grilled emergency lights, almost all of which shone down into the exposed Metro system.

Only, when Summer pressed against yellow police tape, standing high on the toes of her sneakers, she saw there wasn't much of the Metro left under the Mall. Mostly the Mall was one gigantic crater, the Metro tunnels torn out of the earth by explosion, then smashed further into the ground by rogue bits of the fallen Washington Monument. Steam rose from the mix of soil and metal and torn pipes; it rolled back and forth like white fog beneath the lights.

"So much for waiting until after dark," Lolo said. "Spotlights aren't gonna keep the *sluagh* down in their hole."

"I imagine the mortals have other monsters in mind." Barker muted his flashlight. He regarded the crater, then the armed men and women in military fatigues surrounding it. "How did you get in?"

"Not this way," Lolo scoffed. "And it's not the Marines you should be worrying about. It's the one's like her." Casually, he jerked an elbow sideways.

Summer tried to look without turning her head. A woman in a gray trench coat and battered ball cap stood not far away under one of the spotlights. She seemed to be moon-gazing. Then the woman swiveled, looking over the crater and directly at their small group. Summer felt a prickle of unease.

"What makes you think I was worrying about the Marines?" Barker retorted. "Show me how you got in."

Lolo led them away from the crater. He whistled softly as he walked. Summer couldn't place the tune. She trailed behind as they crunched over another expanse of frozen grass, past the Smithsonian Castle. The Castle was dark, but the glow of emergency lights cast spooky shadows over the brick facade, making her shiver.

She wondered what Barker thought of his new freedom. She'd been allowed to visit Winter once or twice since he'd been sent away and she'd always been excited at the chance to explore a different city. But Barker had gone straight from *Tir na Nog* to Manhattan, then lived centuries trapped on the island.

Summer was a little surprised he wasn't running about in mad circles, trying to see everything new all at once. Maybe he thought one mortal city was the same as another. Maybe he didn't feel well enough for enthusiasm or awe.

Maybe he was still mourning her papa.

She buried that thought quickly, squinting hard at Barker's rigid shoulders until she was sure she wouldn't cry.

Lolo turned right just past the Castle. They walked east past the Air and Space Museum. The damage from Richard's bomb didn't extend much beyond the Mall, except for the dust and a few lost chunks of concrete and metal.

"Win's portal wasn't exactly right under the Washington Monument," Lolo explained. "But close enough. Richard must have set off his C4 as close to the *sluagh* hole as he could get. The Metrorail's not as massive as the New York subway system, but it's not small, either. And Richard's tunnel is on the *other* side of L'Enfant Plaza."

He gestured again, this time with his flashlight, as they passed the Metro at L'Enfant Plaza. The station escalator was cordoned off and under guard. Summer felt another unwelcome pang of grief. L'Enfant was Winter's territory and now Richard's stupidity had started mortals sniffing about.

"Federal Center's actually closer to home," Lolo continued. He hopped off the curb, still humming under his breath, then cut sideways across an old alley lined with leafless trees. "And it's got another totally sweet perk."

"What would that be?" Barker asked. The *sidhe* ghosted silently alongside Summer. He'd switched his light back on, muffling the blaze with a wad of his shirt hem, even though Summer knew he could see as well as a cat in the dark.

She tried not to feel sorry for him, in case he heard the sympathy in her head.

"Federal's far enough away it's local cops watching it," explained Lolo. "And they *know* me."

"How's that a good thing?" Summer demanded.

Lolo only shrugged. "No funky fay Glamour required. Just the right words in the right ear."

"Bran," Summer guessed. "He taught you a secret police password, or something."

Lolo made a rude noise.

"Bran's a suit," he said, as if Summer had suggested something dirty. "They're not going to like you, though," he told Barker. "'Specially the demon eyes."

"They won't notice me," the *sidhe* replied. "Lead on."

The two cops guarding Federal Center Station didn't exactly smile when they saw Lolo, but they relaxed enough to make Summer think they recognized him as a friend. When the tiny policewoman bumped Lolo's fist and then slapped him on the back, Summer wondered if maybe they were more like family.

"*Hola, como esta?*" The woman stood proud in her blues, but she was barely taller than Lolo, even in her chunky boots. "What's happening, *mi hijo*? It's not a good night to be out."

"Doesn't matter if it's good or bad," Lolo replied. Summer noticed he kept Winter's gun carefully hidden under his ratty denim coat. "We've got business inside, Mary-Beth."

24

Mary-Beth's bulky partner shifted, but didn't say anything. Mary-Beth looked from Lolo to Summer. Some of the humor left her mouth.

"This weather, every squatter in the Triangle wants to sleep in the tunnels. We've just finished clearing them out, best we can. Why would we want to let you in?" She looked Summer up and down again. "You messing with Georgetown trouble, Lolo?"

"No," Lolo answered quickly. "No drugs, *nada*, you know me better, Mar. Business inside is totally kosher, and it won't take long. Camera's still out?"

"Like the rest of the electricity." Mary-Beth's partner turned his head and spat on the cement, just missing the square of concrete Barker had occupied a few seconds earlier. Barker himself had vanished. "It's not exactly safe in there, and I don't mean the structure. Tunnels are wormy with vagrants, and hookers, and some that *are* looking for that Georgetown thrill. We can't round 'em all up, they mouse back in so fast."

Lolo nodded. "That's why we're here. Summer's lost her brother. Word on the block's he's gone under looking for a high. We just wanna find him and take him home before his *padre* gets wind, or before he picks the wrong dealer."

Summer felt Mary-Beth's stare a third time. She scowled at the toes of her sneakers and tried to look worried. It wasn't difficult. Her stomach knotted every time she thought of Winter.

He's not gone, she promised herself, but the toes of her shoes blurred. *He wouldn't leave me.*

Maybe the cops noticed the tears leaking down her nose.

"Okay," Mary-Beth relented. "But you be careful. And stay away from the blast site. That *will* come down around your ears, you breathe wrong."

"*Gracias*," Lolo bumped the cop's fist again. This time Summer saw the wad of money as it changed hands, a quick flick of green between fingers.

The other cop spat a second time as they slipped into the station's dark and gaping mouth.

"That looked like a lot of cash," Summer said once they were out of earshot.

"Not really." Lolo pointed his flashlight into the depths. Summer saw the prickly slope of a stopped escalator and the impression of squares on the barrel-vaulted ceiling above. "I keep a few Benjamins around for emergencies. Mary-Beth's got a sister in one of those shiny Connecticut coke hospitals. Her family could use the tax-free donation, no skin off my ass. Knew she'd fall for the lost brother story; Mar's got a boner for happy-ever-after rehab stories."

"Lovely." Barker detached himself from the shadows at the bottom of the motionless escalator. *"Your empathy is overwhelming."*

"Talk out loud." Lolo clattered down the escalator. "Make noise. People down here, they don't want to be found. Give 'em time to hide away: no trouble."

Barker watched Lolo with unblinking yellow eyes, but stepped aside and let the boy take the lead. Summer wanted to run back up the escalator and into the night. She took a deep breath and followed Lolo. Barker walked silently at her back.

She'd been in the Metrorail tunnels before, of course. The very first time she'd thought of it as a game; Winter hiding beneath a mortal city, walking among the humans all unknown. He'd given her a tour of Richard's money-train tunnel, served her Thai food in the makeshift kitchen.

He'd been all of ten. She'd been eight. And Winter hadn't let her sleep overnight in the tunnels, not once the trains stopped running and the *sluagh* came hunting. No, come dark she'd been safely tucked away in a nearby hotel with Gabby to guard her dreams.

"Watch it," Lolo cautioned. The beam from his flashlight arced back and forth across the station platform, picking out bits of trash and chunks of fallen rocks. "The third rail's dead, but don't go tripping over it."

Summer stood at the edge of the platform. She looked down at the tracks. More trash and rocks, and in the white circle of her own shifting light: a dead rat.

"Gross. Seriously gross."

"Iron," Barker hissed, more interested in the tracks than road-kill. Summer knew it was a reflexive reaction. Most of the exiles were iron-immune. Centuries of living around mortals and mortal steel dulled the iron-sickness.

But Barker had recently been pierced through by a sword forged of consecrated Church iron. Summer couldn't blame him for holding a grudge.

"Chill." Lolo bent at the knees, then dropped off the platform. He landed in the trench, one foot on either side of the closest rail. "You're cool. Trains aren't running."

Barker seemed to float from platform to dirt. He held up a hand for Summer. She ignored it, hopping into the trench behind Lolo.

"Stinks," she complained. "Like a toilet."

"Pinch your nose and suck it up. Follow me. Don't look to the side, even if they try to make you. Don't engage."

"What are you talking about? Engage who?" Summer stood on her toes and peered over Lolo's shoulder.

Lolo lifted his arm, pointing his light straight ahead. The Federal Center Station platform ended ten feet ahead. Where the platform trench ended, the underground waited, a gaping tunnel mouth. Lolo's flashlight turned the entrance gray, and illuminated a few more feet into the darkness.

"Them," said Lolo, and Summer saw they weren't alone.

2. Broken

Richard woke in stages.

The fingers in his left hand twinged first; useless, swollen appendages throbbing in time with his heartbeat. The painful itch of the Cold Fire burns on his thigh joined the angry chorus.

Grit and gravel and sand had abraded the seeping coldfire blisters when the Dread Host pinned him to the earth on the dark side of Winter's portal. Richard had fought back and in the struggle managed to rip a few feathers from the *sluagh* Prince's ebony wings.

Then the Prince ordered Richard's hand broken as punishment.

"Human bones are fragile, just like human minds," said the Prince, wormy white tongue flicking in contemplative circles as it directed two lesser *sluagh* to hold Richard down while a third smashed his hand with a chunk of rock. "I have need of your mind yet, but your bones will serve whole or in pieces. Touch us again without permission and you'll soon be naught but a sack of jelly."

Richard screamed when they held him prone on the beach. The air burned his throat and the sand stung his flesh. Where the lesser *sluagh* gripped his forearms, Richard's jacket and shirt smoked away and frostbite fingerprints marked his skin.

Aine, standing motionless in a circle of wing and tooth and claw, watched Richard's fingers snap and didn't make a sound.

The hungry, hollow pit of Richard's stomach woke next. They'd had nothing to eat for at least a day, maybe longer.

"There's nothing grows on or near the Dark Waters safe to eat," the Prince explained. Its voice, unlike the rest of it, was beautiful. "Mayhap, when we reach the catacombs, there will be something suitable."

"We'll die without food," Richard argued. "Food and water." He'd still had spirit, then. His spirit, and his fingers.

"You were willing enough to die only hours ago," rebuked the Prince. It had raven wings, dark and glossy, and tall as a man. They moved gently when the *sluagh* inhaled and exhaled. "And this side of the Gate is no place to regain hope."

"What about Aine?" Richard challenged. "She'll die, too."

The Prince clicked its teeth.

"The human *siofra* will need nourishment," it acknowledged. The Prince pulled its wings close, for warmth or protection against the acrid air. "She'll last until the catacombs."

Richard's eyes were sealed shut. Thick, dried crusts glued his lashes together. He rubbed at his eyelids with his good hand, gritting his teeth to keep from groaning when the bones in his other hand shifted. He scrubbed until the crusts fell away and his eyes wept fresh tears, stung by the poisonous air.

He was afraid to open his eyes, but he did anyway. He'd been afraid for most of his life. Until Winter came along and showed him differently, he'd assumed everyone walked through life in a constant state of dread.

He'd fallen asleep on his side, but somehow he'd shifted without waking and now lay on his back. The *sluagh* dimension's round white sun hung directly overhead, shedding a cold gray light. It was high in the sky, which meant half the day was already gone. That was one of the first things Richard noticed; the alien sun kept time with the still running pocket watch on his belt.

Which meant maybe it wasn't an alien sun after all, but the very same Earth star seen through a different filter.

Richard's pocket watch was failing—it was too difficult to wind the spring one-handed—but when he'd collapsed into a nest of gravel many hours earlier, the sun had been setting. He'd slept for far longer than he'd yet managed. Usually the Prince allowed his army only a short break.

Richard sat up carefully, cradling his left hand in his lap.

The *sluagh* Prince crouched only a few feet away. It sat on its heels, clawed hands resting on its knees. The *sluagh's* wing feathers trailed in the gravel. It smiled at Richard, showing sharp teeth.

"The path ahead is blocked," the Prince explained. "We must wait until it's safe again before we move on."

"Blocked?" Richard asked, but the Prince only stared and smiled.

"Water?" the monster offered, polite as a *maître d'* at any four-star restaurant.

Richard was almost overcome by a wave of hatred. He wanted to pummel the *sluagh* until the ghoul's ugly face was nothing more than slime, until those knowing green eyes were jelly on his knuckles. Only the pulsing agony in his broken hand kept him from trying.

"Yes," he said.

The Prince whistled, the sweet trill of a bird in spring. A smaller *sluagh* detached itself from the shadows of a boulder. Richard recognized the *sluagh* by its vacant, one-eyed stare. A warty growth of small tentacles undulated where its other eye should have been.

Richard had taken to mentally calling the one-eyed ghoul 'Water-Bearer,' because as far as he could tell its only purpose in the small army was to lug around a large leather jug full of drinkable water.

Water-Bearer bent at the knees in front of Richard. It unstoppered the jug and held it out so Richard could suck from

30

the leather tit like a baby. The *sluagh* smelled of rotting flesh and moldy soil, and the water from its jug tasted metallic, but at least the water was cold and not poisonous.

Water-Bearer waited patiently while Richard drank, then resealed the jug and took it back into the shadows.

Bracing his injured hand, Richard inched backward until he could set his spine against a boulder for support. The rock was cold even through his clothes, but it was dry, which meant he didn't have to worry. The *sluagh* had quickly put the poisonous lake at their back, marching away from the shore on a well-worn path. Even with the lake well behind, the air remained acrid until they passed into a rocky valley between low hills where the wind died down.

Now he could breathe the air without searing his mouth and lungs. His eyes still burned and wept, but some of the blur was clearing from his vision. He no longer felt like he was watching the alien landscape through a pair of foggy glasses.

The Prince rose, stretching its dark-angel wings. It lifted its chin, opening its mouth, fat tongue quivering between sharp teeth, tasting the air. It hissed, then leapt from the gravel and into the air.

The draft from the Prince's wings smelled foul, but once in the air the monster was graceful, almost beautiful, a misshapen dancer between the white sun and dark hills. Richard couldn't look away. He watched until the Prince disappeared, and he couldn't pretend the lurch in his heart wasn't more envy than fear.

Water-Bearer stirred. As Richard watched, it inched away from its solitary pool of shadow and approached the rest of the Host where they gathered in a knot against the sheltering hill, guarding the changeling. Richard could see only their dark forms, a wall of feathers and grotesquely twisted limbs, but he knew Aine was there among them, guarded by sharp teeth and wicked claws.

At first Richard assumed they were protecting her from the poisons in the air. Now he wondered if it was something more.

The group muddled, parting just enough to let Water-Bearer squeeze through. Richard rolled onto his knees, hoping to catch a glimpse of Aine, but the feathery gap closed again too quickly.

Once he'd eased back onto the gravel it occurred to Richard that he was being ignored. Whether out of curiosity or distrust, the Prince had been his guardian since they'd crossed through the portal. As far as Richard could tell, the rest of the Host had dismissed him in favor of the jewel that was Aine. And now the Prince was gone.

Go! Richard's conscious always sounded an awful lot like his father. *Get your ass up and go! Just like I taught you, Rick! Now!*

He was up and away before he really thought about it, running through the ever-present twilight, dodging boulders and slipping on gravel, leaving the *sluagh* path behind. The resulting pain in his hand made his head spin, but he didn't slow, even when his damaged leg began to drag.

Richard put the lake at his back and limped uphill. As he climbed out of the shelter of the valley, the wind picked up again, stinging. It sucked the air from his lungs and he was forced to slow to a jog, then a staggering walk.

He found a man-sized spear of granite and sank down against it, cradling his hand. The sun seemed brighter from the hillside, the cold light malevolent. He looked back the way he'd come, but saw no sign of pursuit. He could just make out the trail the *sluagh* had worn into the earth. A pale thread through the darker gravel, it ran parallel to the lake and toward the lowering sun.

West, Richard decided. East was where Winter's portal had spat them out, all in a rush, the heat of C4 following them through, singeing *sluagh* feathers and making Aine cry out in terror.

Richard shivered. The explosion had been bigger than he'd expected. Richard's father was infamous for his immolation expertise—or had been until he'd blown both his legs off in one of his own traps. From Bobby, Richard had learned how to build and rewire; he'd repaired old clocks and old buildings, antique phones and rusting gas-lamps. Richard was a tinkerer. Bombs were no more difficult than clockwork.

Something went wrong, Richard thought, recalling the roaring flame and the seismic blast. *It was only supposed to be enough to collapse the Way.*

"Forty thousand tons of stone, Richard. That comes down, there will be real damage," Bran had warned, right before the timer on the ignition clicked down to zero, triggering the accelerant, blowing the tunnel.

"Sorry," Richard whispered to the alien sun. "I'm sorry, Bran."

He used the side of the granite spear to lever himself back upright, even though his legs and eyes ached. His broken hand sent tiny zaps of nauseating pain straight to his stomach. He missed his cane—a cane that had once belonged to Oscar Wilde— and wondered if it had survived the explosion. Last he'd seen it, Aine had been using the long ebony stick as a weapon against the invading Host.

Aine, who'd gone faded and dull since she'd surrendered to the *sluagh*. The few times Richard had gotten close enough to whisper a word, she'd been unresponsive. He wondered if she hated him. She'd sacrificed herself, and all for nothing.

It didn't matter. He'd find a way to rescue her from the Host, just as soon as he recovered some of his strength, and got a good look at the environment, and figured out what sort of materials he had to work with. He'd come up with a clever plan, because he always did, even if a clever plan meant nothing more than tossing chunks of rock at the Prince and its minions. And because he'd promised Aine, in a whisper, that he'd save them both.

Then he'd gone and run off like a coward and a fool.

"Recon," Richard reminded himself. "Recon is good. Always start with recon."

He'd run, but not far. He'd just circle back down the hill, follow the army at a safe distance and wait until an opportunity solidified.

He started back the way he'd come, jogging slowly. He couldn't help but wish for Winter and one of the *sidhe*'s pain-blocking Cants, or for Gabby and her magic healing ointment.

It was a lucky thing Richard was moving carefully, because if he'd gone back to barreling about in fear and distress, he'd never have noticed Water-Bearer in time. As it was, he barely had a moment to step out of the *sluagh*'s half-flying, half-shuffling trajectory, and freeze.

You can't see me, Richard thought, motionless. *I'm not here. You can't see me.*

It was the tiny prayer he'd held close to his heart since Bobby had first tried to break him, when Richard was five. It was every broken child's useless mantra, but for Richard, it always worked.

Water-Bearer loped past Richard, unseeing, exactly as they all did, because Richard refused to be found.

I'm not here. You can't see me.

Bobby, and Bobby's goons. Elementary school teachers. Social workers. The retail clerks on the District streets and grocery store baggers. Tourists, street police, museum guards, fish-eyed cameras, traffic cops. If Richard didn't want to be noticed, no one paid him any attention.

The only person Richard couldn't fool was Winter, and that was because of the *sidhe*'s wicked sense of—

"Smell," said Water-Bearer, just as Richard remembered. His heart jumped into his throat. "I can smell you, Adam's son. I know you're near, I can smell your blood and bones and sweet, sweet flesh."

The monster stopped ten feet up the hill. It turned, wings partially spread, and peered back down in Richard's direction. Its head swiveled, seeking blindly, single eye narrowed, no longer vacant. Then it snuffled, scenting its prey.

"Brave, but naive." It had the Prince's alto tones. "You won't last long without water, mortal. And there's none safe to drink outside the catacombs." It grimaced, tongue flicking. "Only what we carry."

Richard edged sideways. The *sluagh* rotated, following his progress. Its fat tongue flickered gently in the air, snakelike. Richard shuddered. He stood still, wondering if it was the heat of his body it sensed, or truly the scent of his flesh.

"I'm faster than you by far." Water-Bearer minced back down the slope. It had bird feet, bare toes curled under and clawed. It didn't move gracefully on the ground, but Richard remembered the Prince in flight and knew the monster told the truth. "Flee again if you like, but I've caught you, and you'll only work up a bigger thirst in the running."

It paused, head tilted, claws scratching for purchase in the gravel. "But mayhap you ran off to die, a dog abandoned by his pack. Is that it, apostate?"

Richard snatched up a jagged chunk of rock and pounced. He hit the *sluagh* sideways, shoulder-to-shoulder, swinging the rock hard at the monster's head. Skin and bone crunched. Water-Bearer fell backwards against the slope. Richard landed atop the ghoul, sprawled on the creature's chest.

He lifted the rock again and brought it down. The *sluagh* twisted sideways and Richard missed. No longer surprised, Water-Bearer was quick. It squirmed until Richard couldn't maintain a good grip. His hands slipped. Water-Bearer hit him once, hard, with the back of its wing.

Richard rolled down the hill, sliding to a stop on his stomach against a boulder. Water-Bearer hopped after, wings flapping. It landed by Richard, set one foot hard between his shoulder blades, talons biting through Richard's shirt and scoring his flesh.

"Useless animal," it hissed. "I see you now." Dark *sluagh* ichor ran from a gash above its eye. "Kin-slayer and coward, to leave your female alone and unprotected, in the grasp of the Wild Hunt."

Richard bucked against the pressure of the *sluagh*'s foot. Water-Bearer flexed its claws, ripping at his flesh. Fueled by pain and desperation, Richard wriggled sideways and rolled again. He grabbed Water-Bearer's foot in his good hand, squeezing until he felt delicate bones shift and then snap.

The *sluagh* shrieked and spat. It kicked, raking Richard across the chin, then fell in a huddle, wings pulled around its front into a defensive, feathery tent.

Rubbery flesh and a single claw dripped ichor in Richard's hand. An entire toe and talon had come away in his grasp. Where the *sluagh* blood fell on gravel it smoked, and where it stained Richard's fingers blisters rose. Hastily he dropped the grisly trophy, wiping his hand on his shirt.

Breathing hard, he regarded the *sluagh*. Water-Bearer glared back. Its one eye was grass-green, and very bright. One beautiful fairy eye, in an ugly, warty face.

"I'm not leaving Aine behind," Richard said, surprising himself. What did it matter what the *sluagh* thought? "I'll kill you all, and get her back."

Water-Bearer laughed. "We aren't easily killed, mortal. And this time, you've no human technology to aid you." It showed its sharp teeth when it smiled.

"Maybe, maybe not." Multiple agonies threatened to pull Richard under. His body wanted to give up and fall down. But he'd faced pain before, and always beat it back. "I'm resourceful."

"Yes," Water-Bearer hissed. It studied Richard thoughtfully. Clawed hands crept from behind the wing-curtain and fisted in the gravel. Richard couldn't help but notice the elegant fingers attached to those claws. They were Winter's hands, *sidhe* hands, but made grotesque by the addition of long talons.

Water-Bearer caught Richard staring. It laughed again.

"Aye," it whispered, single eye bright. "We were all beautiful once. The queen's glorious Host. Most beloved, most powerful, most dangerous. Until Gloriana grew jealous, and frightened, and we were exiled *here*, a land more poisonous than envy. Here"—it stuck a pale foot from beneath its wings—"here, we change, and fall apart."

Richard swallowed to keep from gagging. The foot wept black blood. A jagged piece of bone showed where he'd torn the monster's claw away. The bone was thin, see-through, and pocked with tiny black craters.

Water-Bearer shrugged its wings and pulled its foot back behind the curtain of feathers.

"I've nearly reached the end of what I was," it admitted softly. "Your blood and gristle are of little use to me. I've forgotten how to hunger." It tilted its head, bird-like. "Just like I've forgotten other things. Tell me how you do it, your magic, here in this place where none exists?"

"I don't know what you're talking about," returned Richard. He took a few steps back away from Water-Bearer. He wondered if he'd best run again, or try to tear the creature to rotting pieces. He wasn't sure he had the strength for either.

"I'm not so close to ending I can't chase you to the boundaries of this cursed prison," the *sluagh* said. "The Prince asked me to bring you back, and so I shall. Far better for us both if you return willingly. Are you thirsting yet?"

Richard licked his lips, then wished he hadn't. His tongue felt thick and fuzzy. Water-Bearer showed its teeth again.

"And hungry," it guessed. "They've fed the female. But you—they've neglected you. They didn't realize what they had. *I* won't neglect you, mortal."

Richard didn't remember sitting down, but somehow he was on his knees in the gravel.

"Shut up," he said. "I need to think." He scrabbled in the dirt for a rock, clutching the chunk in his good fist.

Water-Bearer only laughed.

"A valiant attempt, apostate," it murmured, "but above ground and without water you'll die in a matter of hours. Your wounds have stopped bleeding. You're drying up. Give way."

Richard looked at Water-Bearer. The *sluagh* stared back, one-eyed and calculating. The small tentacles in his empty eye socket stretched and twitched.

"If you perish here on the scree," it said. "You waste a life better spent for your female."

Aine, Richard mourned. Aloud, he said: "You're talking riddles and nonsense. Shut up, or I'll rip off your wings."

Water-Bearer snorted through its melted nose. "No riddles. She's got Mending in her veins. It's not a quick or easy end she'll face, not as a bridge between two worlds. She'll be bled dry, several times over. You've guessed, or why come through in our wake? Slit her throat, spare her the suffering, redeem yourself. *That*'s why you've come."

"I came to save her." Richard's eyes were gooping shut again, lashes drying together in crusts.

"There's no saving either of you." Water-Bearer rose. It shuffled across the gravel and stood over Richard, wings rustling. "But it will be interesting to watch you try."

It bent in a swoop, and before Richard could twitch, it scooped him up in wiry arms, then sprang upwards. The last thing Richard heard as he let go of consciousness was the unearthly whoosh of strong wings beating against poisoned currents.

He dreamed he was drowning, then woke to a trickle of water on his tongue.

"Carefully," Water-Bearer cautioned. "Swallow."

Richard swallowed. The water was sweeter than he remembered. He drank until the jug was taken away. He reached up to rub the gunk from his eyes and a wet cloth was pressed into his hand.

"Use this. Hold it against your eyes until the scabs loosen."

Richard didn't argue. The damp eased his stinging face, soothing.

"I've splinted your hand. The bones are beyond resetting; fingers are difficult. The splint will prevent further damage. Even better if you shield it from notice."

Richard took the wet cloth from his face. He opened his eyes, shuddering as lashes stuck together and tore apart. The world had gone blurry again, but Water-Bearer's one eye glinted clear as day. Over the *sluagh's* broad shoulders Richard glimpsed familiar shifting shadows: the Dread Host.

"Aine?" he called.

"Quiet," Water-Bearer hissed. "Your female still lives. They're preparing her for travel. The path is clear; we're walking on. Now, eat this, quickly."

He took the rag from Richard's hand, replacing it with something small, hard, and warm. Long as a carrot and beet-red, it reminded Richard of a skinny turnip.

"What is it?"

"My dinner. Journey-root. Eat it. I haven't saved you from death on the rocks only to poison you now."

Richard was too hungry to be cautious. He took a bite, chewing greedily. Journey-root tasted like bitter onion. Richard didn't care. He finished the root in four quick bites.

"Hasn't anyone ever told you never accept food from a fairy?"

This time his conscience sounded like Winter. He shook his head, chasing the voices away. It was far too late for warnings or premonitions. He'd left common sense behind the day he'd stolen C4 from Bobby's basement.

"Remember," Water-Bearer whispered as it rose, shedding feathers. "End yourself now and your female will suffer later."

"Her name is Aine. She's not mine."

But Water-Bearer was gone, disappeared into the rocks. In its place stood the Prince, beautifully frightening, and at the Prince's side two tall *sluagh*. They held chains in their clawed hands, short chains made of links of bronze.

Shackles.

"Very stubborn, for a mortal," the *sluagh* Prince bellowed. "Nor entirely without wits." It clicked its long tongue, then dipped its chin.

"Bind him," it ordered, and the *sluagh* fell upon Richard, shrieking with delight.

3. The Queen

Siobahn summoned the remaining exiles to Malachi's Gold Street office. Located on the top floor of a boutique hotel and glassed in on three sides, the small apartment had plenty of light. It looked down onto a narrow cobblestoned alley. Across the alley a pizza joint spat out a constant stream of delivery boys on bicycles.

The office was meant to be modern-eccentric like the rest of the hotel, but Malachi had ignored building ordinances and instead furnished it with various pieces of mismatched furniture he'd collected through the centuries. Stickley and Tiffany competed for space with a faded Chesterfield and Chinese stools. He'd spread Oriental rugs over the original wood floors. Across the rugs he'd tossed skins of the bear and deer he'd hunted over the island before Manhattan became Manhattan.

The apartment also had an all-important back entrance: a fire ladder that eventually dumped into a second, smaller alley.

Siobahn arranged herself in a polished Stickley armchair, Morris standing silent at her back, and watched the open window over the fire escape.

No one ever used the apartment's front door. Malachi had spelled it shut. Even his mortal visitors came up the fire ladder and through the bedroom window.

It was a silly precaution, Siobahn thought as she faced the open window, waiting. A locked door wasn't likely to keep serious busybodies out. But Malachi liked his little dramas and they'd kept him from boredom.

"Tea, m'lady?"

Siobahn glanced at the spread of tea and biscuits Morris had set out for guests on a low, battered table that looked more Ikea than turn-of-the-century.

"Something stronger, Morris. Whiskey. One of the old bottles, from the bar."

"Yes, m'lady." Morris sounded disapproving, but Siobahn didn't care. Morris disapproved of everything. It was why she liked him.

A blast of chill winter air blew in through the open window. Siobahn shivered, pulling the sleeves of the sweater she wore down past her wrists and over her fingers. The sweater had belonged to Malachi. It still carried his scent, as did the Gold Street office, and the penthouse over at The Plaza, and the Italian cafe on Thames Street, and every single pore of her body.

Morris bustled back. He extended a snifter of dark brandy. Siobahn took it, warming it between her covered palms, Morris in position behind her chair once more. Together they contemplated the open window.

"They're late," he sniffed after a moment.

Siobahn lifted her eyes to the clock on Malachi's desk. It was a small carriage clock, enameled, a twin to one she kept in her own bedroom.

"Not yet," she replied. "Give them time to remember."

Morris cleared his throat disapprovingly, but kept silent. Siobahn drank from her snifter. She swirled the liquid around her teeth. She swallowed and considered Morris's bland reflection in the windowpanes.

"Don't you think," she said, "the British butler routine is a tad out of date?"

Morris didn't blink.

"No, my lady," he said.

Siobahn shook her head and took another swallow of liquor. Before, Morris had been in charge of feeding the Progress, a dangerous job few in the Court volunteered to take on. Now he seemed perfectly happy arranging cookies on a tea plate and polishing silverware.

She knew he still wore a knife under his black dinner coat. She wondered if he remembered how to use it for anything other than slicing fine cheese.

The wind gusted again, this time carrying in flecks of snow, and the distinctive, earthy smell of *sidhe*.

"They come," Morris murmured, relieved.

"Yes." Siobahn closed her eyes. When she opened them again, she was ready. "As I said, they but needed time to remember."

They came through the window in groups and straggles, and arranged themselves the same way throughout the apartment, talking quietly amongst themselves, or staring vacantly out through the glass walls. Most were thin and ragged and more than half-mad. A few looked less fay than mortal. Three came in animal form: a cat, a raven, and a gray mouse.

The mouse made Siobahn miss Gabriel. But this mouse easily turned itself into a lean young man. He collapsed into the Chesterfield, pulled his mobile from a pocket, and was immediately engrossed. He didn't once turn his head Siobahn's way.

"Twenty-five," Morris said quietly. "By my count we're missing Katherine Grey, Nightingale, and seven more."

His tray of sandwiches was mostly empty. Many of the exiles lived on the city streets where good food was hard to find. A few had tastes that had nothing to do with mortal fare.

"Katherine Grey isn't reliable. Nor Nightingale. The rest will come."

Morris set down his tray. He regarded the gathering, lips pressed together into a thin line. "Reliability isn't something I'd expect from this lot, m'lady."

"No." Siobahn set her drink aside. She rose, unfolding her long limbs from the Stickley. "But loyalty is."

She arranged the long skirt she wore beneath Malachi's sweater. Freeing her palms, she clapped them together once, sharp. The sound, purposefully magnified, bounced off furniture, walls, and glass. When it hit the open window, it rattled the casing, dropping the upper sash with a bang.

The quiet chatter in the room went silent. Palpable tension rose until their fear and anger pricked against Siobahn's skin.

"When Malachi stood on my right-hand with his sword and strength," she said, "you remembered your place. Was it only the sword that made you bow? Have you forgotten obedience?"

She waited. They went down to their knees one by one, reluctantly at first, then more quickly, as they recalled who they were and where they'd come from. Only the boy with the busy mobile and a petite maid in a whore's fishnet stockings refused to drop.

"Himself is murdered and gone," the boy said without looking up from his phone. "He was the last who believed. There's no Way home for us now. Why should we care who sits on a throne we'll never see again?"

Siobahn crossed the room without moving. The lad at last glanced up from his screen. He had a shock of straight dun-colored hair that fell across his nose. He wore a bowtie and bespoke suit. His feet were bare and dirty.

Malachi would have remembered his name. Siobahn didn't care to.

She flicked her fingers. The phone in his hand turned to a clutch of maggots. They fell from his hand, tumbling across the Chesterfield cushions in tiny pit-pats. When the larvae hit the ground, the nearest *sidhe,* head still bowed, snatched them from the rug and shoved them in her mouth.

The boy's eyes widened, but he didn't move.

"I had half my life on that phone," he said, showing pointed teeth. "All my connections and contacts."

"Connections and *contacts,"* Siobahn scoffed. "How human you sound. What of blood and vow?"

He shrugged, fists clenched on his thighs. "Himself is gone. It was Malachi kept us safe, kept us fed, while you, m'lady, hid away and watched from on high. Just like Gloriana."

Siobahn slapped him, twice. Her hand left a red mark across his cheek. He half stood, then prudently changed his mind and fell back onto the cushions.

"Wise," Siobahn said. She bent and scooped a single missed worm from the carpet, dropping it in the lad's lap. "My patience isn't what it was. Get down on your knees."

He was canny enough to slide off the couch and onto the rug, but not before Siobahn caught the gleam of malice in his blue eyes. He started to bow his head, hair flopping over his forehead, but Siobahn bent in one swift motion and grabbed his chin.

"What's your name?" she demanded.

He kept himself still against the grip of her fingers, but Siobahn could feel the pulse beating under his jawbone. He was frightened, or angry, or both. The single tiny worm had fallen from his lap and squished beneath his knee.

"Carran," he answered, not quite a hiss. "I kept your cloak from the mud, when we crossed through. I carried Himself's helm. Don't you remember, m'lady? I was *his* page. The one who slipped—

"—the poison to the Guard, and the sleeping *draiochta* into Gloriana's cup." Siobahn relaxed her fingers, remembering. He'd been barely a child, then. Now he was grown, like her own son. Grown, but not thriving, like a sapling pruned back.

"You were loyal to my husband. Willing to commit murder and high treason. You kept his blade clean, and you combed the leaves from my hair when we still ran like animals in the woods." Siobahn regarded his bent head. "Yet now you'd rather play with human toys than prostrate yourself at my feet. Once you knew your place, Carran. My husband's death does not change your standing. I am, and was always meant to be, your queen."

"You have the bloodlines." He'd put his hands behind his head as though she held a pistol to his lowered brow. "Aye, that's true. But it was Malachi who treated us as his own, Malachi who held us together." His eyes were cobalt slits through the fall of his hair. "You, you would have let us rot while you dreamed of revenge."

Siobahn hit him again, knocking him flat. She conjured a small bronze knife to her hand, pinned him immobile with a word, and would have spilt his traitorous innards all across Malachi's bear rugs if not for a sudden change in the room.

It was almost imperceptible at first, an inhale and an exhale as the *sidhe* grouped on their knees around the apartment began to stir. She'd held their attention completely and without trying, because it was the way of royalty, but now they were turning away.

Siobahn smelled the danger before she saw it. Not in through the window, no, but under the spelled door, in the gaps around the old frame; a familiar perfume, a hated fragrance, calculation and threat.

Morris rose to his feet. Siobahn wasn't sure how he meant to protect her with only his small knife; still, he was quick as a cat, and spread himself in front of Malachi's spelled door a heartbeat before it burst into splinters and shrapnel.

The exiles rose in leaps and bounds, surrounding Siobahn. Power hummed, and weapons were drawn; pistols, bronze blades, and in one case a sawed-off shotgun. Siobahn felt a surge of satisfaction. They'd protect her even as they chafed under her rule, because it was bred in their bones.

Morris spat a quick Cant as he staggered upright. An orb of amber light spread across Siobahn and her small army.

"Nicely done," the queen said, surprised. "You've a few tricks up your sleeve still, Morris."

"Yes, m'lady." Like Siobahn Morris kept his attention on the splintered threshold.

Around Siobahn and beneath the amber orb, the exiles arranged themselves for battle. Only the arrogant blue-eyed boy and the female in the fishnet stockings refused to join ranks.

Katherine Grey sent her human into the room first, a coward's gambit. He was tall for a mortal, and fit, even after the explosion that had nearly killed him. He walked carefully, and there were sutures still on the right side of his head where emergency room doctors had shaved away his graying hair, but he held himself with the easy confidence of the unafraid.

"Detective Healy," Siobahn purred. "You might have knocked."

He scanned the room with a warrior's quick precision, briefly considering the open window, then smiled at Siobahn.

"I did. You didn't hear me." He kept his gaze on Siobahn, but she knew he was assessing her small army and trying to determine the threat level in the room.

"So you kicked the door in?" Siobahn showed her teeth. "Overdone, Detective."

"Shot the lock," he said, twitching his coat so she could see the holster under his arm. "One of your son's modified weapons." He smiled back. Siobahn didn't like the genuine amusement on his mouth. "I learned the hard way human technology and *sidhe* magic make a volatile combination."

One of the exiles hissed and flapped the tiny black batwings sprouting from her spine. The long blade in her fist thrummed a reaction, shifting from black through all the colors of the dawning sky, then back again.

"An explosive combination," Siobahn agreed. "You're healing well. Liadan must be tending to you personally. Where is she?"

"Here."

Morris spat a curse, whirling away from the door. Siobahn turned more slowly. She was used to the Grey Lady's games; they'd been playing against each other for longer than Siobahn cared to remember.

Katherine Grey climbed through the open window. The curtain shivered at her passing, the worn lace pattern recoiling from her touch. She'd pulled her hair back into a plain braid and wore a black shirt and trousers instead of the overdone couture she usually preferred and Summer so admired.

Carran and his female companion rose from the Chesterfield and ranged themselves at her side. Morris growled, but Siobahn was unsurprised.

"So. You've come to sow dissent?" Siobahn set her hand on Morris' arm to keep him from lunging forward. "I expected the treason, and the theatrics, and even the human. But I find the mourning raiment distasteful. You never loved him; you haven't earned the right to grieve."

"I loved him." Katherine replied. "So much so that I've come to pay you my respects, because it's what he would have wanted."

"Detective Healy." Siobahn paced back to her chair. "You've made your point. Come all the way in, please. Morris, see what you can do about the door before we attract the notice of our neighbors."

Morris nodded. His protective sphere tightened around Siobahn. Bran circled the room until he stood at Katherine Grey's side. The exiles hissed and seethed as he passed.

"Not your usual bodyguard," the detective said. "Where's Barker?"

"Indisposed." Siobahn settled herself on the edge of her chair. "Still recovering from *Buairt's* bite. I've discovered Morris' talents beyond driving."

Bran's eyebrows rose. He set himself at Katherine's Grey left shoulder, alongside Carran, then watched with exaggerated interest as Morris cast a Glamour over the broken door.

"Pay your respects on your knees, Liadan," Siobahn ordered the Grey Lady. "And I'll worry less you've come to kill me."

"I haven't." Katherine set a restraining hand on Bran's arm. She lowered herself to the floor, shoulders bowed. "Come to kill you. My lady."

Siobahn shifted her attention to the human. He rocked on his heels, hands crossed behind his back, brows still raised.

"No," he said. "You're not my queen, Siobahn. You've paid me well to guard your son, but you haven't earned my loyalty."

"Winter has," Siobahn guessed. She felt the shift of attention in her exiles, even as they waited without moving.

"Winter is my friend." Once again the human scanned the room. "Where is he?"

"Not here."

"Not in D.C., either. I've a desk jockey meant to keep an eye on him while I'm away on vacation. My man says Winter's gone AWOL. I assumed he'd come home. For the wake."

Siobahn felt grief take a stranglehold around her heart.

"We burn our dead," she said, sharp. "We don't wake them. I've sent Winter on an errand."

The mortal bristled under his coat. The stitches in his skull stood out against clenched muscles.

"You don't think the kid deserves a break? Maybe a few days to recover? Or isn't he allowed to grieve his daddy?"

Siobahn would have burnt the detective to ash but for the sly smile she glimpsed on Katherine's mouth. The expression was gone as quickly as it came, but Siobahn wasn't fooled.

"My son is Malachi's get, and a warrior." She pitched her voice so it echoed across the ceiling. "Grief is for the weak, and the idle. *Geimhreadh* is neither. He's gone to avenge his father's murder."

"Smith's dead," said Bran. "Brains splattered all over Sixth Avenue. NYPD's still looking for a suspect. I hear Barker's on the top of their list."

"Barker's indisposed," Siobahn repeated. "Michael Smith means nothing to the *sidhe*. He was but a pawn in a larger game."

This time, when the Grey Lady smiled, she lifted her head.

"You fool," she said. "You've actually done it. You've sent a child to best a monster. Your *own* child, Siobahn, and the last prince of the old blood. If Malachi weren't already lost to us, this surely would break his heart unto death."

She rose to her feet, the treason Siobahn expected, garbed all in mourning.

"You're mad," Katherine Grey accused, while around Siobahn the exiles began to stir. "You've been on the edge for centuries, and Malachi's death has finally sent you over."

4. Forbidden

"Crawlers," Lolo said. He shone his flashlight left and right, but looked straight ahead. "Don't stare. It just pisses 'em off."

Barker shifted minutely. Summer felt the stir of power as he muttered a Cant under his breath. She hoped it was some sort of protective spell, because the stares from the tunnel's edge made her shiver.

"Stupid boy," Barker hissed. "You've walked us into a lion's den."

"No." Lolo continued to walk. "Most of 'em aren't violent, just high. They don't want any trouble. They just want their fix, and to be left alone."

Summer wasn't so sure. She knew the effect *sidhe* beauty could have on even the steadiest of humans. The lost group sheltering in Federal Center Station looked anything but steady. Many of the slumped forms were still, caught in their own drug-fueled dreams, but a few took glassy-eyed notice, and one man with a tangled, ginger beard licked his lips as they passed, showing Summer his tongue.

"Lolo!" She hurried to catch up. "Maybe this was a bad idea."

"You said you wanted to see the portal," Lolo said. He dodged a pile of trash and the sleeping man curled around it. "It's down here. They can't hurt us, Summer. We've got Barker."

Summer grabbed a handful of the back of Lolo's coat. For once he didn't make fun of her. She looked over her shoulder at Barker. The older *sidhe* kept his flashlight trained on the curving tunnel sides. His mouth was moving, but she couldn't hear what he was saying.

"What about the *sluagh*?" Summer asked.

"The trains aren't running. If there were monsters about, we'd be walking through a blood bath, not a flop house."

"That doesn't make me feel any better."

"Sorry," he said, but Summer didn't think he meant it. She wanted to hit him, but couldn't make her fingers let go of his coat.

"I smell smoke," said Barker.

"Up there ahead," replied Lolo. "Bonfire. That'll be where the big bosses are crashing."

"Big bosses?" Summer repeated.

"Pushers," Barker murmured. "Dealers. Lorenzo—"

But Lolo was already ten steps ahead, dragging Summer behind.

"Look natural," he said. Summer couldn't decide whether she wanted to laugh or cry.

The bonfire was more smoke than flame, but it gave off enough heat to warm Summer's cheeks as they approached. It burned between the tracks and over, turning the rails warm several inches to either side of the blackened wood, and effectively blocking their way. Folding lawn chairs were set in a circle, exactly as though the tunnel crawlers intended to roast marshmallows and sing camp songs.

Four mortal men sat in a half-circle around the fire. Summer wasn't good at guessing mortal age, but she thought they looked little older than boys, beardless and wiry. Three had tattoos, one was bald, and the fourth had a ring in his nose.

He looked up as Lolo approached, and set the neatly flared hand of cards he'd been studying upside-down into the dirt, safely away from the fire.

"Evening." He smiled. "Shopping?"

"Passing through," Lolo corrected. "*Vale?*"

"Sure. But there's not much past here, except the hole."

"Tourists," explained Lolo. "They want to see the damage."

"Huh." The shifting light glinted on the piercing in his nostril as he wagged his chin back and forth. "People are crazy. Don't I know you, kid?"

Lolo shrugged dramatically. The beads in his braids clicked.

"Could be. Used to mule for Bobby Lorimer some, before I got a better gig."

"Yeah. I remember."

Summer decided the sway of his chin was a tick, or a spasm. She couldn't help but notice the flecks of spit in the corner of his smile. When he caught her staring, she looked away, embarrassed.

"How much you making off this *tourism?*"

"Not enough to pay the rent."

One of the other men shifted in his lawn chair. The bonfire picked out the planes and wrinkles on his face, making him ugly.

"You want to pass, you got to pay the troll."

"Toll?" Barker echoed in clipped tones. He was little more than a silhouette against Summer's shoulder, yellow eyes muted.

"Troll." The ugly man giggled under his breath, then jerked a thumb at his younger companion. "We call him the troll, because he collects the gold."

"Oh, come on," Lolo whined, suddenly sounding his age. "This tourism thing is my gig. I thought it up, I paid off the cops. Let a man make a living."

"It's a good idea, but you ain't no man, *kid.*" The troll held out one hand. "Give us a cut, or you don't get by."

Barker pushed past Summer, Winter's Glock in his fist. Summer wasn't sure whether he'd conjured it to hand or simply plucked it from Lolo's waistband.

He leveled the pistol at the troll's head. "Move aside."

Lolo went very still.

No bullets, Summer remembered.

The troll grinned.

"You won't use that," he said. His three companions rose one by one. Two pulled pistols of their own. The third dragged a shotgun from underneath his chair. "Unless you're stupid. Three against one and now I'm wondering, *hermano,* exactly what sort of *tourist* carries a semi-automatic instead of a camera phone?"

"Hey." Lolo lifted both his hands, palms up. "Hey, hey. I've got nothing to do with—"

The empty Glock spat four times in a row. Summer bit back a scream, then choked on it as the troll fell sideways. He hit the ground, twitching, his foot and the cuff of his jeans scraping through the bonfire. His shoe began to smoke.

"You'll want to move him once we're past." Barker told the troll's frozen companions. "He's not dead, but if you leave him to burn, he soon will be." He nudged Summer, hard, with an elbow, Glock still steady in his hand. "Go. Now."

Summer edged around the fire and lawn chairs. She had to pull Lolo with her, because he'd gone quiet and dull-like. The troll's friends didn't move. They watched Barker and Winter's pistol as the *sidhe* circled past.

Once the bonfire was behind her, Summer began to run. Lolo stumbled after. Barker drifted behind, insubstantial as mist. Summer had forgotten the flashlight in her hand, and now it bounced in her loose grip, sending round circles of light up and down and sideways, dizzying. She thought she heard shouts and angry voices, but she didn't see any more faces against the tunnel wall.

Eventually Barker reached out and pulled her to a halt.

"Steady," he warned. "They've not come after, and I've no wish to get lost in this place. Lorenzo, pay attention."

Lolo was bent in an L-shape, hands on his knees. He coughed and spat.

"You killed him," the boy said without looking up. "You shot him, with an empty gun. *Four* times."

"It was only a Glamour," Summer said, confused when Lolo retched and spat again. "The gun's empty, remember? No bullets. A Glamour, and a sleep spell, right?"

"Of course," Barker replied. "Now." He took Lolo by the arm, hauling the boy upright and around. "Which way?"

Lolo jerked back, out of Barker's reach. He wiped his mouth with the back of his hand, then tugged his jacket straight. Ignoring Barker, he pointed his flashlight at the wall.

"We almost ran past it," he told Summer. "A few more yards this way."

"How can you tell?" Summer demanded.

"I can tell because this is my home turf," the boy said. "But when we first moved in, Win left a mark every ten feet. In case we got lost, or mentally fucked by a psycho *sidhe* who can kill with an empty gun. Look." He stepped closer to the wall, aiming his light left and then right. "There. It's always on the east wall."

A small glyph glittered on the edge of Lolo's light; an amber rune etched into the stone wall at shoulder height, a tiny stick man with a round face and wide, anime eyes.

"Funny." Summer reached out to touch the glowing mark. It felt no different than the stone behind it, but the shine turned her fingers gold.

"They're not all the same. Couple of them are doing some really lewd things. There's one that makes Richard blush." He paused. "Used to make Richard blush."

"Those are more than bathroom humor." Barker continued up the tunnel. "Those are homemade Wards, crafted with an *aes si*'s tutelage. A few yards up, you say?"

"There will be a gate in the wall, on your right." Lolo didn't move. "It's unlocked."

"Are you alright?" Summer asked, puzzled. "What's wrong?"

"Nothing. Shouldn't have dipped in the minibar for dinner, that's all."

"Okay." But she grasped the edge of his coat again, more for his comfort than her own. She supposed maybe they were both remembering Michael Smith fallen on the sidewalk, face ruined by Lolo's bullet.

The gate hung open. Barker had gone ahead.

"Heads up," Lolo warned. "There are rocks and shit on the stairs."

Summer pressed her free hand against the rough wall. She descended one step at the time, counting as she went. Twenty-three steps farther down into the earth. Lolo was right. Chunks of the wall and low ceiling had fallen into small piles on the stairs. She was glad of Lolo's light.

At the bottom of the steps a heavy metal door stood cracked open.

"No me chingues!" Lolo said. "I locked it behind us when me and Brother Dan left. I always remember to lock it. No one knows the code but Win and Richard and me."

He aimed his light at what must once have been a keypad on the wall. The plastic buttons were melted. Summer could see a faint charring around the small rectangle.

"I don't think Barker needed the code," she said.

"Fuck," Lolo spat. "Winter's going to kill me."

The metal door looked heavy. Lolo squeezed through the crack. Summer followed. She smelled rotten food, and damp, and old sweat, and beneath it the faint spicy scent that was her brother.

"Gross." She covered her nose. "Something in here's off."

Lolo grunted. "No electricity. Richard's salami is probably growing fuzz in the fridge, not to mention Win's veggies. Come on, this way. Rest of the tunnel's back here."

Old train tracks ran down the center of the narrow tunnel. Floor to ceiling curtains divided the space into odd little compartments. They passed through a kitchen and several bedrooms. Twice they had to edge around piles of collapsed wall.

"The library's pretty much destroyed." Lolo shone his flashlight between two curtains. Summer caught an impression of jagged rock and shining puddles. "Something came down through the ceiling, brought pipes with it. It's all turned to mud."

Summer thought he sounded like he'd got something caught in his throat. She'd only seen Lolo cry once before, and that was at her father's burning, but she figured seeing his home destroyed might be even worse. Lolo hadn't known Malachi, but he'd grown up in the Metro.

"Sorry," she said.

"Yeah." He swallowed hard, then coughed. "Whatever. We were outgrowing the place, anyway."

Beyond the library the tunnel opened up and dead-ended in a huge pile of junk. Spears of metal and large coils of cable made frightening shadows against the floor and ceiling. Summer almost tripped over a tipped bucket.

"Richard's workshop," explained Lolo. "Guess he built the bomb here, and we never even knew it, *cobarde*, and we never even guessed."

"Do you hate him now?" Summer asked. She guessed he must.

"I don't know."

"Children," Barker's voice rang like low bells in Summer's skull. *"Come down. Cautiously."*

57

"He means the pit," Lolo explained. "There used to be a real path, but it's all fallen over. Try not to step on anything sharp. There's a lot of it."

They picked their way through piles of junk. Summer stubbed her toe on a rusting gear and was once again glad of her tennies.

"No wonder Winter always dresses like a bum. It's a dust-fest in here."

"What?"

"Nothing."

Past the mountain of trash Lolo came to a sudden halt.

"Watch it," he warned. "You don't want to fall in."

"The pit." Summer remembered. She aimed her light into the depths. "Barker!"

"Here. At the bottom."

"This way." Lolo scuffed sideways along the edge of the hole. "There's a path down."

The way down was more of a crumbling slope than a path. The dirt shifted under Summer's feet as she half-walked, half-slid her way slant-wise into the grade. Bits of mineral or glass in the sand glittered in the flashlight beams. She heard dripping water and smelled more damp, and something else that stank like rot and sewer.

"Corpse-stink," Lolo said, breathing through his mouth. "That's the *sluagh.*"

Summer's scalp prickled. "Are they here?"

"No," Barker said from the shadows, making Summer jump and fumble her flashlight. "It's their prison you smell."

"Fuck!" Lolo hissed. "Can you be less dramatic? Almost pissed my pants, you bastard."

Barker murmured a word in the Gaelic. The pit went all bright and white and stark, then black again. Summer blinked, momentarily blinded.

"The Gate sucks it away," Barker said. He sounded mild, but Summer thought she could smell his fear mixed with the corpse-stink. "Starlight. My torch lasted only a moment before the batteries died."

Summer's own flashlight began to flicker in reply. She switched it quickly off, alarmed by the dying strobe.

"Didn't used to do that," complained Lolo. "Always just spat out monsters."

"Where is it?" Summer demanded as Lolo's light faded. "I can't see it. It's too dark."

"Look." Barker took her shoulders. "This way. The moon has mostly set, but you can see a glint off the water."

At first Summer didn't understand. Then she saw it, all at once, a blacker patch in the darkness, and at its center a shifting gleam: faint light off the roll of waves, but so far away it was like watching the neighbor's television one apartment building over.

"I can see it now." She stretched out a hand, but the reflection of moon-on-water stayed out of reach. "It's floating. Winter's portal."

"*Sluagh* door," said Lolo, disgusted. "What's it doing here? Used to be all the way down past L'Enfant."

"It moved."

"No shit. How'd it do that?"

"I'm not positive." Barker tried Gathering starlight again. It flashed and then fizzled, but this time Summer knew what she was looking for, and caught a quick glimpse of the Gate itself: a man-sized tear in the air, no wider than a bathtub, floating at knee-height.

"It needs to be closed," Barker said. "Before it begins to suck in more than light and warmth."

"Like a black hole," Lolo said.

"You can't close it!" Summer argued, frightened. "Not if Winter's in there!"

"Is he? Lorenzo, are you certain?"

"I saw him go in. Dunno if he still is."

"It's a one-way door," Barker murmured. "Shoddily made by a child who didn't know what he was attempting and was lacking in both knowledge and power."

"It can't be one-way. You're wrong. Win wouldn't leave us behind. He promised Mama." Summer made herself speak calmly, one word at a time, willing Barker to understand. "He has to kill the queen, and save Mama. You know he has to. We have the sword, we have Hannah." She wanted to shout, but thought her father would disapprove. "Winter *promised.*"

"Summer." Lolo's hand found Summer's in the dark. He squeezed her fingers. "Calm down. We'll figure something out. Win will figure something out. He always does. He'll find a way back, because you're right, he wouldn't leave us."

She heard Barker shift, Barker who was always sill.

"I'm sorry," he said. "It's possible your brother didn't know. Either way, the Gate needs to be closed before the *sluagh* grow restless again."

"No. I won't let you." To Summer's shame, she felt tears overflow her lashes and drip down the side of her nose. "You can't. I'm Siobahn's daughter, princess of the royal blood. And I'm telling you: leave it open!"

Lolo's hand slid up her wrist, tightening. She thought he meant to pull her out of range in case Barker flipped out. She was wrong.

"Summer," the boy said. "He's right. You've never seen the shit the ghouls get up to. The things they do. It's bad, Summer. They're really bad."

"Your brother spent every moment of the last ten years trying to protect mortals from this gate," Barker said evenly, a low growl in the dark. "His best friend brought down the earth trying to close it. And you'll tell me no, *Samhradh?* Make very sure, before you speak again. Because I'm bound to listen."

"Summer," Lolo pleaded. "You have to let him close it. Win will find another way home."

Summer wiped snot from her face with the back of her arm. "What are the chances of that? Barker?"

He was quiet for so long she thought he wouldn't answer. In the darkness of the pit, alien light shifted on far away water.

"The Dread Host were imprisoned for a thousand human years before Winter cracked a hole in their prison," he said at last. "And they never found escape. But your brother is a constant surprise to those of us who remember astonishment. It's not impossible he will find a way when the *sluagh* did not. Unlikely, but not impossible."

"Summer." Lolo let go of her wrist. "Winter saved my life. But the *sluagh*, they eat babies. Like you and I eat chocolate candies. I've seen it. They. Eat. Babies. You can't let them come back. There's no one left here to fight them off but me."

"No one left here..." Summer repeated. Her father was gone, Winter was gone. Lolo was what she had left, and she could hear the terror in the crack of his voice.

Mercy, Malachi had said, a few weeks before he'd left her. *Remember mercy.*

"Close it," she ordered. "Close it, and this time, make sure it's closed for good."

5. Promises

In spite of himself, Richard grew used to the shackles. He learned how to shuffle, one foot and then the next, so the cuffs around his ankles didn't catch and throw him to the ground. The bronze circles around his wrists were more difficult; they caused the muscles in his shoulders to ache and pull. After only a single stretch of hours on the meandering path, Richard would have done anything for a chance to raise his hands above his head and ease the pain in his back. But the shackles on his wrist were attached to the circlets around his ankles and he couldn't lift his fists past his waist.

The gnawing pain in his damaged hand was so constant it became almost bearable. Only when he was jostled or when he accidentally forgot to hold the limb still did the nerves wake in white-hot agony.

Something had changed. Richard thought the change had to do with Water-Bearer. Ever since he'd tangled with the one-eyed *sluagh*, Richard's place in the alien world had shifted. He was no longer forced to walk on the edge of the feathered army; instead he was nudged along at the very center of the Host, protected from the biting wind and acrid air by a barrier of feathered wings and writhing tentacles.

When the Host stopped to rest, Richard was allowed an allotment of journey-root with his swallow of water. And when, on what he roughly calculated as their fifth day on the narrow path, burning rain hissed in a sheet from grey clouds, the *sluagh* pressed close, protecting with mottled flesh, warming him as he shivered.

Richard realized he'd grown used to their foul smell. When he curled into a ball, reaching for sleep, he was unreasonably grateful for the small furnace of a *sluagh* body next to his own.

"Why?" he dared ask Water-Bearer on the seventh day, when the *sluagh* squatted to offer the water jug.

"'Why' is a mortal failing." Water-Bearer shrugged as it stoppered the water. Its wings ruffled and shed feathers. "The *sidhe* rarely pause to question the intricacies of life. Best you do the same."

"Sidhe?" Richard asked around a mouthful of root. Because he couldn't lift his hands past his hipbones, Water-Bearer severed bits of turnip with its own sharp teeth, then fed them to Richard. Richard hated it. At first he'd gagged and spat, but then his angry stomach had grown used to the taste of metallic saliva and earthy root.

"Sidhe or *sluagh?"* he asked, chewing, although he thought he already knew.

Water-Bearer only grimaced in what Richard had come to think of as a shit-eating smile. Its single eye gleamed. Then the monster wandered off, intent on its duties.

"That one is trouble," the Prince said from behind Richard. "His influence is far-reaching as a poison in the water and if he's taken notice of you, mortal, you'd best wonder why."

"'Why' is a mortal failing." Richard didn't bother look around. He chewed on the root and studied his wrists. His skin had stopped bleeding beneath the bronze circlets. His damaged hand was swollen inside Water-Bearer's splints.

The sun had sunk below the horizon. The Prince didn't cast a visible shadow, but when it loomed, the warmth of its breath spread against the back of Richard's neck.

"I might have killed him long ago," the Prince continued. "But that one had more influence at Court than any of us, and I mean to keep every weapon I have. Alas, his body is finally failing beneath the weight of this world, even if his wits are sharp as ever."

"Dying, you mean." Richard looked past the resting tangle of the Host. He could see Water-Bearer still moving about, bending to offer the jug here and there amongst the pile of lazing *sluagh*.

"Death is a mortal failing," the Prince mocked. "But, aye, he's no hope of continuing."

Richard finished chewing. When he shifted on the cold sand, his shackles rang.

"Can I see Aine?" he asked, as he did every time they stopped.

"Not yet," the Prince responded, as it did every time Richard asked.

Richard imagined leaping up and somehow strangling the Prince with the chains he wore.

Useless, Bobby cautioned. And Winter said, *Be patient*.

So he closed his eyes, the *sluagh* Prince's breath warming his neck. He pretended to sleep.

Richard discovered if he didn't keep his mind busy, terror would creep in, filling the secret places in his head with hopeless, black thoughts. It had been the same when he'd first left Bobby; the fear lived permanently in his stomach until he couldn't eat or sleep. He'd been half-dead with dehydration and malnutrition, more than half-high on the last of the pills he'd taken with him from home, when he'd fallen off the platform at Eastern Market.

He'd been lucky enough not to hit the third rail, a miracle he didn't really appreciate until months later. He'd stood up, brushing dirt and trash from the knees of his pants. No one had paid him any attention at all. The platform was now at shoulder height. Richard wasn't sure he had the strength to pull himself back up.

So he'd turned and walked into the tunnel.

Three trains rushed past while he wandered. The first time he heard the rumble he'd pressed hard against the wall, closing his eyes as the cars screamed by. The second time he leaned an inch toward the train, just to feel the stale wind on his face.

When he saw the lights rushing toward him for the third time, Richard thought about throwing himself on the tracks. He knew it was a quick end. Bobby had murdered one of his backlogged clients similarly, but on an above ground track in Alexandria. Richard had watched it happen. The junkie didn't even have time to scream before the train passed over his head, popping his skull like a grape.

He'd taken a step forward, screwing up determination, when out of the corner of his eye he noticed something interesting on the tunnel wall.

It was a man-sized gate, rusting and secured with a padlock. Obviously old. Possibly antique.

By the time the third train passed, forgotten, Richard had managed to jimmy the padlock with the penknife his mother had given him on his tenth birthday.

The Money Line beyond, and its buried mysteries, was puzzle enough to keep Richard alive. He forgot terror in the enormous effort it took to turn the forgotten tunnel into a home.

He remembered to eat and to sleep. He remembered to live.

There was nothing so obvious as a locked-gate mystery to distract Richard from the enforced march. He was deeply entombed at the center of the small army, and couldn't see much past the mash of wing and claw. The path they walked was interesting only in its enduring sameness. The width and grade seemed to change little, if at all. Pebbles had turned to rocks when he'd fled uphill, but the bits of gravel on the path remained bits of gravel, entirely unremarkable.

The sun rose and set, a white orb in the black sky. The wind blew, the wind eased. There was a time for rest and sleep, food and drink, then wake and repeat. Boredom lead to terror. Terror beat like an angry moth behind Richard's eyes. He caught himself chewing through his lips to keep from howling. The taste of iron coated his tongue.

Somewhere between one step and the next blood trickled down his chin and dripped onto his shackles. Richard watched the blood fall in black beads. It rolled over the metal, spread into tiny rivulets, dripping onto gravel.

He stopped. The *sluagh* walking behind him did not. Richard was knocked sideways. He staggered, almost fell, and was plucked off his feet and steadied.

"You're bleeding," Water-Bearer said without sympathy. "From your mouth."

"Yeah." Richard turned his head and spat. The darkness in his head was retreating, chased back by the gleam of neatly turned bronze manacles. "These are manufactured," he said, turning the links over in his fingers as the Host marched on, an endless tide.

Water-Bearer looked at him sideways, single eye narrowing.

"Manufactured," Richard repeated. "Machine made. No wright made these. They're too perfect."

Water-Bearer paced at Richard's side, claws clicking on gravel. The *sluagh* seemed more interested in Richard's bloody mouth than the shackles.

"No magic, either," Richard pressed. "Look, look! Right here. The whorls, and the grooves. These are the marks of a machine. A *machine.*"

Water-Bearer had eyebrows, fine and black on its pale, misshapen face. It quirked them in humor or curiosity. "Aye?"

"Technology and the *sidhe* are enemies. Even Winter avoids it, and he was born into a manufactured world. So what's the Dread Host doing with machine-made chains? Doesn't that seem...strange...to you?"

He'd forgotten what he was talking to. Water-Bearer grinned toothily, but didn't reply. Richard shivered. He looked away from that horrible smile, clutching the chains between his fingers like a talisman.

The Prince came for Richard on an especially windy slice of time between the rise and fall of the sun. The dark *sluagh* didn't speak. He grabbed Richard by one manacled wrist and pulled him through the Host.

"Hey!"

Richard wasn't strong enough to fight, but he wasn't ready to die. He wriggled in the monster's grasp. The Prince picked him up off the ground, hauling him under one arm like a parcel.

"Stop!" Richard kicked, chains rattling. "Put me down."

He'd spent part of several days trying to count the *sluagh*, but without reliable results. Sometimes he thought the Host was comprised of no more than twenty or thirty ghouls. Other times their number seemed endless. He wasn't sure if the discrepancy was in his head, or if the count honestly changed.

The Prince carried Richard deep into the heart of the march. *Sluagh* bowed their heads and lowered their wings at his approach. The Prince ignored their obeisance, going so far as to hiss and spit when a few of the Host were slow to move out of its way.

It was only then that Richard realized the army had come to a halt. Wings continued to pulse on an unseen draft. Tentacles quivered and claws clicked, and a few of the monsters leapt into the sky, hovering overhead, but there was no longer any forward movement.

"Here."

The Prince flung Richard onto gravel. He rolled, trying to protect both his damaged hand and swollen face. When he came up onto his knees, he was almost nose to nose with the changeling.

"Aine!"

She looked as though she'd barely survived violent battle. Her golden curls were smudged with gray dust. It coated all of her diminutive figure like mortuary ash. Her clothes were torn in several places, and stained with dried blood and old *sluagh* goo. There was a burn healing on her chin and another on her throat.

He'd done that to her, he realized. Aine was marked by his decision, blackened by the explosion he'd engineered. Only her wide blue eyes remained undamaged.

She watched him as he shuffled across gravel on hand and knees.

"Richard," she said quietly. "I thought you were dead."

He sat on the ground at her side, unable to speak. Guilt closed his throat. Aine sighed quietly and laid her head in his lap like a small child in search of comfort. Richard's chains allowed him little movement, but he was able to wiggle his forearms until he could touch her cheek.

She was skinnier than was healthy, more bone and muscle than padding, and she'd been small to begin with. Where Richard touched her skin, the gray ash rubbed off in a greasy smear, showing raw pink flesh beneath.

"Are you alright?" he whispered, even though he knew it was a stupid question.

"Aye. But I'm tired. The food here makes me sick and dizzy." She frowned a little. "It thought it would be over by now."

Richard stroked her limp curls with his good hand. More greasy gray ash came off on his fingers.

"They said it's to protect me," she said, when he shuddered in disgust. "From the poison in the air. It's a salve, very similar to Mistress Gabriel's, I believe. But...foul smelling." She wrinkled her nose.

"Everything here smells foul," Richard replied.

"Doiteain domhain. Cold Fire. This land stinks of it. Little wonder the *sluagh* are half-mad. Nan says the *doiteain domhain* is a double-edged blade, best wielded with care." Aine shifted restlessly. "Even Gloriana is reluctant to employ that magic."

"Nan?" Richard echoed. He didn't like the way Aine's eyes rolled in her head. When he let go of her curls and touched her face, she felt too warm.

"Richard, I'm thirsty."

It was almost a whine and he'd never heard Aine utter a single complaint. He looked about, seeking, until he glimpsed a familiar pair of mange-riddled wings.

"Hey!"

Water-Bearer was curled in a tight ball, chin on bony knees, ugly face further wrinkled in uneasy repose, wings tented around its head. The *sluagh* didn't stir until Richard let loose with a piercing whistle.

"I think she's feverish," Richard said when that single green eye focused on him. "She needs water."

The water here makes that one ill. It was Water-Bearer's voice in Richard's head, only softer, and clearer. *She's too much of the Court still in her blood.*

Richard drew his shoulders up around his ears. He was used to Bobby's nagging in his head, and Winter's wisdom, and his mother's ghostly pleadings, but he'd long ago realized those voices were schizophrenic bits of his own self. Water-Bearer's whisper was real, something entirely not-Richard.

"Get out of my head!"

The *sluagh's* mouth twisted. It rose with a sigh, shuffling across gravel to Richard.

"Here." The ghoul unslung the water jug from its chest, offering. "Don't give her too much. We're almost home. The springs are clearer in *Reilig na Rí.*"

Aine sat upright, almost clipping Richard in the chin with her head.

"Nay," she said, shrill. "I'll not be buried again."

"Aine." Richard couldn't lift his hands to squeeze her shoulders, so he leaned hard against her spine, trying to comfort. "I won't let them hurt you." But he'd been slowly teaching himself the Gaelic, before—before.

"Cemetery?" he translated, scowling at the *sluagh.*

"Burial mound of the kings," Water-Bearer replied.

It was free of fettering chains, and able to steady Aine and help her drink. Richard tried not to notice how gently the monster wiped dripping water from Aine's mouth and how careful it was with its own wicked claws.

"Slow sips, changeling," it cautioned. "Too much and you'll be sick again."

Aine, being Aine, gulped, gagged and spat. Water-Bearer made a noise of dry amusement. Aine licked her lips, then sagged back against Richard's side, eyes closed.

"That one's in better shape than you," the *sluagh* said, looking Richard up and down. "The ointment she wears is dearly come by. We won't let her die before she's useful."

Chains kept Richard from striking the ghoul. Instead, he turned his head and spat blood. Water-Bearer only laughed.

"Don't fret, mortal. I'm beginning to see your worth, and it's not your hearts-blood I'm after. Rest, now. The river's treacherous mid-year."

"River?" Richard asked.

Water-Bearer only smiled and shrugged. It drifted away, jug merrily sloshing. Richard wanted to spit again, but his tongue had gone dry.

"Miach," Aine said into Richard's shoulder.

"What?"

"Miach One-Eye. Be careful, Richard, Miach has run with the Dread Host a very, *very* long time."

The river fell out of broken black cliffs, crashing against boulders, then roaring its way toward the now distant lake.

The path had been winding ever steeper in the last half day, so much so that Richard could feel the grade in his calf muscles. The cliffs shot up to where low hills had been. Richard thought he spotted small twists of shrub and brush growing out of the harsh slant.

"Anything that grows in this place is stunted," Aine said when Richard pointed out a spike of brown flowers bobbing halfway up a cliff face.

Richard thought she was probably right, until the Host pulled to a halt above the river, and he noticed soft green moss curling on wet boulders.

"Look," he said.

Several of the *sluagh* had left the path and had dropped, wings spread, down thirty feet to the river below. As Aine and Richard watched, they plucked at the moss, collecting it from the rocks. Richard saw Water-Bearer in amongst the others, wading in the shallows as they scavenged the plant.

"What are they doing?"

Aine frowned. She leaned against Richard, one hand on his elbow, unbothered by his chains. She was still too warm to the touch, but she'd walked without complaint and appeared to have regained some strength.

"It looks like threadwort."

"What's that?"

"Medicinal herb," Aine said, brow wrinkled. "The *aes si* burn it. The smoke is said to ease pain, and the ashes are mixed with rabbit grease to soothe burns." Self-consciously she lifted a hand to her face, rubbing at the ointment on her cheeks.

"Water-Bearer said the salve was dearly bought." Down below the *sluagh* splashed in the river, feathers and tentacle buffeted by a sudden gust of wind off the cliffs.

"Water-Bearer?" Aine asked.

Richard didn't reply.

A bridge spanned the river, constructed of rough stone blocks and more bronze chains. The Host drove Richard and Aine across it. Many of the *sluagh* crossed the ravine on dark wings, but many more shuffled, stuck to the ground as solidly as their mortal prisoners.

Their army's in bad shape, Bobby whispered.

They're dangerous, Winter cautioned.

Richard shook his head, willing the voices away. Aine looked up, a question in her eyes, but Richard turned his face away. When he did, he caught Water-Bearer watching him from three regimented rows back.

The bridge quivered at its center, rocked by wind. The waterfall roared, muffling any other sound. Aine's hand tightened on Richard's arm. Richard inhaled cautiously, but his nose wasn't wrong. The air tasted of ozone rather than poison, and the spray from the waterfall didn't sting his already singed eyelids.

The stones in the middle of the bridge were slick and wet. Richard was more interested in their shape; rough-hewn and lopsided. Hand-made, he thought, scored with a sharp blade of some sort, or equally sharp claws. The chains that bound them were a twin to Richard's own, only thicker than his arm, and coated in rust.

Still—

"Manufactured," he muttered. "It doesn't make sense."

Aine was too busy setting one foot in front of the other to notice. The bridge rocked from side to side and she staggered. Richard held her up as best he could. Spray from the river rose in visible whirlwinds, skirling over the Host, dampening their wings and ugly faces. Richard lifted his chin, enjoying the cool caress.

On the other side of the bridge the trail widened to twice its previous width, then rose at a steep incline through foothills and toward the mountain. Aine was growing short of breath. The *sluagh* didn't exactly prod her forward, but they weren't gentle with claws and wing. The army had picked up its pace until the march was almost a run. Richard looked at those blank alien faces and couldn't tell if the *sluagh* were eager or frightened.

"Piggy-back," Richard said to Aine.

The changeling blinked, uncertain and remote. She shook her curls, confused.

"On my back," Richard suggested. "Hop on my back. I'll carry you."

He'd only known Aine a short while, but he knew she was proud, and fierce, and determined. He admired the strength in her tiny body. But he was stronger, and prouder. So when she started to argue, he simply stepped in front of her and bent her knees.

"Now," he ordered. "Hands around my neck. Before they knock you over."

"They won't—"

Before Aine could finish, Water-Bearer appeared at Richard's side. The *sluagh* lifted Aine with uncanny ease, boosting her onto Richard's back. Richard's beaten body registered painful protest. He ignored the shrieking pain and straightened before Aine could protest. Her hands locked automatically onto his shoulders. Satisfied, Richard walked on.

"Thank you," he said, but Water-Bearer was gone again.

Aine laid her head in the curve of Richard's neck. Her breathing slowed and Richard thought she'd fallen asleep, even though her fingers gripped his shoulders like a lifeline. His left hand was aching in its makeshift splint, sending spikes of heat all the way up his arm. The path crept steadily upward until the sharp grade felt impossible and dangerous.

Richard counted steps to keep from crying.

Close your eyes if you like, his subconscious said in Winter's gently mocking tones, *but don't turn away. Never let your nightmares see you flinch.*

"Richard," Aine breathed in his ear, awake after all. "Look."

He'd been watching his feet to keep from falling. Dully, he lifted his head.

"Oh," he said, feeling stupid. "Is that it? The catacombs?"

They'd been climbing a mountain and Richard hadn't noticed. It was a mountain out of picture books or movies, wide and jagged at the same time; its final crooked spire appeared to balance the white sun like a golf ball on a thumbtack. Richard thought he glimpsed snow on the highest peaks.

There was an opening in the mountain one third of the way up, a cave or a gate, where the path dead-ended. The opening was black and squat and square—unnaturally so—but tall enough to swallow the front ranks of the army in twos and threes.

Richard stood still, Aine on his back, while the *sluagh* eddied about him.

"Shit," he said, with emphasis.

"Aye," Aine replied. "*Reilig na Rí.* Cemetery of the kings."

6. Crush

Summer knew that it was Barker keeping Hannah from running off. At first she couldn't figure out how it worked and supposed it was some kind of Binding Cant, the sort the First Kings had used to ensure the loyalty of the *sidhe* Court. Summer was suitably impressed, because she'd never believed any of her mama's people were still strong enough to exert that sort of power. Not after centuries of exile on mortal soil.

So maybe she caught herself making eyes at Barker again, even though she knew he wasn't likely to ever notice. He was brave and fine to look at, and a little scary, and the closest thing to a piece of the Fairy Court she had left.

Besides, pretending to fall in love with Barker was much more fun than thinking about Winter locked away in the *sluagh* world, maybe forever, probably forever. And she'd been the one who'd made it happen.

So she spent the entire drive from D.C. through Virginia staring out the window of the embarrassing minivan Brother Daniel had insisted on renting, and she wasn't watching the boring scenery ghost past. Because Barker didn't travel in cars. Barker rode a motorcycle, one of those sleek black machines with tons of chrome and a purr that rose to a growl when he really had somewhere to be.

Her papa had given Barker the motorcycle before Summer was born; she didn't remember a time without it. In her head Barker and his ride were intertwined.

Once, right before her sixth birthday, she'd decided the motorcycle was some sort of mechanical pony, and she'd wanted a ride. Mama had protested vehemently, so loudly even Papa hadn't dared challenge her.

Barker had taken her on a ride anyway, waiting until her parents were out or simply unaware. He'd even found Summer a child-sized helmet, black with pink flower decals, and he'd made her dress in her best leather boots.

"It's like flying," he whispered in her ear as he set her on the seat between the handlebars and his lap. "Only better."

The only flying six-year-old Summer had ever done was in her dreams, and she was quickly convinced that Barker's bike was much more fun. It wasn't like riding a pony at all, it was like dreaming in fast-forward.

Mama found out, of course. Barker limped for a whole two weeks after, so Summer tried not to hug him too tightly so he wouldn't bleed through his shirt.

She still thought that midnight ride through Manhattan, wind screaming over the crest of her helmet, Barker laughing into her shoulder, was the best almost-birthday present she'd ever had.

Lolo interrupted her daydream, spoiling it because he ruined everything, always.

"Man, I'd like to ride that rocket," he said. He made the words sound dirty. He leaned over Summer's shoulder to stare out the window at Barker. "Think he'd let me try?"

Summer pushed Lolo away.

"That's a *Ducati*," she said, smirking. "Barker doesn't let anyone touch it."

Lolo sighed. He shifted restlessly on the bench they shared. Then he glanced ahead at the front of the minivan and lowered his voice.

"Did you notice?"

"What?" Summer wished Lolo would shut up. She wanted to stare out the window some more and pretend they weren't already more than halfway to Yorktown.

"What Hannah's wearing."

Hannah was wearing vintage Versace pulled from Summer's closet because the fancy gown the changeling had been wearing when Winter kidnapped her was pretty much ruined by the time they'd made Manhattan, covered with burns and sweat-stains and ripped in several places. Winter didn't appreciate fashion.

"Vintage," Summer said promptly. "1990s. Christy Turlington wore that shirt and trousers. Pink's not really Hannah's color, but—"

"No, *princess,*" Lolo hissed. "On her wrist. Look familiar? Don't stare!"

Summer wasn't sure how she could pretend not to stare from three feet away. Luckily Hannah didn't look like she was paying attention to anything around her. She'd curled up in a ball on the front passenger seat, feet tucked up under her thighs, head tilted against the car window, long black hair flipped forward, concealing her face.

She'd scooted about as far away from Brother Daniel as she could get, and she was either asleep, or pretending really well.

Summer couldn't help feeling a tiny bit sorry for her. Summer knew what it was like to be the daughter of a *sidhe* queen. Hannah would never have a chance to find out.

"Win says she's a right bitch—" Lolo whispered, rolling his eyes, because he knew Summer well enough to guess what she was thinking.

"Lorenzo," Daniel cautioned quietly from behind the wheel. "Language."

Lolo groaned, then actually leaned forward, plucking at Hannah's closest sleeve, pulling it gingerly up her arm, revealing a thin wrist.

"See," he said, low-voiced. "Fairy handcuffs. Your mother doesn't miss a trick, does she?"

Hannah sighed but didn't stir. Summer blinked. Not real handcuffs like the NYPD carried, but a single thick bangle of seamless fairy amber, gleaming yellow against Hannah's pale flesh.

"Oh," Summer said.

She looked away from the yellow bangle and stared out the window, swallowing hard, because Lolo ruined everything, always.

It wasn't a Binding Cant after all, nothing so romantic as old magic and Barker's hidden talent. It was Siobahn and her vicious, clever parlor tricks, and when Summer squinted through the tinted window, she thought she could see the matching glow of amber on Barker's wrist beneath the edge of his sleeve.

Hannah didn't stir until they turned off Highway 17 and into Yorktown proper. The clock on the dashboard said twenty minutes after midnight. Lolo was snoring, knees pulled up under his chin, garish jacket balled up under his head as a pillow. His beaded braids looked even more like a bird's nest than normal. And he was starting to stink.

"Turn left," Hannah said. She had a voice like sugar, deep and mellow, dripping with Southern charm. Just like Scarlett O'Hara, Summer thought, remembering an essay she'd written in tenth-grade English. Scarlett O'Hara used her voice and her eyelashes and her Southern charm to make men do whatever she liked.

Hannah was *sidhe*. She could make mortals fall at her feet without batting a lash or saying a word. Still, Summer couldn't help be just a tiny bit jealous of that buttery accent.

"Now right," Hannah ordered. Brother Daniel complied without speaking.

Hannah hated the minivan, but not because it was ugly. Hannah hated the mini-van because she thought she was allergic to iron, thought she'd break out in hives or puke or turn into ash all because she was surrounded by steel. Summer had tried to explain to her that iron sickness only applied to the original fay, but Hannah hadn't listened.

The changeling was shivering a little in her seat as she directed Daniel through the city streets. Summer couldn't help feeling sympathetic. She rolled down her window a crack, because whenever she got motion-sick over Morris' Manhattan driving, fresh air always helped.

Yorktown air smelled like salt, like real ocean, and something else, something ancient and muggy. Trees, Summer decided, very old trees. Roots, deep in the sandy soil. And mortal history. Human bones buried under the foundations of two-hundred-year-old houses.

She could hear the ocean and wished it wasn't too dark to see the shore.

"Three more blocks down," Hannah whispered. "Pull up beneath the dogwood."

Summer didn't know what they'd do without Brother Daniel. The friar had managed to insert himself into their adventure without so much as a 'please' or 'thank you.' Even Mama hadn't kicked up a true fuss when he'd insisted on coming with them, and Winter had practically fallen on his knees in relief. Only Summer had noticed *that*.

"You'll need me," Daniel had said, and it turned out he was right, because now Winter was gone and Summer and Lolo really shouldn't drive, and Barker and Hannah flat-out refused to take a train down the coast.

Brother Daniel pulled up alongside a low green hedge, then shut off the van. Barker coasted to a stop behind them. Summer watched through her open window as the older *sidhe* hopped off his bike. He plucked off his helmet, shaking his head.

Even in the dark his wild red hair managed to catch light and shine.

"What now?" the friar asked mildly.

Hannah stretched.

"The servants will be asleep," she said, sounding oh-so-very-bored. "Willa keeps a key under a flagstone by the back stoop. We'll go in that way."

"Maybe we should just find a hotel," Summer suggested, even though she'd grown sick-to-death of cheap mattresses and heavy curtains. "We could come back in the morning."

"No. This is my house. It belonged to my mother, and now it's mine. I want to sleep in my own bed again, and shower in my own bathroom." Hannah opened the van door and slid out.

"Gloriana's her mother, not Darlene," Summer hissed. "And Winter said she practically burned this place down in a temper-tantrum."

Brother Dan only shrugged. He'd traded his robes for street togs, jeans and a t-shirt and motorcycle boots, but Summer didn't think he'd fool anyone. His street tats and gold tooth said gangsta, but the well of calm in his faded eyes said: I believe in something you can't see, and I'm alright with that.

Summer's papa had carried the same faith in his own head. Maybe that's why she liked Daniel more and more every day.

"Lorenzo," the friar said. "Wake up. We're here."

Lolo sighed and stirred. He rubbed his eyes, stretching and yawning, sweet and innocent as the puppy Summer had always wanted but was never allowed to have. Then he woke further and his attention focused. He glanced out the window, sharply observant.

"Where's here?"

"Hannah's house," Summer said. "Near the cave, remember?"

"Of course I do." Lolo unsnapped the seat belt he'd argued about wearing in the first place. "Where *is* Hannah? You haven't lost her already, have you?"

"Out," ordered Daniel. He popped open his own door, unfolding from the front seat.

"Did I miss anything?" Lolo demanded.

"No," said Summer, struggling with the van's heavy sliding door. Lolo leaned over to help. The door burst open, and they both tumbled out, falling on top of each other but managing to keep their feet.

Summer felt herself blushing, until she realized Barker hadn't even noticed their abrupt exit, and then she just felt tired.

"Wow," Lolo said. "Nice place. Gloriana set her daughter up in *style.*"

Summer turned. She saw the dogwood first, a massive tree that surely had been growing since before the exiles were banished. The tree grew up and then out, overshadowing much of the street. It was bare of leaves, its trunk thicker than Summer's ribcage.

Behind the dogwood flowed a large expanse of lawn, winter-brown. Past the lawn a mansion rose out of more manicured shrubs. The house was square with a peaked roof and multiple square windows, aglow even at the late hour. A single old-fashioned gas-lamp burned in the exact center of the lawn.

"I wonder if she knew," Summer said, out loud, although she'd meant to use her inside-the-head-voice.

"Gloriana?" Lolo scoffed. "Of course she knew. What would your mother do, if she had to give you up? Sure as shit wouldn't place you in some DumBo triplex."

"Lorenzo." Brother Dan ghosted up behind them. "Help Hannah."

"With what?" Lolo wondered. "It's not like she has luggage or anything. Winter snatched her up and whisked her away."

"Ayudarla a no tener miedo."

"Fine." Lolo stomped off in the direction of the mansion.

"What did you say?" Summer wondered.

"That Hannah's frightened," Daniel replied. "And that it's unkind to let her wander alone in the dark."

"The dark is not that child's enemy," Barker said from Summer's shoulder. "Ready, *Samhradh?*"

Summer touched the filigreed cross hanging on a chain around her throat: *Buairt*, disguised. She knew Gloriana was still far away, but the sound of waves on sand reminded her that for the *sidhe,* 'far away' was a relative term.

"Yes," she said.

Brother Dan strode ahead. The friar walked with a surety of step that made Summer wonder if Daniel, also, was familiar with the night.

The low hedge ran parallel to the street then cut back up the lawn, squaring with the mansion. Halfway between street and house the boxwood was broken by a filigreed garden gate. The gate was unlatched. Daniel slipped through. Summer followed, Barker nothing more than a familiar whisper against her arm.

On the other side of the gate, a curving flagstone path bisected a dormant herb garden, dodged a dry fountain, and rose in three wide steps to the mansion's back door. Another gas-lamp sprouted from the garden, shedding pale light over clumps of sleeping lavender and dying kale.

Brother Daniel eyed the herb garden with obvious appreciation. "Someone has a green thumb."

"Darlene was a gardener," Hannah said from the top step, her hand on the doorknob. "Before the human stole her. Dirty, smelly hobby. I never did see the point."

Summer agreed, but didn't say so out loud, mostly because Lolo was watching her knowingly.

"Shouldn't you ring the bell?" she asked instead. A lighted doorbell gleamed against the brick, and beneath it a neat little engraved plaque: RING FOR SERVICE.

"That's for the servants," Hannah said, tossing dark hair over one shoulder. "Family uses a key."

She bent gracefully and shifted a loose flagstone in the step. She used the key she found there to unlock the door and stepped over the threshold, chin held high.

"'And fair and stormy, all weather's moods'," Daniel murmured, following after.

Lolo was less pleased.

"Servants," he scoffed, disgusted, as he nudged Summer up the steps. "South of the Mason-Dixon, can't you tell? Bet this house has never heard of the Emancipation Proclamation, huh, guys?"

Neither Summer nor Barker responded. Summer thought human politics were boring. Barker, with his ebony skin and peculiar sense of justice had probably played his own small and private part in the American Civil War. But it had never really occurred to Summer that Lolo might have an opinion on anything other than television or the best way to run a con. Maybe he was finally growing up.

The back door opened into a kitchen, possibly the largest Summer had ever seen. When Hannah turned on the overhead lights, glass and silver and granite sparkled. A gigantic wooden table spread from one side of the room to the other, flanked by heavy-looking wooden chairs. A large crystal bowl filled with cut white roses graced the table's center.

The room smelled like lemon and lilac and silver polish.

"*Hijo de puta,*" Lolo muttered. "How many people live here?"

84

"It's just Grandmama and Uncle Lewis, now." Hannah stood in front of a gleaming restaurant-sized refrigerator, blatantly surveying the room. Summer had the distinct impression the changeling was looking for something. "Plus the housekeeper. I used to have a nanny and a tutor, but I scared them away."

"Burnt them to a crisp, probably," Lolo said. "Winter told us all about your tricks, so don't do anything stupid." He shifted a little, patting Winter's pistol through his coat.

Six months ago Summer would have laughed at Lolo's posturing. Now she was beginning to wonder if she'd missed something important about the human boy. She'd never thought too deeply about her brother's friends, but standing in Hannah's fancy kitchen, surrounded by fragile glass and shine, she suddenly remembered something her papa explained just after Siobahn had sent Winter away.

"Things break, *Samhradh,*" Papa had said as he wiped away her lonely tears with the tips of his fingers, "your brother needs to learn for himself that not everything is his to fix."

Now Papa was murdered and Winter was missing, and Richard had built a bomb and Lolo had shot Michael Smith right in the face, then admitted to running drugs, and maybe he wasn't growing after all, but actually revealing a broken piece of himself no one could fix.

Summer touched *Buairt* on its chain around her neck, seeking reassurance. As she did, she noticed Brother Daniel watching her from his place by the bowl of white roses.

"This way," Hannah said from the other side of the kitchen.

She took a white taper in a silver candlestick from a carved wooden sideboard and lit it with a spark from her thumb.

"Hold this," the changeling said, passing the candle to Lolo. "Grandmama doesn't believe in flashlights. The batteries all go dead."

"Does she believe in light switches? Electricity?" Lolo retorted, but he took the candlestick.

"I don't want to wake anyone. There are guest rooms upstairs. You'll sleep there and in the morning I'll show you the cave."

The last was directed at Barker, who didn't answer. Hannah glided from the room, light on her feet. Lolo followed. The taper in his hand didn't give off much light. Brother Daniel lingered at the wooden sideboard, lighting a selection of similar tapers. He didn't use a spark from his hand; he used a silver lighter from the pocket of his jeans.

"I thought you were supposed to keep her from burning us to ash," Summer grumbled in Barker's direction. "Isn't that what the bangles are for?" She stared pointedly at the amber bracelet around his wrist.

"A single spark does not an inferno make," Barker replied, mild.

"And how do you think a fire starts," Daniel asked, handing a lit taper first to Summer and then to the red-headed *sidhe*, "if not from a single spark?"

Barker scowled. Summer knew he could Gather starlight and turn the entire house to daylight, but he took the candle, cupping the flame with one hand.

"It's under control," he said.

"God willing," the friar replied.

Summer found Lolo behind a half open door on the second floor. The bedroom he'd chosen was huge, three times the size of Summer's own room in The Plaza. An overhead chandelier blazed, crystal teardrops shedding rainbows. He'd switched on the two bedside lamps and the sconces in the adjoining bathroom.

The candle in its silver stick, wick black and snuffed, sat on a roll top desk against the far wall.

Summer

Summer blew out her own candle and set it on the floor.

"Hannah said no lights."

Lolo sat cross-legged on the giant four-poster bed in the middle of the room. He had his backpack open on the coverlet and was sorting through its innards.

"Have you seen this house?" He shook his head and the beads in his hair clicked. "It's ginormous. No one will notice, especially if you close the door. 'Sides, Hannah said her grandma and uncle sleep on the top floor. And the servants—fucking sick if you ask me—have bedrooms in the basement. I need the lights to keep me awake, cuz I'm not gonna fry in my bed."

"Don't be stupid," Summer said, pretending she hadn't just voiced the same fear to Barker. "It's all under control. She can't start a fire, Barker won't let her. Besides—" To hide her nerves, she crossed the room and sat on the edge of the bed, bouncing a little on the mattress "—I thought you liked her. Hannah, I mean?"

Lolo turned his backpack upside down and shook it. Summer watched, impressed, as a variety of knickknacks fell onto the bed. Lolo was like a magpie, attracted to shiny things, and without Winter around to scold he was more likely to pick up things that didn't belong to him. Which wasn't exactly a good thing, because without *Richard* nearby and running interference, Lolo could be tagged for shoplifting.

"What makes you think that?" A Red Bull dropped onto the bed. Lolo grunted in triumph, cracked the little bottle, and sucked the drink down. "She's a crazy bitch, didn't I say so?"

He had.

"But you were being all...solicitous..." It wasn't really the right word, so Summer tried again. "Attentive. *Nice.*"

Lolo grinned, cocky. "Keep your friends close, and your enemies closer. Know who said that? Sun Tzu."

"Okay."

The bed covers were really soft. They smelled like lavender. Summer lay down on her side. Lolo selected a pillow from the mountain against the headboard, and tossed it her way.

"Sleep, if you want. It's late. I'll keep an eye out."

Summer pulled up one edge of the coverlet and snuggled under, taking the pillow with her. She nestled into the mattress and closed her eyes.

"Lolo, what do you think the cave's like?"

The mattress shifted. She thought maybe he was grabbing another pillow.

"It's a cave, Summer."

"Have you ever been in a cave?"

"No," he admitted. Then, after a silence: "It's probably dirty and cold and wet. Like the Metro, you know. But smaller. And without the trash. And without the marks—people."

Summer tried to imagine *dirty* and *cold* but couldn't. She'd never been truly cold in her life, and dirty was something she avoided.

"What about the Fairy Court?" Lolo asked a while later, just as Summer was dozing off. "What's it like?"

"Bright." Summer smiled, more asleep than awake. "Mama says it's bright. Like a star. And warm, and sweet, like lilacs in Central Park in the spring. Papa says there are bees the size of baseballs, and flowers all the colors of the rainbow, and garnets in the trees, and there's dancing in the evenings, and games, and poetry."

She could imagine it so clearly, see it on the backs of her eyelids.

She couldn't wait.

"Huh," said Lolo, incredulous. Summer thought he was going to make fun, but he didn't.

So she followed bees the size of baseballs all the way down into a deep, garnet-colored sleep.

7. Reign

Siobahn met with Carran in a street bakery just off Maiden Lane. She chose a two person table near the dirty window so she could watch the snow fall between the skyscrapers. Morris ordered hot tea and two kronuts, because the pastry reminded Siobahn of Summer. She missed her daughter and was regretting letting Summer go. Winter had long ago lost his claim to the fay Court. Summer was another matter entirely; she needed to be cossetted and kept safe.

But Siobahn, better than anyone else, knew that safety was a very changeable notion.

She nibbled at the kronut as she waited. It was flaky and too sweet on her tongue, but when she followed it with bitter tea, it made a perfect breakfast.

The bakery was busy with locals and tourists, but when Carran pushed his way out of the snow and through the door, the small space emptied out at once, because the young *sidhe* wished for privacy. Even the baker and the sales clerk ducked out into the weather, abandoning ship without a second thought.

Siobahn was impressed.

"Nicely done," she said, as Carran shed his long coat and shook damp from his hair.

Beneath his coat he wore Gucci trousers and an expensive shirt. His feet were bare and caked with mud and snow.

He shrugged slightly, wild blue eyes twinkling.

"Fay business is fay business. They'll go for a nice walk-about, and when they return, they won't recall they were ever

89

absent. Tea, is it?" He slid behind the counter. "I prefer coffee, and—ah!—look at these lovely jammy scones."

Morris, standing against the windows, radiated disapproval. Siobahn smiled into her tea.

"Do you remember, Carran," she asked, "the berry scones Gloriana served mid-spring? For days on end, the Progress stank of ascot berry, until finally she gave up that particular gluttony."

Carran shrugged again. Siobahn noted the way his shirt spread across his shoulders and decided he paid his tailor well.

"I remember the mid-spring massacres," he said. "Mortals and *sidhe* elders mowed down like so much spring grass. Gloriana sang while my mother died. But, no, I don't remember the scones."

He poured coffee into a ceramic mug, added three sugars, and used bakers' tongs to select a plump scone. Instead of rummaging for a plate, he wrapped the scone in a bit of wax paper and took it with him to Siobahn's table.

"So." He sank into the second chair. "I have little information for you so soon, I'm afraid." Setting his breakfast on the table, he dug into his pocket, retrieved a shiny new mobile phone, and slapped it next to his coffee. "It's as you say, she's contemplating treason, but that's no surprise."

"Contemplating?" Siobahn regarded the lad. "We contemplated betrayal long before we found the courage to commit. 'Contemplating' is not yet a death sentence."

Carran's smile didn't quite reach his eyes.

"She shares her secrets with the mortal cop, no others, not yet. Alice is perhaps closer to that inner sanctum yet than I."

"Alice." Siobahn recalled the petite girl in ripped fishnet stockings. "She's not one of mine."

"She's one of mine. She'll do as I ask, when I ask it. It won't be poison this time, I suppose?"

"No." Siobahn didn't like how casually the boy spoke of murder. He'd been unswervingly loyal to Malachi, and he'd played his part well thus far, managing to insinuate himself into Katherine Grey's small entourage, but she thought he hadn't yet realized how infinitely precious was a single exile's life, so long as that life could be made loyal.

If Carran hadn't come to understand that simple fact in five hundred years of forced banishment, he'd been broken to begin with.

She wished she knew how far Malachi had trusted the boy. She wished she had Barker to consult. But Barker had run off, just like Summer. And there was an empty, aching spot in her chest where Malachi used to be.

"There are other ways to put down uprising." She ordered, "For now, watch and wait."

Carran ate his pastry in quick, neat bites, with obvious relish but without lingering. He watched Siobahn all the while. His precious phone belled and beeped twelve times in the ninety seconds it took him to consume the scone, but for once he ignored it.

"Okay," he said at last, drying his fingers on his shirt. "It's your call. But I don't like the cop. He's smart and he's canny and he's watchful, and thanks to your heir, he knows more than he should about killing the folk."

"*Geimhreadh* is not my heir," Siobahn corrected, sharp, angry when the thoughts that had been circling her skull only half an hour earlier were made real by the young assassin. "My daughter will sit on the throne, when the time comes."

Carran's lips set into a thin line. Against the window Morris stirred.

"That's a mistake," the lad said, blunt. "Whatever your feelings for your son, my lady, he's next in line and well beloved."

"He's impulsive." Siobahn clutched her teacup in both hands. "And irresponsible. He poked a hole between two worlds out of hubris, let the *sluagh* run free, and risked exposing us to genocide. Or have you forgotten our history?"

"I haven't," he admitted. "The humans have always feared and hated us; it's true their iron tools tasted almost as much of our blood as Gloriana's whim has. But," he tapped the table top with long fingers, "Winter is your late husband's true get. That streak of impulsiveness seated deep within Malachi's bones. Winter palpably tried to build us a way home. A mistake, but a child's mistake, and one made very much in his father's tradition."

The tea in Siobahn's cup roiled with bubbles and steamed when before it had grown cold. Both she and the sharp-tongued lad carefully ignored the evidence of her temper.

"Malachi did not sit the throne. *I* do. Best for you if you keep that firmly in mind, Carran Kin-Killer."

He didn't flinch. Siobahn gave him credit for bravery.

"I am always loyal to the bloodline, my lady," he replied, bowing his head over his own tea. Dun locks flopped over his pale face, hiding his expression, but his words rang true.

"Swear it," she said. "I want to hear it off your tongue."

"Saol fada chugat," he pledged quietly, lifting his chin. "I have served your family since birth. *I gcónaí is go deo."*

Siobahn nodded. "Go, then. Keep watch and wait."

Carran pushed back his chair and rose, finishing his tea in one deep swallow. Siobahn liked the way his body moved, an economy of muscle. She thought that, if she had been younger and less wise, she might have kept him at her side for beauty's sake.

He pocketed his phone, bowed once to Siobahn and once, perhaps ironically, to Morris. Then he padded barefoot out into the snow. Almost as soon as he stepped through the door, the bakery began to once more fill with mortals.

Siobahn stood as well, tilting her head at Morris. He followed her out the door, two exact paces behind. She wondered who he thought would dare threaten her in daylight, on the street. Michael Smith was dead and gone, and there was no reason to believe Gloriana had sent another in his place. Still, Morris fairly bristled with nerves.

"You're worse than the Kin-Killer," she said over her shoulder. The snow came down in waves, coating her hair and cooling her cheeks. The cold, sharp smell reminded her of home, and she sighed. "Katherine isn't a complete fool, nor fully mad, not yet."

"Kin-Killer," Morris repeated. "Do you hear yourself, m'lady? You've given that young pup a title and a purpose all in one breath."

Siobahn only smiled. Inhaling snow, she increased her pace. Mortals parted before her like butter before a hot knife.

"Come," she said.

"Where?" he asked, falling into step.

"Hunting," Siobahn promised, and smiled wider.

Siobahn walked up Fifth Avenue. The snowfall grew heavier, coating her wrap and turning her dark hair to wet tendrils. Three months earlier the damp would have been an irritant. She'd have spoken a simple warming Cant, as Morris had already, and kept the snow away. Three months earlier she wouldn't have noticed the way the ice on her flesh matched the chill at her core.

"My lady," Morris asked. "Where are we headed?"

"The carousel."

Morris chewed her answer over for two blocks before he spoke again.

"It's likely closed, my lady. In this weather. Begging your pardon."

Siobahn tried not to grimace. Morris was so very, very proper. And always so deeply concerned. About everything.

"I don't plan to ride it." Siobahn paused in a doorway to set a gold *sidhe* coin in the hat of a scrawny beggar. The beggar met her smile, lidless eyes the color of spoiled milk.

"I'm looking for Nightingale," she said.

"It's been decades since *that* roamed about the carousel," Morris protested. "Himself chased it away in the 80s."

The beggar plucked the coin from his hat and secreted it away under his coat. Siobahn strode on. Morris increased his pace to walk at her side. The weather was cowing mortals, the sidewalks beginning to empty out as tourists took shelter in tiny shops and office laborers returned to work.

"My lady," Morris said. "That one hasn't been sighted for so long Himself hoped it dead or moved on."

"My husband occasionally made mistakes," Siobahn answered. "That creature is never far from the seat of my power. It hasn't permission to die or the strength of will to move on."

Morris made a low noise of disbelief, but didn't dare speak his doubts out loud.

At 60th Street, Siobahn turned into Central Park. Snow covered the grass, making the paths slippery. Skeletal trees lined the walk, furred with frost. Siobahn set her hand on Morris's arm because he expected it. In truth she was as sure-footed as a cat and he knew it.

It was only a game the exiles played, an attempt to camouflage what they were and appear more human. Siobahn had been performing the charade for so long she sometimes almost forgot what it meant to be *sidhe*.

"My lady," Morris murmured, patting her fingers with one white-gloved hand. "We're being stalked."

Siobahn showed her teeth. She nodded. "It appears we're not the only hunters about in this weather, Morris."

Summer

They crossed Gapstow Bridge in perfect step, age-old companions promenading where so many had before. Siobahn ran her bare hand over the blocks of stone along the bridge's low wall. Snow crystals dusted her fingertips. She flicked the crystals away like so much fairy dust.

When they reached the other side of the bridge a man detached himself from beneath a skeletal sycamore and joined the promenade. The tip of a half-smoked cigarette glowed red between his first and second fingers.

"Disgusting habit, tobacco," Siobahn said. "I confined Summer to her room for an entire month after I caught her stinking of cigarette smoke."

"Seems a bit harsh, but I agree they're the devil's own habit." Bran Healy replied. "I quit years ago."

Siobahn gave the cigarette in his hand a pointed look. Bran shrugged. He took a long drag, then dropped the butt in the snow and left it to smoke away.

"Settles my nerves," he confessed. "I've needed that lately."

Morris grunted. Siobahn stopped. She looked the ex-cop up and down, from the tip of his battered running shoes, up the faded jeans and cheap sport coat, over gray stubble, and across that long line of stitches on his face. The scar would run from the corner of his right eye all the way to the back of his skull. More stubble was growing up around the incision, but it was growing in as white as the falling snow.

"Yes," Siobahn said, regarding that newborn white streak, "you've had quite a time of it, Detective Healy. Headaches?"

"Some." He looked uncomfortable .

"Katherine can banish the pain completely, you know. She has very powerful healing magics."

"I prefer the more usual cures." He smiled. "Advil, a glass of good whiskey."

Siobahn started walking again. She could see the brick roof of the Carousel in the distance. There was no sound of music. Morris was correct; the ride was closed due to weather.

"What do you want?" Siobahn asked.

"Winter," the human replied, blunt. "Katherine's quite visibly distressed—I'd say frightened, if I hadn't been reliably informed nothing frightens the *sidhe*—but she won't talk to me about it. Just says it's not my concern."

"It's not."

"You're wrong. You made it my concern, ten years ago, when you had me transferred to D.C. just so I could keep an eye on your son."

"A job. Nothing more. I paid you handsomely."

"Winter's a good kid," Bran continued as if he hadn't heard. "He's saved my badge more than a few times and my life at least twice. I watched him grow up, and he grew up fine, thanks to Gabby."

Low hills lined either side of the path and low evergreen brush. The carousel building grew up out of the ground, arches dark, striped brick slick with frost. Siobahn could just make out the carousel itself behind locked gates, carved horses and lions and fantastical creatures motionless.

"Has Katherine told you tales of Nightingale, Detective Healy?"

"No, what's that?" He stuck his hands into the front pockets of his coat, probably to keep his fingers from twitching, and slouched along at Siobahn's side. Morris drifted three steps behind, watchful. "Not another magical sword, I hope."

Siobahn smiled politely. "Believe it or not, enchanted weaponry is a rare thing, even at Court. By all logic, *Buairt* should never have been our problem."

"Right," Bran said, obviously unconvinced. "What's a Nightingale? Other than the obvious, anyway."

Summer

They crested a low hill and looked down on the sleeping carousel. A layer of snow glittered on the roof and on the low evergreen bushes against the building's foundation. Several benches sat nearby, dripping icicles. An empty can of Diet Coke rolled by, clattering along the concrete path, chased by a wind Siobahn didn't feel.

"Goddamned slobs," Bran muttered, "whatever happened to 'Clean and Green?' There's a fucking recycling bin on every corner."

He stepped forward, apparently meaning to rescue Central Park from a single aluminum can, but Siobahn stopped him, slapping her hand against his chest, holding him in place. She watched the Coke can as it reversed directions, bouncing back in front of the carousel, leaving a track in the accumulated snow.

"Wait," she said. "Katherine needs to stay out of my business, Detective Healy. Winter is my business; the tasks I set him are also *my business*, and none of her concern. If she is, as you say, 'distressed' over my children's safety, she should have offered her aid when I asked it. It's not an easy journey I've sent them on. Like as not they'll be hunted the very moment they set food in Cornwallis Cave. In fact"—Siobahn wouldn't let the words stick in her throat—"as it's very likely I've sent the last of my blood to their deaths, I'll admit I find Katherine Grey's 'distress' both laughable and insulting. What does she know of sacrifice?"

The human visibly flinched. "I don't think you understand. What I meant to say," he paused, distracted, squinting down at the dancing Coke can, "is that—"

"Music, yes." Siobahn grinned through her teeth. "Or poetry. It's always been irrationally fond of its own voice."

"Voice?" Bran protested. "That's an aluminum can."

Only it wasn't, of course it wasn't. It was an instrument, as was the unnatural wind skirling in small gusts at the foot of the

97

carousel. The wind tossed the can against brick and concrete, frozen dirt and dead grass. A rhythm emerged, at first dull and thin, but quickly deepening in tone and intensity until Siobahn could hear a veritable chorus of unearthly voices in the aluminum can's clatter.

"Clever," Siobahn agreed. "It was always clever, until it got caught in the politics of our kind and was forced to make a choice of queens. Come, Detective Healy. Katherine will never forgive you if you miss this. Morris?"

"Ready, my lady," Morris answered in that distant, sleepy tone that meant he was preparing defensive magics. "Step cautiously."

Bran drew a pistol from beneath his coat. Siobahn might have scoffed, but she supposed the gun was one of Winter's modified toys, which meant it was possible the weapon wasn't entirely useless.

"Dangerous?" he asked briefly, sighting the dancing can.

Siobahn didn't laugh.

"More likely than not," she replied, and started down the hill to the carousel, Nightingale's odd symphony rising in the unnatural wind.

8. Infection

There were no guards at the entrance into the mountain, only a gaping hole half-again as tall as Richard and wide enough to allow a pair of *sluagh* to pass without scraping folded wings.

"What point security?" Water-Bearer murmured. The one-eyed *sluagh* was beginning to make a habit of answering Richard's questions before he spoke them. "We are the only inmates in this prison."

The passage into *Reilig na Rí* was narrow enough that the Host was forced to walk single file. Richard, trapped somewhere in the middle of the living worm, could see nothing but feathers ahead and hear nothing but the susurrus of labored breathing behind. If he walked close to the wall and stuck his good hand out as far as possible against the manacles, he could brush the tunnel wall with the tips of his fingers. The stone was rough and scored with many shallow hollows, as though it had been scraped with multiple spoons.

Every twenty steps a single patch of cold blue light gleamed in the ceiling. Richard recognized the light for what it was; Gathered starlight, but static and sickly, trapped in the stone. The dim light cast thin illumination: just enough to see by, more than enough to cast strange, misshapen shadows against the wall and ceiling.

"Bones," Aine murmured into Richard's ear. She trembled against his spine, frightened or chilled. "Look, in the walls."

He'd seen the bits of skeleton from the very beginning; long finger bones pressed into the stone, a single femur half-absorbed by the ceiling, a fan of what must be the bones of an entire wing, the puzzle of bones and joints reminding Richard of the dinosaur fossils he'd once studied at the Met.

"*Sluagh* bones." Richard's mouth was bleeding again. He had to spit twice to clear the words on his tongue. "What killed them?"

Aine didn't answer. Richard glanced over his shoulder, looking for Water-Bearer, but it had disappeared again into the press of wings. The *sluagh* behind Richard grunted and shoved, jarring Richard's arm. Pain burst in stars behind his eyes, and he staggered, chains rattling, but managed to stay upright.

He counted steps, breathing shallowly, until agony retreated to a bearable red throb.

"Richard," Aine said, small-voiced and frightened. "I don't want to be alone. Don't let them put me in the wall again."

Richard remembered Aine crucified against the Metro tunnel wall, ensnared by stone and spell. He remembered Winter cutting her free, slicing flesh and hair, spilling blood on the tracks.

"Don't worry," Richard promised. "I won't let them hurt you."

Aine laughed. Her breath was soft and warm against his cheek. Richard shivered in surprise and then, incredibly, felt himself blushing.

"Aye, well, I'm not asking for a miracle," the changeling said. "Only a promise. Don't let them put my body in the wall, after."

Richard knew it was a promise he probably couldn't keep. He hated making promises at the best of times. There was no such thing as certainty in life, and Richard wanted no part of pretty subterfuge.

Doesn't matter, said his subconscious in Winter's voice, *tell the lie.*

"They won't put you in the wall," he said to Aine and Winter both, "I promise."

"Thank you," Aine said, and sighed out relief.

Richard exhaled slowly in echo, briefly grateful for those small, shiny parts of him that had been burnt clean by Winter's friendship.

The tunnel rose straight into the mountain. Richard didn't have Lolo's knack for timekeeping and he'd retreated into that half-aware state where pain and fear were less sharp, so when the passageway suddenly widened and spat the Host into a large, bright chamber, making Richard gasp and blink, he wasn't entirely sure how much time had passed since they'd marched into *Reilig na Rí*.

He thought it must not have been long, because Aine was still safely on his back, and although she was small and light, he knew it was doubtful he'd managed to carry her far.

"This way," Water-Bearer said, appearing at Richard's side. "Come. You can sit and rest."

The cave was oval, shaped like an egg. As the Host spread out, thinning, Richard realized the space was far more than large; it was gigantic. A white fire blazed high in the center, stretching from a circular pit in the floor, disappearing toward the distant ceiling, shedding light and warmth in great pulsating waves. The white flame flickered but made no sound.

"Here." Water-Bearer led Richard ten feet along the curve of the wall. "There. Rest there."

'There' was a niche in the wall, a *sluagh*-sized shelf cut into the stone. Richard grunted, easing Aine from his shoulders. The girl half-crawled, half-climbed onto the floor, stretching on the ground with a sigh of relief.

"It's warm," she said, wonderingly. "Warm but smooth as ice."

Richard sank down against the wall, which was equally warm and satin-smooth. He lay on his side, face turned to the white pyre, and concentrated on breathing. The air in the chamber was sweet, oxygen-rich. The radiating heat off the ground and walls lulled his aching bones and eased Richard toward a half-sleep. He dozed restlessly, but the sharp slashes of pain from his hand and the two forbidding *sluagh* very obviously standing guard to either side of their niche kept him from falling completely under.

Water-Bearer sat alongside Richard's head, wrapping itself in black feathers.

"Watch," it murmured, too low for any but Richard to hear. "Watch, mortal. Your life may depend on it."

Richard was resigned to the fact that his life was a shortened line, worth very little in the grand scheme of things. Still, he shifted and sat up, groaning as his hand protested. It felt as though he'd had a hot knife shoved all the way from the tip of his middle finger to his elbow. He had to swallow hard to keep his stomach from rebelling but at least the agony chased the last of the fog from his brain.

"Infection," Water-Bearer pronounced wisely. "You'll have to lose the hand, I think."

"Shut up," Richard hissed out of the corner of his mouth. Cold sweat trickled across his face. He wasn't worried about his hand. He didn't expect to live long enough for it to matter.

"And if you succumb," Water-Bearer asked, watching Richard out of its one eye. "Who will care for the *siofra?* Pay attention."

Richard tried. The first thing he noticed was the precise shape of the room, an almost perfect egg-curve in all three planes, from the curvature in the walls to the matching concavity on the floor and likely on the vanishing ceiling. The niches in the wall were much smaller, matching ovals, but half-an-egg instead of whole.

"Machine-made." He ran his unbroken fingers over the smooth-as-glass-floor, baffled. "Machine-cut, it must be. Impossible."

"Nothing is impossible," Water-Bearer corrected. "Although in this case you are incorrect. The chamber was carved from the mountain by a very powerful magic, when the Host was still strong enough to work such spells. What else?"

"The white flame warms but doesn't burn," Richard deduced. Most of the *sluagh* had arranged themselves around the white pyre, close enough to the flame that their feathers and tentacles rustled in an invisible vortex. Several of the monsters appeared to be standing half in and half out of the column. It was impossible to tell, but Richard thought those deformed faces wore expressions of pure pleasure.

"It calls to us," Water-Bearer agreed. "Warms old, frozen bones, and recalls us to easier times, before war, before betrayal. Recalls us to hope. We rarely venture far from the center now, not for centuries."

Richard meant to say something scathing about the one-eyed ghoul's sudden chattiness, but his attention was caught by the Prince. The tall *sluagh* stood alone on one curve of the white column, ebony wings held high, shoulders curved forward in longing or anticipation. His monstrous face was lifted and the reflection of fire gleamed inhumanly in his eyes.

"Oh," Richard said, because he'd seen that very same pose before, but on Winter, in front of a much darker, much smaller patch of magic. *Longing*, Richard realized, or *regret*. "It's a portal. A Gate."

"Through which the Wild Host entire was exiled, yes. That is the lingering flame of *Tir na Nog*, which we believed was lost to us until now." One eye rolled in Aine's direction, poignant and pointed, while the cluster of tentacles in the empty socket writhed and curled into small knots. "Some of her blood will go into the

Gate itself, of course, to waken the old magic. The rest shared out between us who remain. The blood spells won't be easy for her and it won't be quick. He'll keep her alive as long as possible, and with the Mending in her veins, that might be a very long time indeed." Water-Bearer showed its pale tongue, amending: "Long enough to send us all through, I imagine."

Richard stared again at the Prince and hated himself for seeing any resemblance to Winter. Winter would never sacrifice an innocent for his own sake, not even if it meant a way home, not even to save his family. Winter wasn't a monster. Winter was good. The lodestone of Winter's goodness kept Richard safe.

Water-Bearer tilted its head, bird-like, *sidhe*-like, Winter-like.

Richard closed his eyes and pressed his uninjured fist to the bridge of his nose. The shackles ground against his wrist bone.

"You're missing the most important observation," Water-Bearer said.

"Why don't you just be quiet and let me be?"

"I have my reasons." The *sluagh* swept out one wing, smacking Richard on his good shoulder, rough but not necessarily unkind, not very differently than how Richard sometimes swatted at a particularly tenacious sewer rat. "Aye, you're canny enough for a mortal, and lucky. But I won't hand it to you on a golden platter. You're not Gloriana, damn her lovely head, and it's not *fidchell* we're playing."

Aine knew how to play *fidchell*, Richard remembered. She'd played the game of chance against the Fay Queen and purposefully lost.

"Purposefully lost," Richard whispered. He opened his eyes.

"Ahh," Water-Bearer hummed. "I could almost come to like you, apostate. Very good."

It took Richard at least three minutes of silence, seconds counted by the throb in his hand. Water-Bearer seemed willing to give him the three minutes but no longer.

"Well?" the monster demanded.

"Are they asleep?" Richard asked, puzzled. Almost every malformed *sluagh* face seemed turned toward the fire, contemplative, basking, worshipping. Even the Prince seemed lost, drawn to the white flame like an overgrown, over-used moth cliché.

The *sluagh* guards were turned half away from Richard, paying him no real attention. The white flames cast shadows in their eyes.

"They're looking away," Aine whispered, startling Richard. He'd assumed she was asleep or passed out. "Richard, they're all looking *away*. Use your knack!"

Richard shook his head, remembering his escape up the alien hill, through unforgiving rock. "Aine, it won't work, they'll hunt us down, by smell. They can smell us."

"Not if I prevent it."

Richard blinked. Water-Bearer flashed its shit-eating grin.

"Go," it said. "Use your 'knack' and go quickly. There's a tunnel on the east wall. It runs further into the catacombs. Carry the girl and go. I'll catch up when I can."

"But—"

"Hurry!" Water-Bearer's grin became even less pleasant. "You're wasting a brilliant and fleeting gift, mortal: Miach One-Eye's goodwill."

"Richard!" Aine reached a hand from the niche, tugged on his torn sleeve. "Please."

Richard shook his head, because he knew it wouldn't work, but he knew not trying would be just another unforgivable thing, so he took a long breath and made the universe think he was never born.

Richard first managed his knack when he was five, on a lovely spring Saturday afternoon when it seemed like most of the world was happy, but Bobby Lorimer was never like most of the world and Richard was scared.

Most of East Riverside was celebrating the warmer weather by sharing front stoops and Coors Lights and over-cooked bratwursts. The old lady in 2275 had Billy Joel on a CD player faced out the window, 'Captain Jack' set on repeat. Nobody complained, because the song was a classic in anybody's books, and also because the old lady's son was a cop, so everybody, even Bobby, tried to stay on her good side.

Richard could hear 'Captain Jack' all the way in the backyard of 2272, where he cowered under the branches of an early blooming shrub, trying to stay out of reach of Bobby's wheels and hands. Bobby was stoned and pissed as hell, because Richard had tripped coming out of the back door and spilled bratwursts and slices of cheese into the dirt, and now Bobby's barbecue was ruined.

The propane Weber Bobby had ordered from Home Depot was so hot Richard could see waves of heat coming off the grill. Bobby kept trying to ram his wheelchair into the shrub, but the shrub kept swatting back, which only made Bobby angrier.

Even at five years old, Richard knew there was no possible way the afternoon would end well. He wished Mama would come home, because at least Mama knew the right things to say to keep Bobby from going off his head and seeing invisible monsters, but Mama was home less and less often recently and Richard was learning not to depend on her rescue.

"Ricky," Bobby screamed, spitting foam. "Come out and take your punishment like a soldier! Come out and take your whupping like a *man*."

Bobby hadn't been a soldier for a long time. Richard knew soldiers, he'd seen parades on television and once in person on the Fourth of July. The soldiers walking down Constitution Avenue were tall and brave and heroic in their fancy clothes and polished shoes.

Richard knew Bobby had never been heroic or brave.

"Goddammit, Ricky! Get your ass *out!*" Bobby shouted, knuckles white on his rims, while Billy Joel sang about tie-dye jeans. The barbecue made an angry hissing noise and Richard twitched, and that was a mistake, because then Bobby managed to get his fingers around Richard's arm.

"Fuck, boy." Richard squirmed, but even without legs Bobby was super-strong, maybe because of the pills. He dragged Richard up out of the shrub and onto his bony lap, locking his other hand on Richard's shoulder, shaking.

"Sorry, sorry," Richard tried, because it was the best word he knew, and one Mama used a lot. "Sorry about the hot dogs. Sorry, sorry."

But Bobby had forgotten all about the bratwurst and slices of expensive cheese. Bobby was angry because Richard had tried to hide. Bobby wasn't brave but he hated cowards.

Richard struggled. Bobby pinned Richard facedown across his stubbed knees, holding him with one hand, wheeling the chair about with the other. Dirt flew up from under his wheels, striking Richard's face. Richard stopped struggling and lay very still, because Bobby was steering toward the barbecue and the air above the grill wavered like water in a bathtub.

Bobby was quiet but for the deep heaves of breath into his barrel chest. When he had his chair against the barbecue, he set the brakes, then hoisted Richard upright until their knees were pressing together and Richard was kneeling on his lap.

"Don't scream, Ricky," Bobby said, almost a plea. "Don't scream, soldiers don't scream."

He bent Richard over the Weber, stuck Richard's face into that wobbly magic air, then lower. Richard screamed. Not because the air was hot enough to burn but because he knew Bobby wouldn't be satisfied until Richard and the barbecue had kissed.

Richard's screams silenced Billy Joel. Bobby swore but his grip on Richard's head.

"What did I say, Ricky? What did I say? I warned you!"

Richard fought but he was only a kid and not very strong. Mama said he was small for his age. He closed his eyes and prayed Mama would come before Bobby cooked his face, and then as waves of heat made his nostrils sting, he bit his lip so very hard and wished he'd never ever been born.

He wished so hard he managed to convince the universe that it was true.

"Faster," Richard said, fighting annoyance. He had his good arm wrapped around Aine's waist, which meant he was bent over and awkward in a tangle of girl and chains and logically he knew there was no possible way they could move more quickly than a snail-paced limp.

But if Aine and Water-Bearer were going to insist Richard perform tricks he generally reserved for Winter, he thought they should at least try to make an effort.

Aine nodded without speaking and tried to hobble more quickly but all she really managed was a drunken stagger. Richard realized with an equally dizzying lurch that she was nearer collapse than he'd supposed.

He hoisted her into his arms, which made his broken hand scream, but in all actuality made it easier to manage his confining chains.

"Sorry," Aine said into Richard's shoulder, breathing shallowly. "Is it working?"

Richard didn't bother reply. His knack always worked. The difficulty wasn't the sneaking away; the difficulty began when someone eventually noticed he'd disappeared and gave chase.

He hoped they'd chosen the right tunnel. He squashed another surge of irritation. He didn't like feeling cut adrift, unmoored. He liked perfect order in his life and worked best when the rules of engagement were familiar. He'd had that comfortable routine beneath the Metro, understood what was required of him, and welcomed the sameness of days and nights under Winter's protection.

"This way." Water-Bearer rolled up from behind without warning, mangy wings spread and beating. It was only then Richard realized how very wide the tunnel was, and when the *sluagh* held aloft a sickly Gathering of starlight, Richard was astonished to see right angles and perfect planes.

"The original Cants have long since disintegrated down here," Water-Bearer said. "This will have to do for light."

"Down?" Richard echoed, dismayed. "Down is not *out*."

"Out is not an option, not yet. Give me the changeling."

Richard stumbled, clutching Aine tight against his chest. "Shove off."

"Oh, aye, very nice. If I planned to eat the child, I'd have done so days ago. Your stubbornness will slow us down. Take the light."

Water-Bearer was strong and agile. It plucked Aine from Richard's grasp and held the girl cradled against one wing. Aine didn't stir. Her head lolled on her neck.

"The light," Water-Bearer hissed. Richard cupped his good hand and the Gathered starlight dripped like molten water onto his palm, then coalesced and spread, growing yellow and bright, hovering like an army of lightning bugs just above Richard's spread fingers.

The beat in Water-Bearer's wings briefly lost tempo.

"Interesting," it said. "You're full of delightful surprises, apostate."

"Richard. My name is Richard."

The *sluagh* didn't answer. Water-Bearer's broken stride covered more ground than Richard had expected. He forced himself to keep up, even though his body was a mass of small pains and larger agonies.

Don't scream, Bobby warned. *Man up, Ricky. Soldiers don't scream, even when they're dying.*

"Shut up," Richard snarled. "Shut up, shut up."

"Richard," Water-Bearer said, rolling the name into a lilt, "pay attention. I can't see the turn if you don't hold out the light. Can you do that?"

The shackles and the voices in Richard's head made the simple task a herculean effort, but he managed. When Richard began to weave because his feet wouldn't go quite where he wanted, Water-Bearer wrapped a wing about his shoulders, supporting him. The feathers tickled, stinking of damp and musk, and Richard should have been horrified. Instead he was grateful.

Then there were stairs, sharp-edged and slippery. Richard started the descent upright, but soon he was on his hand and knees, crawling backwards, chains rattling, and the light he'd been tending had gone out. The world was near black, he'd lost the guiding feathers—and more importantly, Aine—and the stairwell descended steeply down. He slipped and slid, wriggling in the dark like a rat.

Water-Bearer hauled him upright.

"Nearly there," the *sluagh* promised, but Richard was beyond caring.

New light, soft light, red and orange and flickering in a hearth. Richard lay on rough blankets alongside the coals, neither awake nor asleep. Pain was gone, as well as hunger and thirst. He tried to sit up but couldn't find the strength needed to move. He thought he'd been dreaming of Bobby and realized why when he smelled tobacco smoke; cigarette smoke.

"Careful." A shadow squatted between Richard and the hearth. "You shouldn't be moving much, not yet. Here." Hands propped Richard up. "Drink."

The edge of a cup pressed against Richard's mouth. He swallowed the cold liquid automatically. It soothed a throat he hadn't realized was dry, tasting of metal and herbs and faintly of dirt.

Richard swallowed down the entire cup then licked his lips.

"Aine?" His voice sounded rusty in his ears and his tongue felt thick. He wondered how long he'd been out. He wondered at the fuzzy feeling in his head and at the liquid warmth spreading through his bones.

"Gently, now. You're hand's in a bad way and the shackles aren't helping. Swallow more of the *draiochta*, and I'll see about the chains."

It was difficult to keep his eyes open. Richard shook his head, knocking away the proffered cup, causing liquid to splash.

"I need to see Aine."

"The *aes si* is tending your friend. Best leave them to it for the moment." Richard heard the distinct and familiar scratch of a match. Blue flame danced through the air, then caught in the wick of what appeared to be an ordinary hurricane lamp. "I need a closer look at the locks and we'd best not wait until the sun is up. They'll not dare come this way quite yet, the Tattered Cavalry, but I'm afraid your fever's rising more rapidly than I'd like."

Richard blinked slowly, once, then again. If there was fever in his bones, it must be the fever confusing reality, because the small man regarding him in the lamplight was most definitely human, bristly-cheeked and hook-nosed, long black hair tied off his forehead and braided through with colorful bits of rags.

A smoldering cigarette dangled from the corner of the man's mouth, wobbling when his lips curled into a smirk.

"Hello, Richard," the man said, and when he plucked the cigarette from his mouth it was with gleaming metal fingers wrapped outside-in with strange, fleshy bits of wire and gristle-gear, clockwork hand clothed in parchment-thin, *sidhe*-white skin, alien and see-through. "I'm William. Welcome to my smithy."

9. Cornwallis

Lolo woke Summer with a vicious poke.

"Come on," he hissed. "The sun's up."

Summer groaned. She rolled onto her stomach, burying her face in lavender-scented pillows.

"Go away."

"Come *on.*" Lolo grabbed an edge of the coverlet and yanked hard. The blanket fell away, taking with it warmth and comfort. "They're moving around downstairs. I want to see what's up."

Summer managed to leave the comfort of her pillow. She propped herself on an elbow, blinking past weak sunlight at Lolo.

"What time is it?"

Lolo glanced ceiling-ward, as if taking note of the eerie invisible clock in his head.

"6:17. AM. Few seconds past that."

"Shit," Summer sighed, ignoring Lolo's disapproving stare. She didn't swear often, because she didn't see the point when there were more subtle ways to make displeasure known. But 6 AM was a horrible time, especially when she was pretty sure it had been past midnight when they'd snuck through the silent house, candles flickering on polished silver.

Five hours of sleep just wouldn't cut it, she decided, glowering at Lolo. He'd tied his braids up into a single ponytail and looked all fresh-faced and alert, even if he did stink. He already had his backpack over one shoulder. She wanted to hate him for his enthusiasm.

113

"They've started without us," he complained, sliding off the mattress. He practically hopped in place, impatient. "They always start without us. Hurry up."

"What's the big deal?" Summer sat up all the way, rubbing at her eyes. She wanted a shower and her mouth felt like it had been swabbed with vinegar.

She'd been dreaming, she remembered. About bumblebees and treasure, flowers as tall as Papa, and sky the color of blood. In her dream, someone had been yelling about cracks in the earth. Winter, maybe, or Papa, standing beneath the flowers.

"Oh." She reached up, briefly clasped *Buairt* where it hung around her neck in the form of a delicate cross because Barker refused to carry it on his back. "What's the hurry? It's barely light out," she complained. "Can't we have breakfast and a wash first? Go down and see while I...wake up."

Lolo only reached out, grabbing her by the wrist, tugging. "You're coming. I'm not leaving you alone with the creeptastic chandelier. Hurry, will you? I smell coffee!"

Summer groaned and rolled out of bed. Her shirt felt clammy and stale against her skin, and her jeans were sticky. She'd slept in her shoes, and she'd sweated under the coverlet.

"Gross," she sighed, then noticed the scattering of Red Bull cans on the floor. "Did you sleep at all?"

"No." Lolo pulled Summer into the hall. "I said I'd keep look-out, didn't I? Besides, I had some shit to think over."

Summer didn't really want to know what sort of 'shit' would keep her brother's twelve-year-old street con up at night. Then she remembered he'd shot a madman straight in the face, and couldn't help but shiver. She yanked her wrist from his hand, ignoring his puzzled stare.

"There'd better be breakfast," she sulked, ignoring the twinge of guilt guttering behind her ribs. "I'm not going spelunking without breakfast."

"I believe Cornwallis Cave is quite shallow," Brother Dan said from the top of the stairs. Summer figured the friar had been on his way to rouse them out of bed. "No spelunking necessary."

"Still need breakfast," Summer gritted. She pushed past Lolo and Daniel, clattering down the stairs, following the scent of coffee past sun-warmed antiques and into the spacious kitchen.

She paused in the doorway, stupidly shy. She hadn't expected anyone but the usual crew, which was sort of dumb, seeing how Hannah had mentioned a grandmother and uncle. She guessed it was the grandmother seated in one of the heavy chairs against the long table, morning light throwing rainbows off the cut glass flower bowl and across her clawed fingers.

It was those crooked fingers that threw Summer, making her hesitate. *Sidhe* didn't age like humans, didn't twist or shrink or grow infirm. Barker was older than the oldest man-placed stone in Manhattan, but looked barely grown where he stood strong and healthy against the steel Viking oven, stirring eggs on the stovetop.

Sidhe died by curse or sword point. The ebb and flow of mortal time was something Summer preferred to ignore, especially as she heard Lolo thumping down the stairs with all the grace of a hungry puppy.

He'll age, Summer thought, struck by a shiver, *twist and shrink and fail, and I'll have to watch it happen.*

The woman looked up and caught Summer's stare. Mama would have called Summer out on her bad manners, but the woman only smiled sadly and shook her head.

"Come in," she said. "You must be Summer Murray. Hannah, please pass Ms. Murray a plate. She looks hungry."

To Summer's surprise Hannah rose without protest from where she'd been sitting across the table and passed Summer a blue-and-white-flowered china plate. Fairy amber gleamed around her wrist. Hanna glanced from Summer to the bracelet and back again, then showed pointed teeth in a soundless snarl.

"You can call her Summer." Lolo interrupted, slipping past Summer and into the room, bouncing a little on the toes of his shoes. He set his pack on the table. "Everybody does. Murray's just a made-up last name, anyway. You know, so they'd fit in."

"Malachi took the surname two hundred years ago for business purposes," corrected Barker without turning from the stove. "It's as legitimate as your own."

Summer bit back a startled laugh. Lolo had a last name, she supposed, but she doubted even Winter knew what it was.

"If I'm to call you Summer, you will call me Willa." The woman rose from the table. She had smooth dark hair, tied neatly into a bun. Her face was surprisingly youthful and unlined, but there was a sadness in her blue eyes that made Summer want to reassure her that everything would be alright.

Which was silly, because from what Winter had told them, Willa Francis' life would never be alright again.

"You're forgive me if we don't shake hands." Willa's smile softened. "The arthritis is particularly bad in the mornings before my medication has a chance to kick in. Would you like some eggs, dear? Your friend Barker has cooked up enough to feed an army."

"Too bad we don't have an actual army," Lolo snorted. He grabbed a plate from the table, shoving it at Barker. "I'm starving. You're shitting me," he made a face at a bubbling urn of coffee, "it's the fountain of fucking youth."

"Lorenzo!" Brother Dan snapped. "Language!"

Lolo rolled his shoulders, then sighed and peeked hopefully across the room at Willa. "May I please have a mug for the coffee, ma'am?"

Summer saw real amusement touch the woman's expression.

"Cupboard to the left," she directed. "Milk and sugar in the refrigerator. Hannah, show him, please."

Once again Hannah rose from the table. Summer wondered if Barker was walking the girl about with the bracelet like some sort of zombie on an invisible leash, but Barker seemed engrossed in his eggs, unaware.

When she edged up to the oven and passed him her plate, he scooped scrambled eggs into a miniature mountain on the blue and white china. The eggs smelled delicious. Summer's stomach growled, making Lolo snort.

"Black, right?" The boy pressed a mug into Summer's free hand. "Winter always says it's best to take it black before battle, because too much sugar will just make you crash later on."

"Thanks." Summer took her breakfast to the table and made herself stand at Hannah's side. Brother Dan was hovering near the coffee urn. Barker kept scraping at his eggs, although everyone's plate was heaped to bursting. Willa stared at the white roses in her fancy crystal bowl. Lolo was shoveling eggs onto his fork and at the same time sneaking rolls and bacon into the outer pocket of his pack.

Summer figured no one really wanted to talk about what the day might hold. If Winter wasn't lost, if it was Winter meaning to storm the cave, he'd be doing more than drinking black coffee; he'd probably be standing on the table, talking everyone into bravery like some scene out of an adventure movie.

Her brother had a way of making everything seem easy.

Summer wished she'd thought to ask him how he did it.

"Sit down, dear," Willa said. "You don't want to eat your eggs standing up, do you?"

Summer blinked. She folded herself into her chair. Next seat over the changeling was busy pushing her breakfast in circles on her plate. It didn't look like she'd bothered to put any in her mouth.

"You should eat," Summer suggested, because she thought that was what Winter would do. "Barker's a good cook. He used to help out in the royal kitchens, before."

Hannah glanced up at Summer, then over at Barker. She wrinkled her nose doubtfully but began to eat without enthusiasm, studiously ignoring her grandmother.

Summer wrapped her hands around her coffee mug, drawing warmth, and smiled politely at Willa.

"Okay," she said, settling straight to the point before she thought too hard about what the rest of the day held, "can you show us where the magic cave is?"

December in Yorktown was much warmer than December in Manhattan. Summer was almost too hot in her coat, and not just because Barker was marching them along the town streets at a relentless pace. Brother Dan's boots thumped on the sidewalk. Lolo was so busy looking at everything he kept stumbling into cars parked along the cobbled streets. Willa walked up front with Barker, murmuring quietly into his ear, her ruined fingers shoved into fluffy mittens.

Summer noticed Barker was doing his floaty, not-quite-touching the sidewalk thing again, and thought maybe he was showing off, although she wasn't sure for who, because she and Lolo had seen it all before, she was pretty sure Brother Dan was supposed to disapprove of false modesty, and Willa didn't seem to even notice.

"Did he really work in my mother's kitchens?"

Oh.

Summer hadn't exactly forgotten Hannah. She'd been aware all along of the changeling sulking a few strides behind, but she'd mostly stopped giving the other girl much thought, because her grumpy silence was just boring.

"Yeah." Summer peeked sideways at Hannah. "When he was a kid. Before he joined the Guard. He used to tell me stories, when I was little. About how Gloriana would feed entire haunches of meat to her hounds, if her roast was under-spiced or over-cooked. Just knock the dinner settings all onto the floor and let the dogs fight over the food."

Hannah said nothing, but she walked a little closer to Summer. The other girl had dressed herself in sensible jeans and high-top Converses and a warm knit sweater. She'd tied her hair up away from her eyes and hidden it beneath a baseball cap, pulled the brim down over her *sidhe* features.

"Mama says sometimes Gloriana would serve her kitchen staff to the dogs too, if she was in a bad mood," Summer added. "Barker was lucky, really. You know, not to get eaten."

Hannah looked up and away from the sidewalk.

"I don't believe that," she said. "I'm sure *my* mother would never be so wasteful."

"Wasteful?"

Hannah nodded, decisive. "Better to punish the offending staff than lose them. Mortals are easily brought to heel, once they understand what's expected of them." She glanced pointedly at Barker. "I imagine it's the same with lesser *sidhe.*"

Summer gaped. Lolo, lurking a few steps behind, giggled. Barker, without breaking stride or conversation, flicked the fingers of his right hand. Hannah winced and glared at the bracelet on her wrist.

"Does it hurt?" Summer asked, hoping it did. "When he does that?"

"No." Hannah huffed. "It pinches a little." But when she looked back over at Barker, she was frowning thoughtfully, chin lifted.

Summer recognized the calculation and huffed.

"Don't bother," she warned. "You're not his type."

Lolo snorted.

They left the cobbled streets and stepped onto grass and then smooth white sand. Summer supposed the beach was full of people in the hottest months but for the moment it was deserted. A breeze ruffled the water, chasing small foam-topped breakers onto the sand.

Brother Dan paused and looked out over the tossing water, arms crossed over his wide chest.

"Is it the ocean?" Lolo asked. "It smells like the ocean."

"It's the York River," Hannah scoffed. "Didn't you learn anything in school?"

Lolo shrugged, obviously unimpressed. Brother Dan smiled out at the river.

"And that's the Coleman Bridge," the friar said, tilting his bald head at a span of asphalt and metal. "It's a swing bridge, that one." He lifted one hand and gestured, side to side. "The center swings out to let the bigger military ships pass."

Summer caught Barker giving Brother Dan the sort of look her papa had used when he suspected something was not quite right. Brother Dan caught Summer watching Barker watching him and his smile widened, flashing gold.

"I like bridges," he said. "Fantastic examples of *mortal* ingenuity."

"More iron," Hannah spat from beneath her baseball cap.

"It connects with Gloucester on the other side of the river," Willa said, ignoring the changeling. "The cave is this way. Best hurry before the crowds come out for the afternoon, don't you think?"

She strode out along the beach with more energy than Summer expected. Brother Dan left off staring at the bridge and followed, grabbing Lolo by the collar of his jacket and dragging him away from the corpse of a smelly, bird-eaten crab. Barker followed more slowly so Summer was able to catch him up.

"What will happen?" she asked, mouth suddenly dry. "In the cave?"

She'd forgotten how tall he could seem when he wanted to look intimidating.

He quirked an eyebrow, red against dark skin.

"I don't have all the answers, Samhradh."

"Papa thought you did."

Barker's lips twisted into a strange expression. Summer wasn't sure whether it was grief or disgust.

"Your father was wrong."

"It wasn't your fault."

Barker walked for a while without responding. Summer noticed his feet were touching earth again. His boots left indents in the sand. He seemed stronger, more energetic. She wondered if he was finally regaining his strength. She edged closer until their arms bumped, wanting the steady reassurance of his companionship.

"Really," she said. "It wasn't. Mama doesn't blame you. I don't blame you. Papa wouldn't blame you, either. You've served our family long and well," she continued, repeating something she'd heard Morris say at Papa's wake, "you couldn't have done any better."

Barker didn't make a sound when he sighed, but his shoulders moved up and down. Summer linked her fingers around his wrist. Barker didn't protest. They crunched over the sand together. Behind them Lolo teased Hannah rudely about the *sidhe* and running water. Brother Dan drifted past, long legs eating up the dunes without effort. When the friar pulled up alongside Willa, he bent and spoke into her ear. Willa laughed, a real laugh, the first sound of happiness Summer had heard the woman make.

"That one," Barker whispered in Summer's skull, meaning Daniel, *"I don't trust. Himself would say the man stinks of Adam and the angels."*

"But there aren't really any such thing as angels," Summer said wistfully, thinking of the giant Christmas tree put up in Rockefeller Center every December, and of the crystalline angels trumpeting below.

"Not for centuries, anyway," Barker agreed out loud, low as the wind off the river. "You're not thinking it was mankind's canny brain taught the abomination around your neck to eat our people?"

Summer pulled her fingers from Barker's wrist and clenched them around the pendant at her throat.

If Brother Daniel heard Barker's comment, he didn't give any sign.

Willa led them around a swell in the beach then off the sand onto winter-brown grass. A weathered timber fence ran parallel to the strip of vegetation, butting up against a sandy cliff overgrown with tree and vine. The vine was dormant, dull as the winter grass, but a few stunted evergreen trees managed to brighten the dreary scene.

The cliff was weathered and carved by human hands. Five small niches were cut high on the wall, above even Barker's head. Someone had long ago squared off the cave entrance; more recently someone else had installed a black-barred gate to keep curious visitors out. The gate was locked. When Lolo hung on the bars and rattled the door, it refused to give.

"In the '60s and '70s the cave was a popular lovers' retreat," Willa explained. "Trash piled up; it was a horrible insult to our town. Darlene helped fund the drive for the gate. Now it's locked except during regular tour hours, and the local young people mostly find it dull."

Summer couldn't help but agree. She thought the worn sandstone wall and the dead vine looked depressing, and had to suppress a sudden shiver.

"Barker will have to magic us in," Lolo said, shaking the bars until sand fell in a tiny waterfall from above. "This is righteous solid."

Willa smiled fondly.

"Not necessary," she said. "My daughter led the tours for many years. I still have her key. Hannah?"

Head bowed beneath the brim of her hat, Hannah dug obediently into Willa's coat pocket. The changeling was thin and pale against her more compact grandmother. Summer wondered how anyone had ever mistaken the other girl for a human. Hannah pulled a lanyard from Willa's pocket: braided leather in brown and red and black. An unremarkable key hung on a ring knotted to one end.

Hannah slid the key into the lock. It stuck but Hannah was inhumanly strong. The girl wiggled and prodded until the tumblers clicked open.

"This is as far as I go," Willa said. "I haven't set foot past the gate in more than a decade. It's an unlucky place, and I don't plan to make an exception now."

Summer was sure she saw a ripple of hatred turn the changeling's pretty face ugly. Then the expression was gone, quick as it had come, and Hannah's stare was bland. Still, Summer was reminded of the old, wily crocodile kept on hand in the Central Park Zoo. When Barker shifted uneasily on the dead grass at Summer's side, she thought he'd glimpsed it too.

"Go home, old woman," Hannah said. "We don't need you." She let the key on the lanyard slide through her long fingers onto the ground, then used the heel of her shoe to grind it into the soil where Willa with her ruined fingers would find its retrieval painful, if not impossible.

Mortified, Summer bent to retrieve the key. Hannah hissed. Summer smelled ash and smoke and when she glanced up, mid-grasp, Hannah's eyes were bright with anger. Tiny white sparks smoked at the tips of the girl's fingers. Her lips stretched, feral.

"Don't," Hannah warned.

Winter would have set Hannah on her butt, knocked her over with a flick of his wrist. Winter wouldn't stutter in fright and retreat, leaving the key in the dirt. Summer backed away, hating herself as she did so.

"Your brother's spent half his life fighting ghouls," Brother Dan said. He stood at ease behind Summer, spoke quietly over her shoulder. "If you think he didn't turn and run the first time he encountered a monster, you'd be wrong."

Summer forced her shoulders to relax. She watched as Barker picked the lanyard from the dirt and secured the key in Willa's pocket. Hannah hissed again, edging away from Barker and his glare. The sparks on her fingers snuffed out.

"Mama was the first monster Winter saw," Summer said, feeling the twist of sadness in her stomach that always accompanied that remembrance. "He didn't run away, but he did cry."

"Tears are nothing to be ashamed of." Brother Daniel put his hand on Summer's shoulder. Together they joined Barker and Willa at the gate.

"It's not a large space," Willa said, already turning away from the cliffs. "Don't let it fool you. Fairy tricks."

"Mortal failing," Hannah retorted, spiteful. "Simple minds, easily manipulated."

Willa looked once at the changeling, long and hard.

"Be careful, girl," she warned. "Whatever awaits you on the other side..." She shook her head, gray strands of hair sticking to her cheek. "Well, it's never quite what one expects, is it?"

"Fairyland?" Lolo asked eagerly, still hanging halfway up the gate.

"Life," Willa said. She crossed herself once, nodded to Barker and Summer and Brother Dan, then turned and started back down the beach, head and shoulders rolled forward against the wind and spray.

Summer was afraid to look at Hannah, so she frowned at the friar instead.

"She made the sign of the cross. Does she think her mortal god will protect us...or her?"

"It's habit," Barker said. "Like touching a tree for luck, or picking up a shiny penny. Superstition."

"Like fearing iron," Brother Dan said. "Dreading the acquisition of a soul. Superstition."

Barker scowled. Brother Dan smiled back. Barker grunted, turned away, and pulled the gate open. The vertical bars left grooves in the sand but the gate moved outward without sticking. Lolo hopped off the bars and onto the beach, shifting from foot to foot in anticipation. Summer didn't feel eager at all.

"Make some light," she said to Barker. "It looks dark."

"No, it doesn't." Lolo was already forging ahead. "It's barely dim at all. And the old broad's right. It's *small.*" Still, he managed to disappear completely inside.

"Lorenzo," Brother Dan called after, chastising.

"Sorry. The old *mujer.*" Lolo's laughter echoed on sandstone. He sounded far away already, down a deep hole or across deep water, although that couldn't possibly be.

Summer shivered.

Brother Dan had to duck to pass into the cliff. Hannah hurried after. Summer wondered what the other girl was expecting to find.

Summer

"Bees the size of baseballs," Summer had promised Lolo, *"and flowers all the colors of the rainbow, and garnets in the trees."*

But what if that wasn't quite right?

"Barker." Summer turned to Papa's old friend, clutched the edge of his leather coat. She wouldn't beg like a spoiled brat, but she couldn't help asking one more time. "Just a little ways in? It's not dark."

He sighed and shook his red head, and wouldn't meet her hopeful stare.

"Samhradh, it's not the shadows. There are things here, on this side—"

"I know," she assured him quickly, biting down on her tongue to keep tears back. "Mama needs you. I *know.* But just walk me in? I'm afraid." She whispered the last word, staring at the toe of her sensible shoes, scuffing at the sand. *Buairt* felt heavy on the chain around her neck, but not as heavy as her heart. Her heart was a rock behind her ribs, pressing her lungs into large gasping butterflies.

"Summer."

That surprised her into looking up again, because Barker never used her everyday name. She didn't even know the *sidhe* version of his. But when she tilted her chin at the sky he must have seen something unusual on her face, even though she was trying very hard to keep her mouth still, because he sighed again, a long, angry puff of air, and then nodded.

"Just in," he said. He took her hand properly, squeezed her fingers. "Just in, but then you have to do the rest. Alright?"

"Aye," Summer promised, in the old way, and that made him almost smile.

Fingers linked, together they followed Lolo's laughter off the white sand beach and into the cliff.

10. Nightingale

The aluminum can abruptly switched directions and rolled across concrete, onto grass, then uphill toward the Chess and Checkers House. Siobahn arched her brows.

"Morris?"

"It's playing a game, m'lady. That's all."

Siobahn wasn't so sure. Nightingale, by its very nature, was unlikely to play games with royal blood. It was a very well trained toy, tuned to the kings and queens of Court by the very same wrights who kept the Progress running.

Nightingale could show a bit of temper and had done so on numerous occasions, but by all accounts it shouldn't be able to flagrantly disregard a royal summons.

Mayhap she hadn't made her wishes clear. Mayhap Nightingale had forgotten. Mayhap the creature was finally driven mad by too much time spent in the mortal realm.

But Siobahn didn't think so. It was too exquisitely engineered to fail under even the most unbearable of circumstances.

The Coke can jumped into the air, singing against rock and tree trunk, against the brick of the chess house, and then up onto the roof. It spun on the roof tiles. Siobahn thought she heard fairy pipes beneath the clatter, a ballad she remembered from childhood, a war time dirge.

"Stop," she ordered in the same tones she'd used earlier to request tea: polite, quiet, firm. "Enough."

Bran had his laughable pistol pointed at the spinning can on the roof. Morris' softly glowing bubble protected Siobahn from falling snow or unlooked-for harm.

"You have my coin, or you wouldn't be here," Siobahn said to the empty chess house. The building was a smaller version of the carousel: brick, six-sided, and steepled. The benches and tables behind were empty, encased in a layer of snow.

"Show yourself, singer."

If her clipped command wasn't enough to cow the creature, the lineage in her blood should be. Siobahn yanked off her gloves, set a sharp tooth to the meat of her thumb.

"No need, Lady. The binding in your veins is potent even without breaking flesh."

Brain's aim shifted down from the roof and over to a shadow against the nearest brick arch. Morris murmured and the barrier around Siobahn doubled, took on a white sheen.

"Stay back," Siobahn told Bran as the shadow began to solidify and spread. "Don't let it touch you."

The human's mouth curled without humor. "Thanks for the warning."

Bran backed up until he stood alongside Morris. Siobahn stepped forward, imperious. The music in the wind and stone stilled, breath held. Metal chimed as Siobahn's gold *sidhe* coin rolled back along the path, spinning when it hit the barrier of her shoe.

She snatched the coin up. It was cold in her hand, colder even than the snow, chill as the grief around her heart.

"My condolences," the Nightingale said. "He was a good man, Malachi."

Bran made a rough sound, clearing disgust or disbelief from the back of his throat. Nightingale glanced at Bran, across Morris, and back to Siobahn. The perfect bow of its mouth stretched into amusement; mundane brown eyes—human eyes, once—grew wide and round in a rusty mimicry of surprise.

"You've brought witnesses," it complained. "Are you quite sure that's wise?"

Shadows against the building pulled away from the brick, following Nightingale as it limped toward Siobahn, a stretch of black mist coalescing in muddy puddles around the creature's feet, crawling up across pale toes, vining up under loose trousers and disappearing, only to burst forth again beneath the white flesh of bare torso and arms, then diving deep between ribs and beneath clavicle.

"Holy Hell." Bran licked his lips. "What the fuck is that? Electrical wire?"

Siobahn ignored Bran, but Nightingale wasn't as well mannered. It took another step forward and where the roiling shadows in its wake dripped off concrete and touched grass, dormant blades smoked and died.

"Close enough," it said, thoughtful stare resting on Bran's bruised skull. "Catastrophic weaponry is not exclusive to humankind." Unbelievably, its smile grew even wider. "Pray tell me, sir, whose dog are you? Nay, wait. Let me guess." It lifted hands and wiggled fingers; black filament webbed those fingers knuckle to knuckle, and ran back under the parchment-thin flesh at the base of the creature's wrists. Nightingale inhaled deeply, pointed tongue protruding between pink lips. "You've the pretender's scent about you, friend, but your loyalty is divided. Best be careful."

"Enough!" Morris ordered. "Or have you forgotten your place?"

The pointed tongue disappeared on a tiny inhale. Nightingale bowed its head in exaggerated submission then dropped to its knees, kneeling in a puddle of shifting black. It was so thin Siobahn could count its ribs, and see the knots in its shoulder blades where Angus had broken an already crooked human skeleton and crafted it back together, entirely changed, for the pleasure and protection of the Court.

Brown eyes watched Siobahn through a mop of tangled curls.

"I am yours," it said, simple and true. "If I wasn't always, I will always be."

Siobahn felt a twitch of pity. She squashed it ruthlessly away. "I do not require you to be clever," she rebuked. "Only useful in war."

It shrugged, resigned, waiting, shedding dark miasma on either side, and where that stain brushed, life smoked away.

"My husband saw little need for you in this world," Siobahn said, more for Bran's benefit than Nightingale's. "Despite all appearances, Malachi was a soft-hearted man, determined to save every one of our people, deserving or otherwise. I'm less sentimental, of a more practical mind." She turned on her heel, setting her back to the Angus' monster, and met Bran's watchful stare over the barrel of his gun. She could feel Nightingale's gaze between her shoulder blades. She clenched her fists to suppress a shudder. "Tell Katherine Grey this: Malachi is gone; I am no longer tempered by his grace. I've no patience for pretenders-to-the-throne, not in *Tir na Nog*, and not on Manhattan. She's to stop fomenting rebellion, or I'll put her down exactly as she deserves."

Siobahn had to give the human credit for courage; he stood firm in the wake of her threat. Her son had chosen well, taking the detective for a friend. Winter wouldn't forgive her if Bran fell in her squabble with Katherine. But Siobahn had never concerned herself with collateral damage and she'd long ago given up her son's goodwill.

Yet—

"A demonstration," she decided. "Watch carefully, Detective Healy, and take what you see in detail back to your lover. Convince her to bend the knee."

Siobahn turned back halfway, tipped her head in permission. Nightingale smiled, sweet as the child-man it had been when it had first been stolen from Whitehill House. Pointed tongue licking restlessly across pink lips, it lifted one long finger, black filaments flexing, bent and pressed the very tip to the dormant grass at the edge of the walk.

Immediately the grass wilted, withered to ash, and dissolved. The tiny destruction spread from one blade to the next, swelling from a blotch to a puddle to a creeping pond. Small shrubs blackened and crumbled. A lone maple burst into a cloud of white ember; ash snowed over the blackened hillock, and where the ash touched, blight spread, a conflagration without flame or heat.

"Malachi compared it to atomic disintegration," Siobahn said, cold. "I've never cared much for human sciences, so long as *sidhe* magic serves. My father used to call it 'poison shadow.' Everything living falls beneath the taint. *Everything living,* Detective Healy."

"Okay, right," Bran said, watching as the black death raced behind the Chess and Checkers House. "You've made your point, flexed your fucking muscles, Siobahn. Stop it now."

Siobahn smiled prettily. She watched the roll of destruction, distantly pleased. In truth, she'd forgotten the taste of obliteration; a heady rush of gratification made her pulse pound again after days of suffering ice in her veins.

"Could you call Hiroshima back?" she asked, gently. "My Nightingale is a weapon, not a game. Once deployed, I've no rein on the results."

Bran was too well trained to let horror mark his expression, but he wasn't entirely impassive. Siobahn noted the flexing of his jaw, and the flush of blood along the stitched seam in his skull.

"There are children—" He stopped, and cleared his throat. "There are people on the other side of the hill, Siobahn. Families on the grass."

Families on the grass. Siobahn remembered Winter and Summer playing in the park, catching snowflakes on their tongues and eyelashes. She shook her head, chasing the old sentiment away.

She allowed her eyes to widen, gave the detective the full force of her disdain.

"What's a point made unless it etches the heart?" she asked, gently. "Bring your naive horror back to Katherine Grey, Detective, and remind her I've little left to lose."

Bran turned and ran. Siobahn saw the moment the human almost put his foot into the dark stain. He recalled himself just in time, foot hovering an inch above the ground, then dodged his own death and sprinted along the concrete path instead. A safer choice, but far too indirect. Olmsted and Vaux's rolling park was meant for gentle rambling and not urban warfare.

"He's too late," Nightingale said without inflection. It watched Bran disappear behind the blackened hill.

"Hope springs eternal," Siobahn returned, mocking.

Nightingale bowed. "So it does."

"M'lady," Morris interrupted. His protective bubble continued to pulse around Siobahn, his concentration unshaken. "If I may ask, what now?"

"Now we return home," Siobahn said. She heard the distant wail of sirens. Someone mortal had phoned for help. "Dispel your Cant, Morris. I'm in no danger. This particular tool is tuned to royal blood."

"My lady," Morris protested, swallowing hard. "I haven't your confidence. Even the finest sword cuts both ways."

Siobahn squashed a twitch of impatience. She hadn't time for fools. But Morris was like a wolf puppy, so eager to test his growing fangs.

"Bind it if you like," she allowed, because it was easier than arguing, and she could see the flash of blue and red lanterns over the hill. "But not on my account. Nightingale is loyal to my desires as my own beating heart. Am I not correct?"

Nightingale bowed again, meeting Siobahn's stare, ignoring the loop of blue fire Morris conjured around its wrists: fairy manacles.

"I am ever at your disposal," replied the monster. It smiled, gathering black miasma about its heels and shoulders like a cloak. "Lead on, Majesty. I'm eager for a proper home."

Nightingale made itself comfortable in Malachi's study. Siobahn stood on the threshold and watched as the creature wandered her husband's bookshelves, scraping a long finger across stamped spines, stopping here and there to examine one of Malachi's small keepsakes or a framed photo.

She'd given Bran Healy a fine fright and she hoped he'd take his horror back with him to Katherine's bosom. The truth of Nightingale was somewhat less terrifying, if only one realized that Angus' living weapon was a finely crafted work of art, perfectly capable ofkeeping its destructive abilities contained. Central Park had survived Nightingale's presence for centuries, just as tourists and bustling natives had survived its walk down 64th street and through the hotel lobby.

"I've had a wee bit of practice," it said now, reading Siobahn's face rather than her private thoughts. "Living amongst mortals. Not one sparrow falls to my touch that I don't take time to grieve." Its lush mouth twisted into a toothy, pink-tongued grin.

Siobahn wasn't amused. "Stay here until I've need for you." She paused, struck by sudden uncomfortable doubt. "Do you require sustenance?" She couldn't recall and the realization made her shift uneasily on the edge of Malachi's study.

Its skeletal hands paused, hovered in front of a book-laden shelf, then gently plucked a framed portrait from its place between spines. Nightingale brushed away a thin layer of dust. Summer and Winter looked back at it through the glass, young faces frozen in time. Nightingale studied the photo thoughtfully, a faint frown settling above human eyes.

"Tea," it said after a moment. "Good English tea. It's been a very long time since I've tasted English tea. Also, music. Any sort of music. I'm not picky. A pen and paper with which to scribe."

Siobahn almost bowed. She stopped herself just in time.

"As you wish, Nightingale. I'll have Morris see to it."

She turned away, then hesitated, reluctant to lock her latest triumph away. Katherine Grey, she thought, should be cowering by now in her Central Park lair, rethinking her rebellion.

"My father called you by your given name," she said as another old memory teased. "When I was a child. You sang whilst he played *fidchell* in the garden, and recited the old ballads, and he called you..." She pursed her lips, narrowed her eyes, tried to recall. *After*, Malachi had always called it only by its title, but Malachi had always been plagued by superstition. But, *before*—

"Alexander." It gave the photograph of her children one final dusting, then set it back in place on the bookshelf. Black mist swirled between Nightingale's bare toes as it wandered on, insubstantial black fog wrapped like a cloak across its shoulders. "Alex, if he was pleased. But I've learned to prefer the title earned at Court, Majesty. Nightingale will do."

Summer

Winter

The thing about blood magic is it wasn't always forbidden. In fact, until my mother and her exiles decided to try and change things, it was pretty much standard fairy operating procedure. Probably it would have stayed that way if Gloriana hadn't gone a bit wacked and started sacrificing fay left and right, just to keep the Progress fed.

If she'd done it right, kept the Menders healthy instead of burning through them one by one, maybe things would have turned out differently. But maybe not, because most of the time I'm sure Siobahn would have used any excuse to try and win back the throne. Handy for my mother she found a cause the *aes si* were willing to get behind: self preservation.

But I think somewhere along the way Siobahn began to believe her own propaganda. By the time she'd lost the rebellion and been exiled with the remnants of her army, blood magic was verboten in truth, worse than poison, and she'd no lack of enforcers ready to punish any poor fool stupid enough to spill a little blood for strengthening Wards or Summoning meat or Gathering flame for warmth.

I don't know what my father thought, not exactly. Malachi wasn't afraid to lop off a transgressor's hand or ear by way of reminder, but just as often he'd stay his sword and ignore Siobahn's call for punishment. And I'm not one hundred percent certain, but I think he may have tried a few forbidden magics of his own long before I was born, pricking his thumb or slicing his palm as he spoke the words he hoped would shake Gabriel from her mouse form.

Didn't work, obviously. Maybe if he'd had a Mender to drain almost dry again and again until the spell was strong, viable. Maybe if he'd had Aine. Maybe if I hadn't kept her under the radar just to spite Siobahn, just because I could.

Maybe things would be different.

"Winter." Gabby's voice in my head, shaking me back from the precipice of angst. I blinked and the cave wall came back into focus. I'd been staring at it for a while, just scowling helplessly at the rock while Gabby prepared our next move.

Usually I was the one making the plans. It felt sort of nice not to have to pretend I knew what I was about for once. Over the years I've gotten really good at baffling everyone with my bullshit. Could be I'm more like Siobahn than I'm willing to admit.

"Are you ready?"

She stood over me as best she could without knocking her head on the ceiling, throwing a darker shadow over the cave's natural gloom. I realized I didn't like that she was taller than me. Easier when she was a mouse and I could nest her in my pocket and pretend she wasn't watching me with wise, sad eyes.

"Depends," I hedged. "How do I know once we leave this hole you're not going to"—I waved a vague hand at my head, bit back a hiss as blisters stung—"make me march back through the rift like some fucking puppet."

Gabby's never liked it when I swear. I could feel her disapproval radiating between my ears.

"The Horn's gone into the mountain," she said, and she said it out loud, as if to make a point. If I'd been half-expecting a squeak, I was disappointed. Gabby sounded as easy with English as any Washington socialite. Even my father had carried a trace of *Tir na Nog* in his tones. Gabby didn't. "There's no reason to protect you from its call."

"Right." I rolled up onto my knees, testing. Everything stung but nothing was agony. As usual, Gabby's healing touch was strong magic. "Care to explain a thing? What's the Horn doing *here*, in *sluagh* world?"

She looked worried. She wrinkled her nose as she thought and for the first time I saw an echo of the rodent she'd been. "I don't know. "

"Fuck."

"Winter," she cautioned and I could imagine her non-existent tail twitching in distress.

"Fine. Okay." I climbed from my knees to my feet, bending a little to accommodate the tight space. "Richard and Aine are here somewhere. We need to find them. Bring them back home."

"If they're still alive."

Gabby's always been a worrier, which is probably why Siobahn chose her as my guardian. Generally I ignore her less-than-positive attitude, but looking out past the mouth of the cave at the malignant atmosphere, I couldn't quite dredge up a cheery retort.

"They have to be," I said. Probably I sounded as miserable as I felt. "It's my job to keep them safe."

We needed more of the *draiochta* before we could leave the cave. We painted the blood-reddened lotion over my exposed flesh, using a bit of wadded fabric torn from Gabby's robe, sponging the thick liquid up from a shallow, natural bowl in the cave's wall. The amount of remaining *draiochta* in the bowl didn't escape my notice, nor the fact that while the blood magic had tasted like honey going down my burning throat, it smelled of salt and tears as it dried on my skin.

Gabby didn't paint herself, but she did wrap her cowl across her nose and mouth. I eyed her up doubtfully even as her blood itched on my face.

"Don't tell me you're immune?"

She made a sound of wry amusement deep in her throat. At first I didn't recognize the vibration for what it was, and I admit I stared, entranced. For a second all the noises around, great and tiny, seemed to swell. The drip of water in the back of our hole became a roar, and the wind outside the cave the howl of imagined hurricanes, the rasp of sand beneath my shoes like the scrape of fingernails on an elementary school chalkboard.

I was eight years old when my mother made me deaf. My brain remembered how to translate sound, but maybe not how to adjust the volume.

I clapped my palms over my ears. The fairy amber in my earlobes felt cold against the heel of my hands. Gabby leaned even closer.

"Winter?"

My ears popped and everything was all right again. Slowly I took my hands from my ears.

"Fine. It's fine." It would be, so long as it didn't happen again. The wave of noise left me shaking. "We're wasting time."

Gabby preceded me out of the cave, but only because I paused to scuff grit over our little hollow of blood magic. There wasn't much of the ointment left, but I sure as shit didn't want any wandering ghoul coming upon evidence of our presence there on the wrong side of my rift. Dirt swallowed the thick liquid, turning it into a red sludge.

The orb in the sky had set and the landscape was black ink, hill and lake and horizon indistinguishable. The wind had died with the vanishing moon. I clenched my teeth and breathed carefully through my nose. The air smelled acrid and tasted poisonous, but I was able to inhale and exhale without pain. Without the punishing wind my eyes stung but didn't water.

"Which way?" I turned in a small circle: black ink all around.

Gabby was a gray shadow at my side. She Gathered a handful of starlight and cupped it on her palm, shielding most of the silver glow with her fingers. Even so the gleam was bright as a laser in the night.

"Without light we'll lose our way very quickly," she replied to my grunt of disapproval. "Fall into the lake or over a ravine."

"With light we're a walking target."

"Aye, likely," she agreed calmly. "You've got a better idea, do you, child?"

I didn't, and of course she knew that. The ground sloped away from our mouse hole. It wasn't a difficult incline, but grit and gravel shifted under my feet, making the ground treacherous. Above our hiding place the cliff looked solid and slippery, although it was difficult to tell without more light.

"Down, I suppose?"

Gabby nodded. "There's a path below. Pay attention, or we'll miss it. It's not more than a scuff on the land."

We slid together down the slope, Gabby's starlight the only hopeful sight in all that dour landscape. Gravel threatened to catch under the edge of my pants and in my shoes. I could hear the eddy of the lake not far beyond our little hill, the slap of fingerling waves against rock. I wondered what chased the water into waves without the wind.

We found the path without trouble, mostly because Gabby has an excellent sense of direction. It wasn't really all that difficult to recognize, not if you were looking for the right signs, and I'm an expert on *sluagh* spoor. They tend to drop bits of themselves behind, ooze droplets of Cold Fire. Their poisonous fluids will char rock almost as easily as flesh; the Metro tunnels are pitted with marks of *sluagh* blood spray.

Also, they stink like dead meat. The caustic atmosphere and Gabby's ointment combined had done a number on my nose, but I've had years of practice. I squatted as close to the path as I could without subjecting bare skin to damp gravel and sniffed carefully. My mother's generation are said to be as scent-canny as bloodhounds. I'm not quite that talented, but I was able to make out the sweet-salt reek of rotting corpse beneath the perfume of the alien air itself.

"They were here, alright." I took a moment to try and orient myself. Without the moon it was difficult. But I thought I'd come from—

"Rift's that way," I decided, jerking a thumb vaguely east. "Too black to make it out now. Trail seems pretty straight forward. They're going west. What's west?"

Gabby's pale globe of starlight floated just above her head, revealing a small patch of rocky ground. An army of ghouls could be lurking just out of sight, and we wouldn't be able to separate them from the shifting shadows. Her small magic was no good against the pitch black horizon.

"I don't suppose it matters," she replied. "Unless you plan to change your mind and turn back?"

"Absolutely not. Only I've got no magic, and no weapon. I'd just feel better if I knew what we're walking into."

"Danger," my guardian answered with a small huff of disappointment or nerves. "When have you ever been able to resist it?"

She turned and walked west. I limped in her wake. Without the comfort of clear sight I had to rely on my new ears, and that was still frightening. The rattle of a kicked pebble made me jump while the back and forth hush of the waves on the lake seemed muffled and too quiet.

"Feather," Gabby murmured, stopping suddenly. She bent over the ground and came up again, a long black pinion clutched in one hand. It looked glossy as satin and when I snatched it away the individual barbs felt soft as silk but unforgiving as wire.

"*Sluagh* prince." I ran the feather between two of my fingers. "Great, winged, ugly monster. Bigger than the average *sluagh*. I've seen it and others like it in the tunnels."

Gabby made a noncommittal noise. When I frowned at her, she only shrugged.

"Does it molt like a parakeet?" I wondered. "Or, could it be, is Richard leaving us a trail of bread crumbs?"

"I doubt he'd have the chance." But Gabby sent her light spinning low to the ground as I squatted and shuffled about, seeking clues. *"They have no reason to keep him alive, Winter. He's worth nothing to them. It's Aine they want."*

I didn't bother with an answer. She was right, of course, and I knew it. I just didn't like to think about it too hard. I couldn't find any other feathers on the ground, any evidence of Richard or Aine or metaphorical bread crumbs. Maybe the feather was just a feather. I stuck it in the waistband of my jeans, rose, and walked on.

The *sluagh* had worn their path as straight east to west through the landscape as possible. It did meander some, around sharp rocky protrusions or sudden inclines, but never more than a few long strides off compass line, which suggested the Dread Host had no desire to spend more time than necessary out in the open. That realization made the hair on the back of my neck rise and prickle. Gabby also was unusually quiet, Gathered starlight held tight and close.

Really, the unspoken sense of doom was so thick I'd happily have cut it with a knife—had I been smart enough to bring one.

Summer

It was difficult to keep track of time, but I thought we'd been walking for at least an hour when the path began to curve up and into the hills. It was gentle at first, just enough of a slope to make me have to dig my heels into gravel for balance. Soon it became a real hike and I had to put my hands down on punishing hunks of rock to keep from staggering. Gabby made the climb without any visible effort. She was sneaking glances over her shoulder back the way we'd come and it was pretty obvious she hadn't yet adapted to life back in a human body because her sneaking really sucked.

"What?" I demanded, nervous and trying not to sound it. As much as I hate to admit it, I felt crippled without my magic to call on—far more crippled than I'd felt in years of deafness. "Is something following us, Mistress?"

"Nay." She pressed her lips together and I swear the tip of her nose twitched. "Not that I can tell. It's only—"

"What?" I insisted.

She stopped, turned around, and looked back east, down the hill we'd been carefully climbing. I wasn't sure what she was looking at; I couldn't see anything past the globe of starlight. Then she sighed and that small noise was like a punch in the gut, because for all her nattering and worrying, I'd never heard such a bleak sound from my guardian.

"I can't feel it anymore. I'm sorry, Win, but I think...Aye, well, I'm sure it's gone."

At first I thought she meant the *sluagh* army. But that didn't make any sense, because we'd been tracking the ghouls west and Gabby's attention was focused in the opposite direction. West, from where we'd come, and there was nothing much back there but our hidey hole and the poisonous lake, and beyond that—

"Oh." I swallowed hard. "Are you sure? I mean, how? *Gone* gone? Are you sure it hasn't just moved? I mean, it has been, hasn't it? Moving around?"

She set her back to the east and regarded me with worried brown eyes. "This world is not so large I wouldn't be able to feel a tear like that no matter where it opened: east, west, south, north or in between. It aches likes a rotten tooth in my head, it always has done, since you forced it open. Nay. The gate's gone from this world. Closed."

"Closed." Richard had tried to blow it shut and failed. I'd begun to think maybe it was something only I could do, shut the door I'd summoned. It smarted my pride a little to be proved otherwise. "There's no one out here but us." I gripped my elbows tight to hide a shiver and then shuddered anyway because Gabby's blood ointment made my fingers stick to the fabric of my shirt.

"Closed from the other side," Gabby said gently.

"From the other...*galla!* Shit!" Realization hurt worse than poison in my lungs, it was an actual physical pain behind my ribs where I thought my heart lived. "Why?"

Gabby didn't reply. Either she really didn't have any answers, or she didn't have any answers she wanted to share with me. Either way, things were definitely looking grim, mostly because I hate being helpless. Usually, even if I don't have all the answers, I can at least pretend.

"Fine." I shrugged. "I'll just open a new one, once we've rescued Aine and Richard. No big deal. I've done it once, I can do it again."

Gabby still didn't answer, and now she looked at the toes of my boots or the center of her globe or even the black as tar sky. Anywhere but at me. And that's when I remembered I'd lost my magic.

Summer

We trudged uphill as the eerie white moon rose at our backs. The moon or sun or whatever it was reminded me of *sluagh* flesh, more dead than alive and ready to combust at any moment. The higher we climbed the easier the air was to breathe. The trail narrowed along a cliff ledge and then widened suddenly into a horseshoe-shaped plateau, ringed on three sides by stone. Even if the place hadn't been littered with black feathers and bits of fetid ooze, I could have guessed the Host had spent some time there, resting or reorganizing or whatever it was it needed to do.

The ground was drier, protected by the ring of low stone. The gravel was disturbed, scraped into many large hollows. They'd made themselves shallow nests against the wind. Yes, they'd slept there, and eaten too. There were crumbs mixed in with the gravel, bits of oat and grain that reminded me of nothing so much as granola.

"Not ghoul food," I let a handful of grain and gravel run between my fingers as we paused to catch our breath. "The *sluagh* prefer blood and bone and sweet meat. Gristle and muscle in a pinch."

Gabby tilted her head to one side. "More bread crumbs?" she suggested.

"Maybe." I shrugged. My feet hurt and Gabby's salve was beginning to peel and fall in flakes from my hands and neck and face, baring my tender skin underneath. We were far enough away from the poisonous lake that maybe it wouldn't matter, but I still shuddered a little in anticipation of pain. "This is as good a place to stop as any."

Now Gabby looked surprised. Probably she could walk on forever. Probably she expected me to stagger on in pursuit until I dropped of exhaustion. Not so much earlier I might have, but ever since I'd learned my best friend had nearly killed himself trying to fix a mistake I'd made in haste, something inside me had grown cautious.

"I need to rest," I said. Sleep would be good, but I wasn't sure I'd manage that miracle. "And think. I need a plan."

Gabby opened her mouth and then shut it again. Probably she knew, as I did, that it was difficult to come up with a plan when there was no indication at all of what lay ahead.

"I could use sleep," she admitted, surprising me. She glanced around, eyeing the ring of stone with resignation. "This place will do. Wake me when you're ready to move on."

She settled in a hollow that had been dug from the gravel by *sluagh* claws, bending delicately in on herself, draping the fold of her gown over the lower half of her face, using her clasped hands as a pillow. It was the curl of a rodent and not the *sidhe* she now was. I had to bite my lower lip to keep back a nervous snigger.

I sat on the ground against a curve of rock. It was warmer down low, away from the shine of the rising moon and fitful, acrid breezes. It wasn't exactly comfortable, but at least I was off my aching feet.

I propped my chin on my fist and considered the *sluagh* debris left behind amongst the shale and wondered what I was supposed to do next.

11. Threshold

The cave wasn't very big. Summer, who wasn't tall, had to duck her chin to keep the ceiling from scraping the top of her head. Barker had to hunch his shoulders and bend at the knees. She was glad of his fingers still linked with her own because she knew any moment now, he would let go and send her forward by herself.

Lolo's excited chattering drifted back from up ahead. She couldn't make out what he was saying, but he didn't sound frightened at all, and his excitement made Summer want to grind her teeth. She was meant to be the brave one in the group, the princess returning to Court. Instead she was breaking out all over in goosepimples, shivering even though the seaside cave was anything but chill.

"Did it hurt?" she whispered. "When you came over?"

It was dim in the cave, but not pitch black. Filtered light fell from above onto the narrow, sandy path, picking out bits of buried sea glass in the walls and turning Barker's red hair orange.

"We didn't go willingly," he said, looking ahead down the gently winding path. "So, aye, it wasn't pleasant. This should be different. You're crossing between worlds of your own accord."

"Should be." Summer rolled her eyes. "You've got no clue, have you?"

"No," Barker admitted. He smiled slightly. Then he released her hand and Summer was on her own. "Ready?"

The shards of sea glass embedded in the cave wall were blue and emerald, but Summer thought Barker's eyes were greener. He crossed his arms over his chest and tilted his chin in

146

the direction of Lolo's drifting laughter. The sandy path curved down and around like the inside of an empty nautilus seashell, only the crooked walls were sandstone and jeweled glass instead of smooth pink.

"Yes." Summer stood as tall as she could without bruising her head on the low ceiling. "Tell Mama"she gulped back a sudden urge to puke right there in the magic cave and on Barker's fancy biker boots—"tell Mama we'll fix it."

A wrinkle appeared on Barker's forehead, not quite a frown, but close. She thought he sighed but she only really heard the sound in her head. Then he awarded her a stiff half-bow, the same sort he'd always given her papa. He turned and walked away.

Summer stood rooted in place, watching as Barker disappeared up and around the spine of the nautilus. She touched *Buairt* on its chain around her neck. She couldn't hear Lolo anymore and that realization made her turn and hurry in the direction her companions had gone. More than anything she didn't want to be left alone with the weight of her burden.

The path dipped sharply down, the turning becoming so tight Summer had to shift herself sideways and edge between sandpaper walls. She wondered how the bull-like friar had managed to make it through. Sand trickled from the ceiling in tiny golden waterfalls. It occurred to her at last that there was no possible way the soft slant of light from above was natural and she felt stupid for not recognizing the magic at once. When she stopped and looked up, shading her eyes with one hand against the rivulet of trickling sand, she found the chips of fairy amber buried in the sand alongside sea glass and broken shell, a wide constellation of honey-colored stars, together bright enough to mimic the fall of mortal sunshine.

Uneasy, she looked away and continued her sideways scrape down into the earth.

Summer

"Summer!" Lolo's excited screech made her jump and knock her scalp on the ceiling. She yelped, the sudden bump bringing tears to her eyes. More sand crumbled from above, dusting her shoulders. "You won't believe this! There's an entire 'nother cave down here. *Massive.*"

All at once Summer knew she should turn back, wriggle her way backwards along the spiral until she reached the shelter of the upper cave, then turn and run away into the morning. She'd throw *Buairt* into the sea, as far past the waves as she could manage, and she wouldn't let herself care if the necklace sank or washed ashore hours later. She'd walk into town and take a cab to the airport and a plane to the West Coast, or maybe even Europe, and she'd never once look back.

Because her papa was murdered and her mama had honestly never been quite right in the head, and their odd little family had always been Winter's unspoken responsibility, but now Winter was gone too, probably as good as dead and Summer didn't really feel much of anything at all except that driving need to run away.

"Hey." Lolo poked his head around the inside of the nautilus. He was grinning wide and white and eager and his braids were sparkling with traces of amber. "You're not stuck, are you? I mean, it's tight, but you didn't eat that many hotel chocolates."

"Shut up." Summer dug her fingernails into the palms of her hands, grinding until the pain chased away the constriction in her chest. "I'm coming."

The rest of the way forward was a wriggle and a pop and the narrow passage spit her out almost on top of Lolo. He caught her as she stumbled, gripping her elbow to keep her upright. He was stronger than he looked.

She glanced around for Hannah and Brother Dan and was relieved to see they hadn't moved far from the mouth of the nautilus. They stood together on Lolo's other side, the changeling hunched in upon herself, shoulders drawn up against her ears. The friar stood with his feet spread and his knees bent, his mass tilted forward. He reminded Summer of a tree buffeted by strong wind, but the air in the cavern was stale and calm.

"What's wrong?" She clutched *Buairt*, bracing for the worst, but saw only an enormous underground cavern, dripping pale stalactites, pocked here and there with flat blue puddles of still water. The ceiling disappeared overhead, black as the night sky, but the sandstone walls glittered with helpful amber light.

"I don't remember this place," Hannah said, hushed.

"Why should you?" Summer retorted. "You were a baby."

Hannah opened her mouth then shut it with a snap. Brother Dan seemed stupefied by the ceiling. Lolo hadn't let go of Summer's arm.

"Well." Summer shook Lolo off and took three brave steps into the cavern. It was easier to be brave if she pretended she was Winter, so she tried to mimic his cocky swagger. "Now what?"

For once none of her companions had an answer. Even Lolo kept his mouth shut. Summer scrubbed frustrated fingers through her hair, wincing when she dislodged sand. Then she crossed her arms over her ribs and glared.

"Where's the Gate?" She scowled first at Hannah and then at Brother Dan. "There should be a Gate, right?"

Hannah's blank expression didn't change. Brother Dan let his bushy brows rise and fall.

"I'm no expert in fay magic," he replied. "But I've an eye for measurement and you might think about the ceiling."

"What about it?" Summer flicked a glance upward and then away. She didn't like the darkness floating above their heads. It made her remember that caves usually came with bats.

Brother Dan flashed a dry smile. He shoved his hands into the front pocket of his jeans while he studied the perimeter of the cave. "We're maybe thirty feet into the earth," he said casually. "Not very deep, not really. Thirty feet below sea level."

Summer shook her head. She didn't know what the friar was getting at and she didn't like not knowing. Lolo caught on before she did. He fished around in the pocket of his jacket and came up with a penlight. She should have guessed he'd be carrying one; he'd lived most of his life sleeping underground.

He flicked the light on and pointed it straight above their heads. The beam was white and narrow and surprisingly strong. It pierced the closest shadows only to get lost again. Summer couldn't help feeling as though she was looking down into an inky abyss instead of up in search of the ceiling.

"Fairy tricks," Hannah hissed. "Remember? Willa warned us."

"She also said the cave was small." Lolo waved the penlight around, trying to catch a glimpse of anything overhead. "This is the size of a movie theater. It can't have changed that much in ten years…could it?"

"There are more things on heaven and earth," Brother Dan murmured. The friar gave up watching Lolo test the shadows and instead crossed to the nearest puddle. Summer trailed after. Brother Dan gripped her sleeve before she could dip a finger in the smooth water.

"Careful."

"Doesn't look very deep." She could see the bottom of the pool, muck and glittering fairy grit.

"Fairy tricks," the friar echoed. "Fall in and find yourself drowning, maybe."

Hannah squatted and plucked a stone from the cave floor. Still crouched, she flicked the stone at the puddle. Her aim was perfect. The stone split the surface of the water with a soft plop, sending rainbow ripples to the edge of the puddle. Brother Dan was busy watching the stone as it sank, but Summer found herself staring at Hannah's still outstretched hand and the amber bracelet hanging on the other girl's wrist, shocked by a sudden realization.

Barker and his matching bracelet were no longer part of the group. Summer's own magics were barely strong enough to muffle her footsteps on a leaf littered street.

"Hannah Francis is crazy," Winter had warned Mama in Summer's hearing, just before he'd let the changeling into their Manhattan penthouse. "Not the useful sort of crazy, either. She likes fire, and she hates everyone who isn't Hannah Francis, and she'll crisp us to grease and bone if she thinks she can get away with it."

Summer pressed her lips together to keep back a worried squeak. Hannah, still on her heels in the sand, smiled back. It was the sort of smile that wasn't friendly at all and had way more teeth than necessary.

Not for the first time since she'd watched her papa murdered on Sixth Avenue, Summer wished she'd spent more time learning the Cants he'd tried to teach her and less time with her nose buried in a Vogue magazine.

"It's gone," Brother Dan said. "Disappeared five seconds after it split the surface." He took a step away from the edge of the water. "Lorenzo. Don't try it. Stay away from the puddles."

Lolo paused, penlight dangling dangerously over a second puddle. He scowled at the back of the friar's head. Summer was darkly impressed. Brother Dan seemed to have Winter's talent for anticipating Lolo's mischief.

"We might need the light later, stupid," Summer said before Lolo could toss the penlight into the water just to make a point. "Use your brain. Come on, let's find the Gate. Brother Dan, could you—you and Hannah—take the far half? Lolo and I will take this half." She knew it was a cop-out to put the changeling under Daniel's supervision, but she couldn't bring herself to care.

"Maybe we're supposed to jump into the puddles," Lolo suggested hopefully. "Maybe that rock disappeared because it fell right into Fairyland."

"Nay," said Hannah, startling them all. She rose to her feet. "*Uiscí nimhiúil*. Poison. The priest's right, stay away from them."

Lolo's eyebrows bounced comically over his glare. "Thought you couldn't remember nothing."

"I cannot," the changeling replied, smug beneath the brim of her cap. "But I have a nose. I can smell the poison. Any *sidhe* could. The waters stink of iron and blood. Pain."

Summer opened her mouth to disagree, then shut it again, uncertain. She could smell salt and sand and Lolo's constant sweaty musk and a bit of damp, but nothing at all from the puddles. Lolo must have noticed her hesitation because he made another face, then shrugged.

"Come on, day's not getting any longer. If there's a way between here and there, we'd better find it."

It felt to Summer as though they searched for hours, tip-toeing around the edges of the *uiscí nimhiúil*, patting and scratching at sandstone walls, trying to ignore the eerie darkness hanging above their heads. Brother Dan borrowed Lolo's penlight and used it to peer into fissures no wider than the width of his thumb. Lolo got down on his hands and knees and brushed his palms over the ground like he hoped the door was somehow buried beneath a thin layer of grit. Summer gave up trying to follow him and walked the length of the west wall for the fifteenth time. Hannah, having given up on the search stupidly early, sat criss-cross-applesauce beneath a large stalactite, scowling.

"There's nothing here." As usual Lolo was the first to grow impatient. He climbed to his feet, brushing sand from his jeans. "Either Willa and the rest of them are mental, or someone's having a neat little giggle at our expense." The last was directed at Hannah, along with a rude gesture.

The changeling stared back. Cut sideways by the shadow of the stalactite, Hannah looked pale and fragile, like one of those fancy Lladro sculptures Summer used to covet as a child. She'd wanted a porcelain swan more than life when she was seven, made Winter walk her past the Fifth Avenue boutique window every day on the way home from school.

Then one day Winter was gone, and so was the Lladro swan, because the display shelf was switched over to kitchen mixers and stainless cooking utensils, and Summer lost all interest. She forgot to want the swan because it was more important to want Winter, but even years later she sometimes dreamed of that curved porcelain neck and the sharp beak, painted black, and when she woke, surprised, she felt no bigger than eight again.

"There's nothing I desire more than to leave this place and return to my rightful home," Hannah told Lolo. She sat still as sculpted porcelain and watched him through narrowed eyes. "If I thought I could find my way without *her* you'd all be dead and burnt." She licked her lips, darting a quick glance between Summer and Brother Dan and back again. "I don't know the way."

"Neither do I," Summer retorted. "And don't you dare try. I see one single spark and I'll smite you into dust."

It was a bluff, of course. Summer expected to be laughed at, but Hannah sighed and shivered and licked her lips again. Brother Dan switched off Lolo's light and returned it to the boy with a shake of his head.

"I'm out of ideas," the friar admitted. "It's gone late afternoon above. Back to the house, I think. God willing, Ms. Francis will have our answer." His tooth flashed brilliant in amber light. "Maybe she's got her caves mixed up."

They were almost ten steps back up the spiral path, Lolo jogging ahead while Dan shuffled Hannah along behind, when Summer, bringing up the rear, realized maybe Willa Francis hadn't got her caves confused at all.

"Wait!" she gasped, tangling one hand in the back of Dan's hoodie. "Wait, stop!"

The friar paused, tugging Hannah to a halt at his side. Even Lolo slowed and turned, scooting back along the narrow trail.

"What is it?"

"The walls." Summer couldn't quite make herself speak above a whisper. Small hairs rose along her forearms as she peered overhead. "Look. Look at the walls."

A person with less aesthetic inclinations might have missed the change in the sandstone, but Summer always noticed the beautiful things in her world, and once seen the patterns in the walls were hard to miss.

"The amber rocks." Lolo caught on quickly. "It's different. They've changed." He stood on his toes so his sharp nose almost brushed the lacy spread of shining yellow stone. "It's art. Is it art? Like tree branches or vines or snakes or some shit."

Dan did touch the closest wave of the amber mosaic. Summer didn't really expect the human to melt or burst into ash but she was relieved when nothing happened.

"Warm," the friar reported thoughtfully. "Brighter."

"Whole," Hannah corrected. "Smashed or scattered before, weren't they? It's obvious, use your brain. Easy as that after all. 'Crawl down, turn around, clap your hands thrice.'" The changeling laughed, delighted. "'Scurry up, hasten up, comes quick the blood-red nights.'"

"Creeptastic," Lolo sounded impressed. "Is it a song?"

"A nursery rhyme," Summer agreed, heart pounding behind her ribs. "And a game. Papa used to play it with me. Like tag only—" She paused when Hannah's mouth curled in a secret smile. "Different. The way out's different. Did we pass through the Gate without even knowing?"

"Only one way to find out." Brother Dan pointed his chin back up the nautilus path. He sounded eager as a boy. "Forward and upward."

The nautilus path seemed endless. Summer knew it was her nerves making time seem to pass slow as syrup, and maybe she was dragging her heels a little bit too. She couldn't quite make the fingers of her right hand release the charm that was *Buairt*. The edges of the filigree cross dug into the palm of her hand. She wondered if maybe she should magic the necklace back into sword form, wondered if they'd need a weapon the second they stepped into fairyland.

But the rapier was longer than the curving path was wide and she thought such a large weapon in a small space would probably cause more damage than not. She imagined the great gleaming blade stuck in sandstone like Excalibur and King Arthur, only unlike Arthur she wouldn't be strong enough or wise enough to pull it free, and their quest would be over even before it started.

Lolo glanced Summer's way. He didn't have Winter's talent for reading minds but he was pretty good at guessing faces, especially Summer's.

"Chill," he said and he sounded almost like a grownup, calm even as his eyes gleamed in the amber light and his fingers twitched restlessly. "I'm packing, remember? It's fine."

"An *empty* gun," Summer hissed and pretended not to see the hitch in Dan's step. "Is not *packing*. Besides, *Barker* has your gun."

Lolo only clicked his tongue. "Whatever you say. You didn't think I'd let him keep it? It belongs to Win. *Besides*. It's just bumblebees and flowers on the other side, right?"

Hannah snorted. "And my mother the Fay Queen," she said, scratching nails along sandstone. "And her noble Court of warriors and sorcerers, more powerful than anything you've yet imagined, human child. Your gun and your sword are useless against Gloriana's might. She'll crush you with a word."

Lolo muttered under his breath. Summer bit her lower lip and shoved past him, scraping her shoulders on the rough walls. One more turn around the nautilus and she was out, the first returned to the surface. She was panting a little from nerves when she stepped back into the cave and couldn't help but squeak a little in surprise.

"It's night." Lolo squirmed free of the nautilus and stood blinking thoughtfully at Summer's side. "Is it night? *Madre de dios*, that's wrong."

Sea glass still glinted in the walls and ceiling. Instead of blue and green the shards flashed red and yellow, reflecting torch light. Not the sort of electric torchlight Summer was used to, but real flame in small bronze bowls hooked somehow into the cave walls. Summer counted ten of the bowls, set at eye level around the small cave. They smoked and spat in and Summer's eyes immediately began to sting.

"Three hours, twelve minutes, fifteen seconds," Lolo complained, stepping aside to let Hannah and Dan into the cave. "That's how long we were below. Shouldn't even be lunchtime yet. And I'm never wrong."

"Reset the clock in your head," Dan suggested. He turned in a half circle, hunching his shoulders and drawing his neck in to avoid the torches. "Might be midmorning in Yorktown, but not here. I can see the moon through the mouth of the cave."

Lolo whooped in triumph. "You're shitting me. It worked. We did it." His grin flashed in the light of the flickering flames, wide and silly. "Told you, Summer. No *problema*."

Summer might have hugged him in gratitude and relief if Hannah hadn't chosen that moment to make a break for it. The changeling elbowed Summer in the ribs, knocking her sideways, and whirled to claw at Brother Dan, raking the friar across his face with her fingernails. Dan grunted and grabbed at his cheek. Summer staggered and caught her balance against the cave wall between two burning bowls. Hannah was already halfway to the cave opening, hissing like one of The Plaza's old steam radiators, when Lolo tackled her around the legs. The changeling went down in a twist of denim and long dark hair, her baseball cap tumbling into the sand. Lolo sat on her spine, knees pressing against her ribs, but Hannah was inhumanly strong and they'd all made the mistake of forgetting her magic.

The changeling bucked Lolo free with a shift of her hips. Streamers of flame came off the wall at her whispered Cant and Gathered on her palm.

"Stupid, hateful *runt.*" Ribbons of red and yellow heat wreathed her fingers. The amber bracelet dangled on her wrist, useless without Barker's twin manacle. She smiled, showing pointed teeth. "I'll make you scream, mortal boy."

"No," Summer said. *Buairt* was in her hands, blade shining. She didn't remember saying the words that turned the sword back into a weapon. She wasn't a warrior like her father or a queen like her mother. Still, the rapier felt light and easy in her grasp.

"Stop. Now." She took one threatening step forward, hoping no one would notice the trembling in her legs. "Or I'll make you stop, I will. *Buairt* will. This sword, it eats *sidhe* like you for supper."

12. Amputation

For a while Richard pretended he was getting better.

Aine was visibly improving, made stronger by the odd potions William mixed over his fire and Water-Bearer forced down her throat. The changeling slept deeply while Richard couldn't. When she woke again she was lucid if subdued, able to sit up on her own and clean the gray mixture of ashes from her skin with one of the smith's many rags.

She was quiet but calm. When William the wright provided them both with bowls of journey-root stew she ate heartily, picking chunks of boiled root from the salty broth. Richard ate with less enthusiasm. The wright had freed him of his shackles, using hammer and chisel and carefully applied flame to break through the bronze, but the fire in Richard's hand hadn't eased at all. In fact, it seemed to have spread through his entire left side, making his stomach roll with nausea. Besides, the broth in the stew was certainly animal, not vegetable. Richard hadn't seen any evidence of life other than *sluagh* and vegetation since he'd thrown himself through Winter's Gate.

Water-Bearer, as usual, seemed to pick Richard's unease straight from his skull.

"We once rode a variety of beasts, large and small," it said, green eye shining in the light off William's small forge. "They were changed in exile as we were. Some of them still inhabit the mountain, living and breeding as best they can."

Richard looked into the bowl. "Horses?" he asked with vague ideas of fiery manes and tails. He swallowed and set the stew aside.

William laughed. The wright stood over a small table set just out of the forge's heat. His hands, both the normal one and the ghoulish clockwork imitation, were busy with a mortar and pestle, grinding something that crunched as it broke.

"A long time ago, maybe," he said. The bits of his hair that weren't bound in rags fell into his eyes. He had a blunt nose and a wide mouth and he watched Richard with obvious amusement. "They've devolved since, those beasties, gone small and lost their hooves and fangs. I call them marmots now, when I snare them with my traps."

"*Who* are you?" Aine demanded with more strength than Richard could muster. "I thought I knew all the wrights, aye. Those that built the Progress and those still alive to see it fed. But you're none of those."

"Once I was," William replied. His clockwork hand was holding the pestle and Richard could see the joints in those gruesome fingers shift back and forth. Richard thought he could hear a faint click of metal against metal as the wright twisted his wrist. "No longer."

Aine scowled. Richard's head was beginning to ache and it took him longer than he liked to voice the realization: "But— you're *human*."

Water-Bearer made a sound of dark amusement. William smiled as he released the pestle, then carefully tipped several teaspoons of ground brown powder from the mortar into a small bronze pan. He walked the pan to the edge of his forge, setting it close to the coals to warm. He dusted his hands on his tattered trousers and crossed the cave to Richard's side.

"The *sidhe* can't work their own machines." He plucked the bowl of stew from Richard's lap without asking, then held out his left hand, his normal hand. "Nor build them. Fay magic and industrialization are uneasy mates—"

"As our apostate well knows," Water-Bearer said with false cheer.

"—and the Fairy Court relies heavily on smithy-men stolen from the mortal kingdom to keep their machines running. And an endless task that is, eh, Miach? Things tend to regularly fall apart; it's the unnatural strain, I suppose. Here, lad, show me your wound."

"Mechanics," Richard realized. The idea was terrible and beautiful all at once, and a wonderful distraction from pain. "You mean mechanics. You're a mechanic?"

William shrugged and smiled and wiggled his fingers. "Hand, lad."

Richard sighed and complied. He'd taken to not looking at the damage. He could smell it, after all, and it was somehow easier to pretend it wasn't his own flesh rotting away if he didn't look.

"Gangrene," Bobby deduced with some satisfaction. *"Blood poisoning, sepsis. You're up the creek this time, Rick."*

"Shut up," Richard hissed back, forgetting in his fever not to speak aloud. Aine turned her head in his direction but didn't speak. Water-Bearer blinked its one eye. William bent over Richard's hand in his own, making thoughtfully noises.

"It's well splinted," the wright said. Then he shook his head. "If you'd been able to clean it out, possibly. Or if you'd got here sooner. It's not the broken bones that's the worst. It's the sand in the torn flesh, the *doiteain domhain*, gone too deep."

"Will he die?" Water-Bearer sounded bored but the *sluagh* drifted close, feathers rustling as it leaned across William for a better look. "Look, there." It traced a long claw along the inside of Richard's wrist. Richard, still looking steadfastly away, felt the brush and bit back a groan. "The poison stops there, just below the elbow. If you remove the limb there, will he survive?"

Richard groaned again and swallowed hard. Aine managed to get her stew bowl in place a second before he puked up what little nourishment he'd managed to get down. She held the bowl as he coughed and gagged, then set it aside and went in search of a rag.

"No," Richard managed past the sour taste on his tongue. He wasn't sure if it was bile or horror. He tried to pull his hand back but the wright held it firm and struggling only made Richard's head swim. "No, let it be, leave me alone. I'd rather die."

"Not your choice, I think." Water-Bearer bent too close, his wings blocking light and heat. The *sluagh* stank almost as badly as Richard's hand. Richard shivered, teeth grinding helplessly. "I wish to keep you alive. We'll cut it off."

"No," Richard repeated as Aine reappeared and tried to daub at his face with dampened flannel. "You *need* me." He wasn't sure why or how, but he was beginning to realize it was true. "Cut it off and and I won't—whatever you want—you can't make me, no one ever can, not for years. No one can ever make me again." He forced himself to smile, breathing past pain and nausea, matching Water-Bearer's toothy grimace with his own.

"Find another way," Richard said.

For a time he dozed, waking and falling again in fits and starts, more unconscious than asleep. Aine brought him cold, clean water and helped him drink from a cup that tasted of bronze. She washed his face and cooled his fever and spoke to him in odd strings of encouragement.

"You're strong, Richard, and clever," she told him as she lay another dripping cloth across his burning brow. "And aye, very brave, if a bit stubborn. You will not succumb to a few broken bones. I will not let you."

He found her words comforting, even as he knew they were nonsense. The fire in his left side had spread to consume his entire body and he thought only the sips of water and cold, wet cloths kept his poisoned blood from boiling.

He stirred when William cut away the binding and splint, crying out as the shock of it made his muscles clench and shudder. While Richard lay on his side and quivered, face turned away toward the light of the forge, the wright grasped his hand and dipped it into a bowl of warm, thick brown sludge.

"To draw out the Cold Fire," William said, but he didn't sound hopeful. The mush numbed Richard's hand and for several heartbeats he could breathe normally. William paused, took the dampened cloth from Richard's face, and held it up against the firelight.

"What's this?" the smith demanded. "Yellow tears?"

"It's only the amber," Richard explained, distantly aware he probably wasn't making any sense. "The Wards shattered and got on my hands and in my eyes. You remember, Aine? It's only the amber." For some reason it seemed very important he make the wright and the *sluagh* understand. Maybe so they wouldn't take his eyes along with his hand. "It's nothing."

Aine hushed him, replacing the old flannel with a new. She pressed him gently to the floor when he tried to sit up.

"Let him be," she scolded. "He's right. It's nothing."

William hummed but turned back to Richard's soaking hand without further comment.

Richard drifted away again. He dreamed of the homeless man the *sluagh* had murdered in the tunnel pit, only this time it was Winter begging for mercy and Water-Bearer doing the killing. Winter gurgled as he died, head lolling on a broken neck.

Richard woke with a gasp. Aine was patting gently at his shoulder, whispering.

"I won't be gone long, Richard. We're just going down the tunnel, aye? To check for signs. William says they won't have found us yet, but very soon. Miach wants to make sure and take a look for himself."

Richard managed to struggle onto his hip. "Aine, no! Don't be stupid. You can't possibly trust the old ghoul. It's like as not to eat you as anything."

"I said I'm not hungry," Water-Bearer retorted from somewhere deeper in the cave. "And, forgive me, but you're in no position to argue, I think. Best learn how to make her own decisions, hadn't she, if you've decided to die?"

"It's fine." Aine patted the top of Richard's head. "William says it's fine. Don't fret yourself. I'm feeling much better. Besides, I still have my knife."

Richard groaned and fell back onto the earth. He knew he should be panicking, shouting, angry. He was failing Winter and Aine both. But a feverish lassitude made him feel as numb as his soaking hand.

He kept his eyes squeezed shut when Aine and the *sluagh* left the cave in a rustle of feathers. He kept them closed when the wright sat at his side and carefully lifted Richard's hand from the bowl of cooling mush.

"I'll wrap it," William suggested quietly. "Keep the poultice secure. I'm afraid it will do you no good. You're far beyond hedge magic. The stain is creeping up your arm, lad. Much further and we'll have to take the entire limb if we're to save you. Once it reaches your heart you're naught but a meal for the Progress, if you catch my drift."

"I don't. And you can't."

"Take the arm? Sorry, lad. If I were my own man I'd not argue, but I'm not, am I? Miach says keep you alive; I'll try my best to do as he says."

"Because you're its slave."

William snorted, but Richard thought it was a sad sound.

"Nay. Because I'm his friend."

When Aine and Water-Bearer returned Richard was propped up against the cave wall in an anxious fugue of fever and imagined disasters. William had retired to the hearth and was busy with quiet packing. If Richard hadn't already guessed they'd be moving on again fairly quickly, the wright's deliberate shuffling of rations into a canvas bag would have convinced him before Aine and the *sluagh* returned.

"By sundown, no later," Water-Bearer told William without preamble. "They're working top to bottom and soon our prince will recall he's left you too long without supervision."

William smiled grimly and tossed the *sluagh* a small loaf of hard bread. He sent another spinning in Aine's direction. Aine caught the bread absently, her attention focused on Richard.

"I assume you've a plan?" William rose and began sifting through the instruments nearest his anvil. He rolled a few small irons into a rag and used another to wrap a cleaver. The bundle went into his bag.

"They're working their way deep, we'll climb the spire." Water-Bearer's wormy tongue lapped at the air. "There are ways and means through this mountain forgotten. We'll make use of them while we can."

"Richard can't walk," said Aine.

"Richard is no longer of any worth," Water-Bearer retorted, unconcerned. "We leave him behind." The *sluagh's* wings rose and fell with the rasp in his lungs. He used the left pinion to draw Aine close against his side. "You, on the other hand, are still valuable. Come. Will, bring your light."

Aine sputtered a protest, shoving against black feathers with both fists, but Richard spoke over her.

"You won't leave me behind." He'd never been more certain of anything in his life, even with fever shaking his bones and poison spreading toward his heart. "Aine might be valuable, but I'm still a mystery you want to solve. That hasn't changed. A mortal with magic tricks up his sleeve in a world where magic's stopped working. Am I right?" Richard was panting with pain and distress and trying not to show it. Aine scowled around Water-Bearer's wing. The wright was edging carefully closer. Richard finished in a rush before the pity on their faces stopped his tongue. "You can't even make Gathered starlight work properly if I'm not there to hold it. Or have you forgotten?"

Aine squirmed and kicked at the *sluagh's* malformed feet. Water-Bearer ignored her. It looked past Richard at William, single eye narrowed. Whatever it saw on the wright's face made it mutter and deflate, the arch of its wings drooping until Aine managed to break free. She darted forward and stood over Richard protectively, knife clenched in one fist.

"I'm not leaving Richard behind," she proclaimed. "We two, we stay together."

Water-Bearer threw back its head and laughed. The monster's merriment was beautiful; Richard heard silver pipes and ringing bells and the promise of spring in the *sluagh's* gasping peals. Aine stiffened, obviously frightened, but Richard thought he'd never heard a more perfect sound in his life.

"Enough," William interrupted. He sounded gruff. "We're walking on. Aine lass, you'll carry this lamp and I'll walk ahead." He snatched a wicked hand axe from the tools hung around the forge and smiled grimly. "For caution's sake."

Aine stuck her knife in her belt and tried to help Richard upright. It was an exercise in agony and embarrassment. Every time Richard managed to roll onto his knees the ground seemed to tilt and only Aine's grip on his good shoulder kept him from falling sideways into the dirt. After Aine's second attempt, William swore out loud in the Gaelic and made an aborted move to help, but Water-Bearer knocked him away.

The *sluagh* struck quick as a snake, graceful for all its mottled, clumsy flesh. Aine yelped and slashed out with her knife. Water-Bearer ignored her. The monster cradled Richard close against its chest, wrapping him in black feathers, holding him immobile. Richard's head lolled helplessly, ear pressed against Water-Bearer's bony chest. He could hear the steady bump of an alien heart through linen and flesh and muscle and the fog in his own head.

Water-Bearer snorted. It shook Aine's knife from its thigh as a man might shake away a particularly aggressive house fly. The little buck knife spun in the dirt, scattering drops of smoking *sidhe* ichor. Aine reached to retrieve it and Richard meant to tell her to be careful but somehow his lips were going numb and his tongue struggled uselessly against the back of his teeth. The world was leaching away, color dripping in gray smears, until even the unwelcome tent of feathers went white and bright and fell away to nothing.

"You can't die," Winter says. He's sitting on the edge of the pit, bare feet dangling over the edge. It's dawn and Richard can smell Sayid's sausages through the grate above and hear the bustle of D.C. waking. "I still need you."

Richard's standing between Winter's straight spine and a maze of collected junk, and he's holding wire cutters in his good hand. There's something he's meant to be repairing back in the tunnel, but he can't leave until Winter says he's free to go, and he hates Winter for being the tidal pull behind his ribs even as he loves Winter for keeping him anchored.

"I don't know what to do," Richard admits. "I don't know what to do next."

"Don't die." Winter wiggles his long white toes over the abyss. He sighs and it sounds like feathers rustling. "That's all I'm saying. And maybe don't blow anything else up. Oh," he pauses, glancing back over his shoulder and smiling, "maybe stop dripping on my floor. That stuff's poisonous."

Richard follows Winter's pointed gray stare to the puddle of sluagh goo pooling at their feet, spreading at an alarming rate, overflowing the edge of the pit and creeping quickly in Winter's direction. The ichor hisses where it touches ground, sending puffs of noxious smoke skyward.

It's running in enthusiastic rivulets from Richard's left arm, caressing the ragged stump where he used to have a hand. It doesn't hurt, but shock has him bending double, dropping the wire cutters. Scattered droplets hiss against his shoes and his pants, eating through leather and fabric. The inside of his nose and mouth are burning, it hurts to breathe, he's suffocating.

Richard screams.

"Hold him down. You need hold him still. I can't—*Dias inn!*—secure the knot if he's rolling like a snared trout."

"God has no place here, Will. Best leave Him out of it. And if I use all of my strength I'll only snap him in two. Work faster."

Richard couldn't make his eyes or mouth or hands work but he could still hear the hiss of ichor on earth. The taste of smoke lingered on his tongue, a cleaner, hotter scent: metallic. Pain rolled across his limbs, a constant thing, and his heart fluttered, pulsing worriedly in the base of his throat.

"Richard. Richard, you need to lay still. Lay still and let us help you. Richard, be still."

"Good, lass. Talk to him. Can you put this in his mouth, between his teeth?"

A wad of fabric choked Richard, muffled his cries even as it protected his tongue from his teeth. They were gagging him, bottling his screams even as they whispered words of encouragement.

They were going to take his hand.

"*Íosa logh dom.* Yellow tears, Miach. You never do anything by halves."

"He's *weeping*, my lord. You said he was beyond fear or pain."

"He soon will be, if we don't hurry. The blade is hot enough?"

"As hot as I can get it halfway up the Long Stair. It will do. Now. Hold him quiet."

"Be still, Richard," Aine whispered in his ear, past the noise of his pulse. "I've got you. Be still."

"You can't die," Winter says. He's sitting on the edge of the pit, bare feet dangling over the edge. It's dawn and Richard can smell Sayid's sausages through the grate above and hear the bustle of DC waking.

"Rick," Bobby shouts. He's crouched in his wheelchair, head bobbing as he taps his fingers restlessly against his thighs. There are bits and pieces of wire and metal and C4 scattered on the carpet around his chair. Bits and pieces of a bomb. "Come out and take your punishment like a soldier! Come out and take your whupping like a man."

William's axe made a sound like a sigh when it split the air.

13. Poetry

Katherine Grey came to see Nightingale for herself. She interrupted Siobahn at breakfast, making Morris quiver and spit until—at Siobahn's gesture—he remembered his place and went in search of another place setting and more toast. To Siobahn's carefully camouflaged surprise Katherine came alone but for the little German dog she'd taken to carrying with her in the city. The dog walked at the end of a pretty leather leash. Jewels gleamed in its collar.

"Lost your latest lover so soon?" Siobahn stabbed at a piece of bacon with the tines of her fork then made a show of enjoying the morsel of meat as the sausage dog watched, ears pricked.

"I wouldn't let him come." Katherine took the seat across from Siobahn. Her skirts rustled as she sat. She wore silk and ruffles and the heels of her boots were sharp as daggers and the jewels on her fingers matched those on the little dog's collar. "Not when you've got Angus' favorite toy sleeping on your sofa. Honestly, what were you thinking? Far better for all of us if you'd left it dormant."

Siobahn set down her fork. She leaned back in her chair. Behind Katherine Manhattan woke to cold rain, sounding horns, and sirens.

"Have you forgotten already?" she demanded. "Must I remark upon your manners a second time?"

Katherine stilled. Her little dog growled, lifting a lip to show tiny fangs in a long snout. Katherine hushed the small hound with a word in the Gaelic, then slid from her chair to her knees on the carpet. Morris reentered the room just as Katherine bowed her head. His jaw flexed but he stepped around the kneeling woman without comment, deftly arranging china on the table.

"That animal tasted Gabriel's flesh," Siobahn remarked once Morris departed. "Why is it still alive?"

Katherine kept her head bowed. "Longfellow knew no better, my lady. He hunts the squirrels in the Park. He's only a dumb animal, innocent in the way of all mortals. The fault was mine own, and I did what I could to remedy the mistake."

Siobahn regarded the dog. The dog paid her no more notice. It sniffed around beneath the table for scraps and then tried to climb beneath its mistress's skirts, tail wagging.

"Do you remember Lámhfhada's great hounds?"

"Aye, my lady." Katherine's Upper East Side twang softened in remembrance. "Big as horses they were, and short of hair. Tails like a serpent's. Wily hunters, if I recall, and brave."

"Lámhfhada had a weakness for fierce, delicate things. You're much like him." Siobahn gestured. "Rise, and sit. Have you come to make peace?"

Katherine Grey scooped her dog into her arms and sat herself again at the table. Her pet sniffed at the plates but resisted temptation. Katherine licked her lips then lifted her chin and met Siobahn's gentle inquiry without flinching.

"I said you were mad before. I never thought it would come to this. That creature was never meant to wake. Angus should never have brought it through in the first place and Malachi was wise to let it lie."

"Malachi didn't have an uprising to put down."

Katherine looked away. Her hand crept up, fondling the little dog's ears. Siobahn took a sip of her tea, considering. Katherine was stubborn, but Katherine had never been *stupid*. It was Katherine who had counseled surrender once Gloriana discovered the exiles' mutiny. Surely Katherine would see the wisdom of humility again, once it was made clear.

"Come, Liadan." Siobahn pushed back her chair and rose. "I imagine Healy didn't do it justice."

Katherine actually blanched. Color seeped dramatically from her already pale cheeks. Siobahn wondered if the other woman would actually dare refuse. But the Grey Lady, for all her foibles, had never been called coward. She pushed back her own chair, tucked the sausage dog under one arm, and stood.

"As you wish."

Nightingale had made itself comfortable in Barker's empty quarters. Siobahn hadn't questioned its choice, although now as she walked the corridor, Katherine at her heels, she wondered if she should have. Barker's rooms were spacious; bedroom, small study and en suite. Barker's rooms were also located on the northwest corner of the penthouse floor and looked out almost directly across Central Park. The walls were mostly window and Barker had refused blackout curtains, preferring airy glass and sunlight.

Nightingale, Siobahn thought as she threw open the door to the suite, had chosen an excellent vantage point if it wanted to watch the mortal world go round. She strode into the room, wondering if she would catch it doing just that, and had to blink fiercely against an assault of bright light.

Siobahn knew Barker had a phobia, of course she did. She occasionally remembered to feel empathy when she caught the red-headed *sidhe* flinching at shadows. None of the exiles had survived the transition between worlds unscathed. She hadn't thought to ask Malachi from where Barker's particular damage stemmed. She hadn't particularly cared so long as Barker was loyal. He did his job and he did his job well, no matter what traumas lurked in his past.

Traumas could be overcome. Siobahn knew that better than anyone.

Still, as she stood in the threshold between corridor and penthouse suite and surveyed a forest of individual and varied table lamps, Siobahn wondered if she should have at least asked Malachi about his friend's eccentricities.

"Well," Katherine Grey said, dry as dust. "Barker, is it? As exile madness goes, I suppose this is mostly benign. Hotel can't be pleased, though. Electricity isn't cheap, not on this island."

Siobahn curled fingernails into her palm. At first count there were twenty lamps in the sitting room alone, set on table and chairs and floor, strung on extension cords like fruit to a vine. She could smell the heat of the manmade light even as the windows beyond were blurred by cold rain.

"Morris!" She tossed the summons into the corridor then stalked into the room, tip-toeing over cords. "Nightingale!"

She found it in the bedroom, spread on its belly atop Barker's wide bed, surrounded by another twelve lamps. Its round chin was propped in two thin hands, its bony knees bent, feet waving in the air. The pose recalled to Siobahn's mind a young Summer lying in the grass in springtime, watching the robins in Hyde Park. But Nightingale's narrow toes were bound all in living black wire, the joints of its knees metal beneath too-thin flesh. She could see black ichor pulsing in its veins like oil.

It was watching Barker's television with obvious fascination and its mouth twisted in irritation when Siobahn clicked off the closest three lamps, one after another. It covered its distaste quickly and rolled onto its haunches, pulling black vapor about its shoulders and thighs.

"Majesty," it said, shaking curls from its brow. "Are my services required? Poetry, verse, murder?" It glanced past Siobahn and its breath caught. "You've brought me a visitor."

Katherine's little dog growled. Katherine hushed it with a murmured word.

"Liadan, now called Katherine." Siobahn traced the nearest extension cord to its outlet and yanked the plug free. Sparks snapped at her fingertips but four of the lamps went dark. "Perhaps you remember her?"

Tiny wrinkles spread from the corners of the creature's human eyes when it smiled. "I remember. You liked to dance, once. Do you still?"

"No." Katherine's shoulders rose and fell on an exhale as she gathered her courage and approached the bed. The sausage dog still growled quietly, muffled by her fingers around its muzzle. "I've no time for dancing. I remember your voice in the halls, when you were first come to *Tir na Nog*. Before."

"Before Angus and his wrights worked their magic?" Nightingale tucked its deadly skirts beneath its legs, politely keeping Katherine and her pet from disintegration. It tapped a finger against its cheek and Siobahn couldn't quite keep from staring as black wires flexed and released.

Katherine Grey was one of those women who managed to look elegant even in a temper. "I didn't know Angus had brought you across, singer."

"He kept it quiet, I suppose. Gloriana insisted, you see. Tuned as I was to Angus, I imagine she thought I was more dangerous in *Tir na Nog* than out." Nightingale's attention drifted back toward the television. Pictures of the D.C. crater rolled across the screen as a flushed and angry political pundit rattled on in the background. The scrolling banner read INTERCEPTED EMAIL IMPLICATES SYRIA and IRAQ DENIES ALL KNOWLEDGE and PRESIDENT TO SPEAK NOON EST.

"He should have used you when he had the chance," Siobahn said. She ignored Katherine's barely hidden disgust. "Well, Liadan. You can see your detective spoke true, while *I* can see you've grown bored and careless. Desperate. I understand. But after all this time the throne is still mine by right of blood, and I haven't kept it through war and exile only to relinquish it now."

"This...thing...obeys your command, now Angus is gone?"

"It does indeed."

Katherine blew a breath through pursed lips. "You frighten me," she said. "You do realize you've sent our only possible defense against this *ghastly* creation away with your children? What if it turns on us?"

Nightingale didn't look away from the television but Siobahn sensed its sudden attention. The tiny hairs on the back of her neck prickled warning. The dog in Katherine's arms made a sound of distress.

"It won't turn," she said with more confidence than she felt. "The royal blood runs within me. It will do as I say." Deliberately she turned her back on danger and faced Katherine Grey instead. "It has to. Do you wish me to provide demonstration?"

"Nay." Katherine remained unbent but her eyes glistened. "I've seen a queen's wrath before, I've no desire to see what remains of our people suffer so again. They are my friends."

"I need your word," Siobahn told the other woman as Nightingale began to hum quietly in time with a television commercial. "I need to know I can trust you when Winter opens the Gate and we storm Gloriana's Court. I am meant to rule, and I shall."

Katherine shifted minutely on the balls of her feet. She stared, not at Siobahn, but at Nightingale. Then she nodded.

"You have my word."

Barker apparently thought he could sneak home like a dog in the middle of the night, tail tucked, but Siobahn was too canny to miss his arrival and too proud to ignore his lapse in manners. She met him in the purposefully darkened foyer, sprung upon him as he tried to slip unnoticed into the apartment, and knocked him up against the wall, both thumbs buried in the hollow of his throat, strangling and scratching at the same time.

He fought briefly back, bringing his knee up in automatic defense, arching his spine to throw her off. But Siobahn was stronger and the shadows were on her side and Barker's knees buckled. He slid down the wall, overturning the little side table Summer so loved, sending antique knick-knacks crashing to the floor.

His blood was warm between Siobahn's fingers.

"My lady." All at once he recognized her and went limp. "Majesty. *Trócaire.* Mercy!" He wheezed, trying to draw air past her clenching fingers.

She followed him down, crouched over his lap, put her lips on his brow in benediction even as she squeezed the air in hoarse puffs from his throat. She didn't mean for him to die, he was far too valuable still for that. But she did mean for him to suffer. He twitched, suppressing his body's natural urge to fight back even as his eyes rolled in his head and it was that impressive mastery of base instincts that had Siobahn releasing him at last.

"Mercy, then, you fool." She climbed off his lap and sat on the floor against his long legs. He was slumped almost prone, his hands resting open-palmed on the carpet. The glint of amber around his wrist was barely visible in the dim light. "If only because Malachi so loved you." She watched as he cracked his eyes and sucked in great gasps of air. Her fingers had left marks, she knew, and there would be blood on his fancy leather coat. "But if you ever defy me so again, I'll have your head with my tea and biscuits."

He shook, rattling the overturned side table, then croaked. "Yes, my lady. May I?"

She nodded once, sharply, and he pulled starlight into a globe above their heads, lighting the foyer and chasing back fingers of darkness. In the shine his eyes were very wide and very wild. Siobahn looked him up and down with displeasure, noting the grime in his hair and the road dust on his boots.

"Chased them all the way, did you?" she asked. "You didn't used to be so difficult. When did you know you were free to run?"

"I didn't." Barker cleared his throat. "Not at first. Not until…I guessed, my lady. Something felt…different. The city felt lighter."

She spat in his face, watched with satisfaction as her spittle dripped along the side of his jaw. He didn't react.

"Was it the sword that changed you?" she demanded. "Or the interfering priest and his baptism ritual?"

Barker appeared to give the question some consideration. Then he shook his head, baffled. He looked crestfallen.

"I don't know. I…I cannot tell, my lady. Does it matter?"

Siobahn hopped to her feet. Snorting, she held out a hand. "I haven't decided," she said. She hauled Barker upright. His hand was cold and dry against her palm. "But it could be very important indeed. Freedom from this island, access to the Cornwallis Gate? You should have told me at once, Barker. Immediately."

"As I said." Very carefully he righted the table and replaced scattered knickknacks. "I wasn't entirely sure until I tried, my lady."

Siobahn turned and left him to follow her into her library. She conjured flames to the hearth with a word and sent Barker's starlight to lurk in every corner of the room, forcing darkness away. She wondered if he would reach for the light switch. Now that she realized the extent of his madness she found herself looking for indications she may have missed, a cat searching sideways for sign of a lingering mouse.

But he ignored the switch and wandered to the bar where Malachi used to keep his fine Irish whiskey and cheap tequila. Siobahn didn't protest when he blew dust from an unused crystal snifter and poured out five fingers of her dead husband's expensive liquor. He drank the whiskey down in one swallow then coughed lightly.

"Subjecting the remaining exiles to forced baptism is probably unwise," he said after a moment, sounding more like the man Malachi once relied on. "Even if the reward is passage off the island. Adam's god has no love for our kind."

Siobahn paused in front of her writing desk, surprised. She hadn't really supposed the friar's ritual of oil and water anything more than empty platitudes or ritualized human sorcery. But Barker's hand trembled as he poured himself a second drink, making the amber bracelet on his wrist glitter, and she couldn't help but wonder what else he might be keeping to himself.

"Surely you don't believe that ex-convict managed to somehow gift you with a *soul?"* She laughed aloud at the very sound of the words on her tongue.

"No," Barker answered quickly. "Of course not."

Siobahn scoffed and seated herself at her desk. "Good. I'd hate to suppose you sentimental as well as foolish. Report, if you will. Tell me of my children. Tell me you bring glad tidings."

Afterward, Siobahn didn't know whether to howl in rage or in triumph. Winter had failed her again; for the third time since he'd sprung shrieking from her womb, he'd done exactly as he'd wished instead of bowing to her greater wisdom. The son she'd once had such high hopes for was finally lost to her and she refused to let herself mourn him.

"Summer will do me proud," she declared at last, past an unwelcome lump in her throat. And then, reluctantly: "Mayhap you should have gone with them. She's never swung a sword in her life, that one."

He was watching the flames in the grate, thinking his own private thoughts. The fall of his hair was very red against the slant of his cheeks and she knew that once she would have found him attractive. Before Malachi. When she was still capable of seeing beauty in any man other than her prince.

"They're safer without us," he replied at last. "Gloriana would know the moment one of the exiles returned. She'd send what resources she has immediately in my direction, the moment I stepped through the Gate. Your quest would be over before it was begun."

"Summer's quest," Siobahn corrected. She tried to imagine her shallow, delicate daughter facing down their greatest enemy and couldn't. Summer had always loved pretty things and in *Tir na Nog* the prettiest things were deadly.

I've lost, she thought, and turned her face away from Barker so he wouldn't see her fury.

Of course he thought she was grieving her children.

"My lady." He had a deep voice, gone deeper as he tried to reassure. "Don't give up quite yet. Summer's a good girl, a brave lass. She takes after her father."

The highest compliment Barker had to give, Siobahn supposed, and laughed again at his earnest expression.

A shifting in the banished shadows interrupted her scorn and sent her once again to her feet. Barker, sensing her alarm, wheeled toward the door, speaking as he did the Warding words that conjured a bubble of silver glow about them both.

Nightingale paused halfway into the room, its noxious cloak bound and gathered at one shoulder, the smoky hem trailing about its heels.

"Oh," it said, guileless as a child. "You're busy." It smiled, glancing from Barker to Siobahn and back again.

Barker went rigid and his Ward flickered dangerously. Nightingale smiled wider, showing blunt human teeth. Barker recoiled and Siobahn found his reaction very interesting indeed.

"Enter and be welcome," she said, although in truth she wished the horrific creature would keep itself well out of sight. "Barker. Dismiss your Ward. Nightingale means me no harm."

For three solid heartbeats Barker didn't move. Then his Ward vanished with an angry crack. He turned and walked away to the library windows, stared out through the rainy night at Central Park. Siobahn pretended ignorance, even as she took silent note of his every twitch and exhale.

It hadn't occurred to Siobahn to warn him. She simply hadn't thought, not even when she'd found Nightingale gone to ground in Barker's quarters. Now she was glad of the misstep. In fact, she was delighted. Barker deserved to be punished for harboring secrets and there was no more fitting punishment than heartbreak. Siobahn knew that firsthand.

"You've come for one of my collection, I suppose," she said, gesturing at her shelves. "I recall how you always so loved your books when you first came to Court. Especially those old volumes of poetry. Do you remember, Barker, how he'd entertain Angus with his own verse? Make us all weep, he would."

"It," Barker corrected, too soft, too calm, as he regarded the rain. "*It* made us weep."

"'Changed as he was, with age, and toils, and cares,'" Nightingale quoted softly. Then: "I am as your people made me. Much improved for the original, I'm told. Poetry has no place in war."

"Choose your book and go," Barker said.

Nightingale tilted its chin at Siobahn. She nodded permission and dismissal both. It shrugged and ghosted into the room to stand before Siobahn's corner of shelves. It walked its fingers over leather spines. Siobahn kept a delicate potted orchid in a silver pot between Conan Doyle and Dickens. As Nightingale browsed Siobahn's selection the orchid withered and turned to ash. Siobahn bit back her annoyance.

Nightingale ignored several volumes of good poetry and instead settled on Tom Clancy. It clutched the book to its concave chest and bowed first to Barker, who ignored it, and then to Siobahn.

"Thank you, Majesty."

It departed soundlessly, trailing curls of miasma. When they were alone again Barker turned from the window and frowned at the ruined orchid.

"It did that on purpose, you realize. It has more control than it pretends."

"I have two teenage children, Barker. I recognize a tantrum when I see one." Siobahn crossed the room and sighed over the lost plant. "It wasn't pleased to see you, I think."

"Be careful, my lady. That one's never completely forgiven your father for stealing it away."

"None of them do," Siobahn replied. "Have Morris book you a room in the hotel. Nightingale's commandeered your own, Barker, and I doubt you want to join it in dreaming."

Her dead husband's best warrior stiffened in insult at the demotion. Siobahn waited, pretending patience even as her knuckles turned white around the orchid's empty pot. She could hear the rasp of his breathing, smell his distress. Surely he wasn't stupid enough to protest, not when she'd only just forgiven him his disappearance.

He wasn't.

He cleared his throat. "Aye, my lady. Of course."

"Goodnight, Barker." She stepped aside to let him pass.

He left exactly as Nightingale had, trailing silent displeasure. When he was gone she set the silver pot back between Conan Doyle and Dickens, making a mental note to send Morris out for a new cymbidium in the morning. Her knuckles ached from the clench of suppressed rage. She crossed her arms and tucked her hands in her armpits and stood in Barker's place against the windows and looked down onto the lights of Central Park.

14. Bromeliads

Hannah lay in the dirt on her back beneath the point of Summer's sword. Summer didn't let *Buairt* touch the changeling, not quite. The silver chain Summer had used to string the filigreed cross around her neck had broken when the cross switched back into a sword. It lay coiled in the sand next to Hannah's fallen baseball cap.

"Please," Hannah said. "I'm sorry. Please. It hurts."

Summer blinked. The sword felt very light, easy in her grip. She was strong in the way of the fay, but she'd never been athletic. Her papa had put a training blade in her hand once or twice when he'd still planned to bring his children up like *sidhe* legends, before they'd discovered Summer was about as coordinated as a mule and Winter preferred video games to fencing.

Buairt didn't feel at all like a training blade. *Buairt* felt like it belonged in Summer's hand and it was beautiful, the most beautiful thing she'd seen since Elle Tahari introduced resort-wear in 2013.

"Please," Hannah whispered. Her hands flopped in the sand as she struggled to slide away from the sword, but she seemed to have lost control of her arms and legs. Summer stared down at her, but it was Papa's face she was seeing, Malachi as he contorted on the pavement, unable to escape *Buairt's* curse.

Then Brother Dan grabbed Summer's wrist and wrenched the sword from her grasp. She struggled briefly, automatically, even though she'd never wanted *Buairt* in the first place. She had to grit her teeth to keep from lunging after it.

Hannah curled in on herself, nose to bent knees, and covered her ears with her palms.

"You've quick reflexes and I can't argue she needed a reminder," the friar said. He gripped the rapier's hilt between blunt fingers, letting the blade prick the sand. "But I think you made your point."

Summer looked down at Hannah. She felt a pang of guilt. She'd meant from the beginning to make the other girl her friend and instead here she was, no better than Darlene Francis, using the sword as a threat.

"I'm sorry," she said quickly, speaking to the friar but looking at Hannah. "It's just—you scared me. Give it to me. I'll turn it back. It's better when it's changed, isn't it? Not as bad?" She bent to catch up the broken chain and Hannah actually flinched, sliding in the sand.

"No," Dan said. "If we've crossed over, the sword's valuable. Who knows what we'll meet in *Tir na Nog*. Better to keep it close at hand, although maybe not at Hannah's expense. Lolo, give me the scabbard."

Lolo, Summer saw, was more interested in what might be beyond the cave mouth than Hannah's wellbeing. He was dancing from foot to foot, quivering in excitement. He dug into the pocket of his jacket and plucked free a fist-sized roll of brown leather. Summer's stomach clenched. Morris had done a neat job sewing the rubies back into place and the leather really didn't resemble human skin, but she still couldn't look at the scabbard without feeling frightened and sick.

Dan didn't seem to have the same problem. He took the roll from Lolo and pulled the soft scabbard over the sword. It went on a bit like a loose sock and Summer recognized it for what it was: decoration, fashion, except for the part where the sorcery of mortal flesh and blood somehow blunted the blade's powerful curse.

A stiffer piece of notched hide was attached to the top of the scabbard. While Summer gaped, Brother Dan unfastened his own narrow belt, tugged it free of his jeans, and slotted it through the scabbard. Then he crooked a finger at Summer.

"We'll knot it around your waist for now, I think. Lorenzo, stop fidgeting and help Hannah up, please."

Hannah whined in protest. Summer was busy watching Dan's hand as he looped the belt around her waist and deftly knotted it in place. It was like being mauled by a gentle bear. He smelled of sea salt and a little bit of clean sweat and of something that made Summer think of Christmas.

The belt was some sort of canvas webbing, striped in red and blue and yellow and far too preppy for an old friar, but it was just flexible enough that they managed to make it work, even if the very tip of the scabbard banged against Summer's heel.

"You'll get used to it," Dan said. "Keep one hand on the hilt and you'll soon figure out how to keep it from catching."

Lolo had somehow managed to coax Hannah upright. He let the changeling lean on his shoulder and stared at Dan like he'd just then noticed something fantastic. Summer had seen Lolo look like that once before, when he'd stepped into The Plaza's golden elevator.

"What's a priest know about swords?"

"Not a priest," Dan corrected patiently even though he must know Lolo was only making the mistake to piss him off. "And I wasn't always a Franciscan."

Lolo scoffed. "They don't let you have swords *in prison.*"

"You're right," Dan agreed. "But they do have cable. I watched a lot of movies. Learned all sorts of things thanks to Hollywood."

"You're shittin' me," Lolo retorted.

For once Brother Dan didn't bother correcting Lolo's language. Instead he shrugged and looked only at Summer.

"Well," he said. "*Niña.* Are you ready?"

Summer wasn't, not at all.

She made her mouth smile and then she nodded, because really she didn't have any other choice.

Lolo was the first one through the mouth of the cave and he was quickly back again, holding a hand up in warning.

"Watch it. We're up high. Like, right up with the moon, and the moon's a fingernail, which isn't right at all." He scrabbled in a pocket, humming in triumph as he retrieved his penlight. "Dark out there. Summer, can you do like Win? Make a light? And you're right," he was babbling in unconscious excitement as Summer and Dan and even Hannah stared, "it smells like flowers."

Summer could Gather starlight, although she had to gnaw on her lip in concentration before the shining globe appeared overhead. But after that it was easier, the globe swelled and expanded just as she thought they might need more light, and it was almost as good as city street lights. She felt a surge of pride.

"Lorenzo's right." Dan said from just beyond the cave. "Come, there's a ledge, but it's narrow."

Summer didn't mind heights, and she was glad of it, because when she edged after the friar and got her first glance of *Tir na Nog* it was a a lot like stepping out onto Rockefeller Center's observation deck. Her heart jumped into her throat, not in fear, but in awe.

Fairyland's version of the Cornwallis Cave opened not onto gently sloping sand and restless seas but onto a very narrow stone balcony, surely no more than four feet wide, and beyond that emptiness. The crescent moon illuminated racing clouds, fat and silver, and behind the cave, high rolling hills. Summer's light was brighter than the moon and when Summer sent it dancing like lazy fireworks above her head the mountainside revealed itself in stark black and silver silhouette.

There was a path, a switchback trail dropping sharply from the ledge and also rising in more gentle curves up and past the cave mouth. Summer thought they were very high up, but the mountain grew on past the cave and the uppermost trail followed swells and curves until it undulated out of sight. The lower path disappeared at the edge of Summer's light where the mountainside spread away into darkness.

"We're at the top of the world," Lolo breathed, impressed. "It's like Everest or something."

"No," Hannah said, surprising them all. "Taste the air, mortal. It's warm and soft. I smell growing things. We're closer to earth than clouds. It's only the night distorting the horizon." And then she conjured her own light with an indolent twitch of long fingers and sent a second globe orbiting Summer's.

"Foothills," Brother Dan agreed. "Sizable foothills, but not palisades. I hear water."

Summer heard it, too. Not the rush and recede of ocean waves but the steady roar of a river. It sounded distant still, beyond and below their ledge.

"Maybe we should wait here until the sun comes up," Summer suggested. "The trail will be easier in the daylight. At least here we've got shelter."

"Sounds good, but I'm not sure we want to stay." Lolo tugged at Summer's sleeve. His knee bumped *Buairt* and Summer felt the vibration of the blade against her thigh. "Look." He pointed.

Tall grass and small plants grew in pockets along the trail and in the slope around the cave. The grass looked thick and sharp, wide as Summer's thumb, black and white in the night. The plants were jagged and bore tiny spines and strings of fat flowers. Summer thought they must be some kind of dwarf cactus. The sleeping flowers gave off a heavy, sweet perfume like honeysuckle.

There were bones scattered in the grass. Old bones, Summer realized, white in the starlight, except for where they were brown and splintered. Not animal bones, because there was a humanoid skull, partially hidden in the grass, and a hand, four fingers and a thumb still attached, caught against a cactus.

"I don't think we should stay around here," Lolo offered. "Look, there's more over up there, on the hill. That skull looks chewed on. And that's a femur."

"Maybe whatever chewed on it is down below," Hannah argued. "Maybe we're safer here. Back in the cave, at least until dawn." She twisted her ponytail in one hand, tugging.

"Is it a graveyard?" Summer suggested hopefully. She'd counted five skulls, now. "Maybe it's a graveyard."

"There's no char," Dan replied. He plucked at his lower lip. "The *Tuath De* burn their dead." He grimaced and Summer thought again what an ugly man he was. "No, this is a feeding ground. Lorenzo's right, that skull's been gnawed. The bones further up the hill look yellow."

"So?"

"Newer," the friar explained. "Fresh. Not yet sun-bleached. I think we'd better move on."

Summer agreed. She couldn't help but imagine something large and hungry watching them from the grassy rise above the cave. A bear, or a big cat, or something worse. She gripped Sorrow's hilt and took the first step off the ledge and onto the crooked path. When her foot crushed the grass a burst of honeysuckle perfume rose and made her sneeze. The path wasn't as steep as she'd supposed, but the empty air all along the outside made her shiver and lean away from the edge as she picked her way.

She didn't mind heights, but that didn't mean she wasn't afraid of missing her step in the night and falling off the mountain.

Lolo edged along behind Summer. The friar took up the rear and Hannah walked between. They traversed the first three tight switchbacks in silent concentration until Lolo, as usual the first to grow restless, asked,"Were they going out or in, do you think?"

"What?" Hannah sounded short of breath even though they'd been walking downhill and Summer thought it had been barely ten minutes since they'd started.

"The bones, the dead people. Which way were they going, do you think, before they were eaten? In or out of fairyland? I mean, they must have been using the Gate, right? I mean, because there's nothing else up here."

Hannah didn't reply. Summer shook her head and for once even Brother Dan didn't offer up a suggestion.

It didn't take long for Summer's feet to start complaining, and soon after that her knees. In spite of Dan's assertion that they were descending foothills and not an actual mountain, the zig-zagging path was steep and muddy. Summer's fashionable tennies were practical in the city, but they weren't meant for hiking, and she could feel the blisters forming. The mud and the grass made things slippery. More than once she almost fell. Just like Dan had predicted, she had to crook *Buairt* at an angle to keep the sword from catching in the grass or in the cactus-plants.

They're getting bigger, Summer thought when she had to turn almost sideways on the path to keep from catching a shoulder on glossy leaves. The spiny plants grew straight out of the hillside, crowding the path.

Lolo swept his pen light back and forth as he walked. The little torch was brighter and better focused than the two globes of starlight bobbing overhead, and when the narrow beam caught on round red flowers Summer saw the furled petals were beaded with drops of clear fluid. Once Lolo stretched out curious fingers but the friar stopped him with a sharp sound.

"Strangers in a strange land," Dan warned. "I'd be cautious if I were you."

"They don't smell dangerous," Hannah muttered, but Summer hadn't missed the way the changeling edged around leaves and thorns and walked worryingly close to the path's edge, as far away from the plants as possible. "Darlene kept some similar plants in pots in the kitchen, before she died. She called them bromeliad."

Summer didn't care much about plants unless they were especially beautiful. If the specimens on the hillside were any indication, bromeliad were ugly, and she didn't know why anyone would want to keep them in pots. As they trudged further down the trail, the moon sunk in the sky and her feet began to scream in protest. The air grew warmer and the hillside became a carpet of bromeliads pressed so close together they might have been one plant. The high grass became sparse and the honeysuckle perfume gradually faded. The ground became more a sluggish stream than a path, a thin muddy puddle between the plants and the cliff's edge.

"Water's getting louder," Dan said when they stopped to rest. The path was just wide enough to sit if Summer didn't mind soaking her jeans completely through. She hated the idea of wet denim clinging to her thighs and butt. Her feet hurt so badly she caught herself eyeing the carpet of spiny plants, wondering if she could possibly somehow crouch without getting pierced.

Lolo peered over the side of the cliff. "Are we getting closer?" he asked wistfully. "Summer, send your light down. I want to see. We've got to be getting nearer to the bottom."

Summer started to say she wasn't sure she could keep starlight Gathered at a distance, but then she didn't have to because Hannah sent her own glittering orb twice around Lolo's head and then darting over the side of the hill and down. Lolo gasped in delight and Summer had to suck her tongue to keep from doing the same. Hannah showed her pointed teeth in a mocking grin.

"It's easier, here, don't you agree?" the changeling said. "Like sparkling wine in my head, in my lungs. If not for the sword I'd be bursting with it."

Summer didn't respond. Her own lungs ached with too much walking. The beginnings of a stress headache itched behind her nose. Her magics felt as unreliable as always and she knew she didn't have the practice needed to make starlight dance and pulse and whirl the way Hannah had.

Frowning, she turned her back on the changeling and joined Dan and Lolo at the edge of the cliff, standing sideways so as not to smack them both with *Buairt's* unwieldy length.

"Oh," she said. "Is that the bottom?" It still seemed very far away.

"Treetops," Dan decided. "We must be above a forest. And, look, there, that sparkle? There's the river we're hearing. Not a large one, I think. Still, it's water. Hopefully fresh."

"Oh," Summer said again. "Water." It hadn't occurred to her before then, even as she'd licked her dry lips and sweated. She'd been too worried about the bones in the grass and the blisters on her feet to pay attention to her growing thirst. "We'll need water."

"And food," Lolo agreed. "Willa's rolls and bacon won't last us forever."

Hannah's starlight bobbed up and down against the sheer hillside, tracing the switchback ahead.

Summer

"We're walking a tributary," the changeling said. "Look. It gets steeper and faster before the end. It will be slippery, dangerous. Summer had the right idea. Better to wait until the sun comes up."

"We could be standing here forever," Lolo protested. "It's just a little waterfall. Where's your sense of adventure?"

"Dawn's near," Dan said. "Moon's gone down behind the hill. Hannah's right. For all we know the water gets deeper as we go. Too difficult to tell in this light. We'd be smarter to wait."

"No way," Lolo groaned. He looked at Summer, a challenge.

"We wait," Summer decided, not only because she knew Hannah and Brother Dan were right, but because she thought if she had to walk any further right that minute she'd start to cry. "We're going to get wet, aren't we?"

"Soaked," Hannah replied. She sounded viciously pleased.

"At least the air's nice and warm," Summer said. Then she sat. Cold, dirty water immediately trickled over her ankles and swirled up the legs of her pants. She had to hold *Buairt* in both hands up at chest height to keep it from getting wet. But her miserable feet practically gasped in relief.

Ignoring Lolo's giggle and Dan's sigh, Summer closed her eyes and waited for the sun to rise on *Tir na Nog*.

At first she wasn't impressed. Dawn came to fairyland slowly and in stages of gray and pink. They heard the birds first, before even the first faint light crept across their hillside. Summer, who was sitting still in the muddy stream, *Buairt* balanced safely on her bent knees, opened her eyes at the first piercing birdcall. She was prepared to be frightened or impressed by alien plumage or even a gigantic specimen, but the fat grey birds cooing and roosting on the bromeliads looked an awful lot like Central Park pigeons.

Brother Dan was still standing. He saluted the sunrise by sketching the sign of the cross in the air: spectacles, testicles, wallet, watch. Then he took a deep breath of morning air and let it out in a slow hum. Lolo grunted from where he sat on his heels almost on top of the bromeliads but didn't open his eyes. Hannah hugged herself tightly and shivered even though the air was heating as early morning broke.

The pigeons made a racket as they roamed the hillside. Summer gave up on dozing and staggered upright. Mud and water clung to her jeans and threatened to drag them down off her hips. She tugged them into place and adjusted her sword and then joined Dan, blinking. Her feet squished unhappily in her shoes.

Together Summer and the friar watched the light spread. Dan was right; there was a forest beneath their mountain, green treetops as far as Summer could see. And there was the waterfall, scarlet in the new day, frothing merrily as it fell toward the forested valley.

"We're in a bowl," Summer realized. There were more mountains across, and on either side. They were high and sharp and dangerous looking, capped with white.

"Yes," Dan agreed. "Although it's difficult to tell for certain from here. Distance, like moonlight, tricks the eye."

"It's just forest," Summer said.

"Did you expect skyscrapers and highways?" Hannah squelched through the mud and looked down into the valley. She made a rude sound. "The fay Court is always moving. You'll not find it rooted in one place for long."

"Then how are we supposed to find it?" Summer demanded. "How are we supposed to know where to look?"

Hannah shrugged. Brother Dan pulled on his lower lip and regarded the treetops without expression. Summer felt panic swelling like vomit in her gut. Then Lolo pulled himself upright with a curse and a groan.

"How do you find your way around any place when you're a tourist?" He hoisted his backpack from its perch atop a cluster of bromeliads and swung it over one shoulder. "You ask."

"Ask?" Summer wondered. The sun hadn't yet shown itself but dawn was almost a solid thing, a pastel brush bringing the tiniest details to attention. The pigeons, she saw now, had iridescent beaks and red-tipped tail feathers. "Ask who?"

"Them." Lolo pointed away and to the left where the waterfall settled and widened into a blushing ribbon and disappeared into the trees. A plume of white smoke rose between the water and the forest, orange against blue and green. "Whoever's down there, frying up breakfast."

"There's someone down there!" Hannah's mouth made an 'oh' of surprise. Then she whirled away and started down the path, slipping and splashing as she went. Lolo tossed Summer an excited grin and trotted after her, backpack slapping against his spine.

"Well," Dan said, resigned. "He's got a point." He nudged Summer gently forward. "But better stop those two before they give us away."

He needn't have worried. They were still miles above even the waterfall. Lolo and Hannah tired quickly, eagerness muted by the downward slope and the water rising around their ankles. The light grew stronger and the sun finally burst into view between the eastmost curve of the mountains. As if on cue the pigeons stopped warbling and began to call in an eager, purring chorus, wings flapping. Summer watched the birds out of the corner of her eye, amazed. The fat pigeons in Central Park never spent so much energy on anything.

The sound of the waterfall had grown to a low roar when morning finally slanted across their hillside, flashing on the stream and on the beads in Lolo's hair and the rubies on *Buairt's* scabbard. Summer couldn't hear the pigeons anymore, not past the sound of falling water, but she noticed when the birds took flight all at once, a startling disruption of gray and scarlet.

The bromeliad carpet was blooming, plump red flowers swelling, reaching on great funneled stalks toward the sky, petals opening as if to drink in the new day. The stalks swayed in the still air, twisting of their accord toward the light. The flat, broad leaves rustled, thorns scraping.

"Shit." Lolo froze and then backpedalled toward Summer. "What the hell, Summer? They're waking up!" He looked so honestly terrified Summer giggled. "Jesus, don't laugh. What if they're—" He lowered his voice to a whisper. "What if those bones—what if the plants—what if they're *carnivorous*?"

"Keep moving," Brother Dan suggested. "If they are hungry, you'd make a perfect mouthful."

Lolo yelped and clutched at Summer's fingers where they rested on *Buairt's* hilt. She knew she shouldn't laugh. His wounded scowl said she'd managed to hurt his feelings. Even Hannah slowed her step as the living carpet continued to wake and stretch, blooming red against the lightening sky.

"Disgusting," the changeling said. "Worse than Darlene's specimens."

"I think they're gorgeous," Summer argued, because they were. Alien and dangerous-looking and not like any other flowers she'd seen and that was why, even though their sway and whisper made her heart race and her knees go weak in fear, she thought the stirring bromeliads were the most wonderful thing she'd ever seen.

15. Machine

Five days before Richard's eighth birthday Bobby was hospitalized for a bedsore gone bad. It was Richard who phoned 911 after the pain of the thing got so impossible that even Bobby's best narcotics couldn't provide more than an hour of peace. Bobby spat and swore and threatened to sue the paramedics if they dared lay a finger on his wheelchair but even that little rebellion left him shaking and sweating. So he gave in and let the three men hoist him onto a stretcher, then down the steps to the street, and into the back of their ambulance.

Richard followed the stretcher into the van and curled himself in a corner out of the way, between rattling equipment and the folded jump seat. He propped his chin on his bent knees and wrapped his hands around his ankles and watched as Bobby fussed and groaned. Richard spent the short ride to St. Luke's trying to guess whether the cords and tubes and beeping machines were of any good to a man with a weeping sore on his ass and too much oxy already in his blood.

The ride-along medic didn't notice Richard because Richard didn't want to be noticed. Neither did the ER attendant with the tired face and pictures of puppies on her blue scrubs. A busy doctor and her young assistant eventually took a brief look at Bobby's coccyx and a longer look at his blood work and soon after that Bobby had a room in Detox.

Richard tagged along because he was curious and reluctantly hopeful, but it became clear when he saw the hospital room that Bobby would do a runner once he could sit in his chair again without pain. First, there was a painting of Jesus on the wall beneath the silent television, and Bobby had no place in his life for Jesus. And second, it wasn't a private room: there was an old man sitting in a chair by the window, hooked up to a placidly beeping machine.

Bobby hated people even more than he disliked Jesus.

There was a tray of food on a rolling table near what must have been the old man's bed, because the nurses lifted Bobby into the other cot, the one closest to the door, before they pulled the separation curtain. Bobby yelped and whimpered as the nurses turned him on his side so as to protect his recently bandaged ass. Richard waited until Bobby settled into heavy breathing and a light doze and the nurses went off to do more exciting things. Then he took a square of Jell-O and a carton of OJ off the forgotten tray.

He had to slip past the curtain to do so, but the old man in the chair by the window didn't notice. Instead of crossing back to Bobby's side of the hospital room, Richard sat on the floor with his stolen dinner. He ate the Jello-O slowly, savoring each cherry-flavored bite. When he was finished with the square he sipped juice out of the cardboard container. While he ate he eyed up the old man and tried to guess what he was in for: pills, like Bobby, or booze, like Derida from the corner market? Eventually Richard noticed the purple marks and old scars up and down the man's right arm, not the arm attached to the IV machine but the other one, the one resting limp in the old man's lap, and decided two things: the man was scram-handed, just like Richard himself, and he was the kind of addict who liked to shoot up.

Eventually Richard grew bored. He closed his eyes and recited pi in his head as far back as he could remember and then he dozed. When he woke again he had a stitch in his neck from sleeping against the wall. Bobby was snoring and the old man was reading a book.

Richard only really paid attention to the book because it had what looked like a drawing of a very old train, or maybe parts of a very old train, on the cover and Richard liked trains, especially the above ground trains that groaned as they hauled freight past Virginia Avenue.

The book was called *Simple Model Steam Engines*. Richard knew about steam trains from television cartoons. Just from the title and cover Richard thought the book might be even more interesting than Thomas the Tank Engine. He'd outgrown cartoons just a year earlier. Books were quieter and easier to squirrel away. Richard was learning to love books, so long as he could sound out the long words.

Eventually the old man with needle holes in his left arm shuffled to his cot and went to bed. As soon as the man was asleep, Richard stole *Simple Model Steam Engines* and took it with him to the hospital cafeteria.

Thanks to the *draiochta* William kept secured in a flask in his pack, pain was a distant irritation. Richard knew agony lurked on the edge of awareness, a monster waiting to pounce and shake and rend, but the sickly-sweet concoction the wright made him swallow at regular intervals kept that threat at bay. William was careful with the draught, either because too much of the drink would send Richard into a complete stupor, or because the medicine was too dear to waste.

Richard thought it was the latter because as it was he spent more time drifting in Water-Bearer's grasp than climbing under his own power. They hadn't managed to sever his forearm without blood loss, and with the blood loss came shock, and it seemed even *sidhe* magic couldn't prevent that entirely.

Richard lay with his ear against Water-Bearer's chest and stared between dark feathers at the ceiling. He counted steps by the lurch of the *sluagh's* hips. The ceiling brushed the tips of

Water-Bearer's wings. The passage was more tunnel than corridor, the walls smooth and the steps shallow. Aine's lamp shed an orange bubble six steps up and six behind, and beyond that the world was black. Water-Bearer hadn't bothered to try and conjure more light and Richard was glad of it.

He didn't have two hands to cup and grow the light, not anymore.

As he watched the ceiling drift by Richard knew fury lurked along with agony in that distant, muffled corner of his head. If not for the lassitude of the *draiochta* in his system he thought he would have tried to kill Water-Bearer and William twelve times over, rip them apart with his one remaining hand and his teeth together, kicking and clawing and screaming until they had no choice but to end him.

He wanted to howl now but his body betrayed him with hiccups and giggles, little mirthless squeaks of laughter that reminded him of Bobby on a bad day.

Fifteen hundred steps and they stopped to rest. Water-Bearer's heart was pounding against Richard's ear. Aine was breathing in shallow pants. Only William seemed unaffected. The wright took Aine's lamp and held it over Richard and Water-Bearer. Richard looked away from the ceiling and into the flame.

"Not still bleeding, at least," William sighed. "Cautery's holding, for now. I'll check under the bandages next time we rest. He's lucky. Any longer and we'd not have gotten it all."

"He'll never forgive you," Aine said between breaths. "He'll never forgive us. Richard works with his hands. He builds things, beautiful things."

"As do I." William moved away, taking the lantern flame with him. Richard blinked. "He'll adjust. If he lives."

"If he lives," Water-Bearer said. "If they catch us, he won't. None of us will. Keep climbing."

Summer

Richard wanted to ask what they'd done with his arm, whether they'd left it behind for the *sluagh* Prince to find, there at the bottom of the Long Stair. He wondered if the Prince and its army would stop and look and guess at that lonely severed limb or whether they would sweep past and over Richard's lost flesh and bone without a backward glance, trample it with claw and tentacle.

He shivered and giggled between clenched teeth. Water-Bearer adjusted Richard's weight against its front and began to climb upward.

Two thousand more steps but then Richard began to lose count because pain was waking to agony in the stump of his elbow and each jolt of Water-Bearer's body was lightning through his left side. Richard clenched his jaw. He stared hard at the ceiling, but he couldn't keep silent tears from overflowing, nor move to wipe them away. Eventually Water-Bearer noticed and called a halt.

They arranged themselves as best they could on the steep stairs. Water-Bearer crouched sideways between two risers, spreading its great wings for balance. The *sluagh* cradled Richard between foul- smelling thighs as William rummaged in his pack for *draiochta*. Aine sat on the step above Richard, lantern extended. She wouldn't look at what remained of Richard's elbow, but she eyed Water-Bearer's rotting feet with honest fascination.

The *sluagh* hissed at her attention and curled its toes but couldn't hide its ruined flesh away without the use of its wings. Richard felt a twitch of embarrassed sympathy and quickly squashed it with remembered hatred.

"Drink." The wright tilted his flask against Richard's mouth. The *draiochta* was sweet and thick as honey and gritty against Richard's teeth. He wished he had the courage to spit the medicine back into William's face, but the growing agony in his side frightened him into swallowing eager gulps.

"Slowly," Aine cautioned. She set a light hand on Richard's brow, petting gently like one might soothe a dog or a child. She liked him well enough, Richard knew. He thought she even considered him a friend. He supposed she was grateful he'd come after her through Winter's Gate. But as he met her concerned stare he couldn't help but feel a gulf stretched between them.

For all she was human Aine had grown up in the fay Court, had thought of herself as *sidhe* for most of her life. D.C. had shaken her, Hannah's appearance had filled her with self-doubt, the *sluagh* army had frightened her, but here on the steps beside Water-Bearer and William she seemed to grow straight and solid, more herself than Richard had yet seen her.

She was comfortable, Richard realized. Water-Bearer and the wright didn't alarm her the way automobiles and apartment buildings and the Metro trains had. Even as she petted his brow and made sounds of sympathy, he thought she was remembering he was a lesser being, mortal and fleeting.

William took the flask away and scraped missed droplets of medicine from Richard's chin with clockwork fingers. Richard turned his face and closed his eyes so he wouldn't have to see Aine's pitying expression.

"Another hour," William said. "Maybe two, until we reach the spire."

Water-Bearer shifted beneath Richard's cheek, feathers rustling.

"They'll climb quickly," it said. "I'll need time, once we reach the top."

Richard could feel the wright looming, blocking the light of Aine's lantern. The gears in his fingers clicked in the silence.

Richard cracked one eye and saw William was tapping that unnatural hand against his pack in absent thought.

"It's the Long Stair to the spire or no way at all," William muttered. "Block the Stair, you'll have time."

Water-Bearer coughed in dry amusement. Its wings shifted in pointed reminder. William wasn't deterred.

"Even if your brothers and sisters are yet strong enough to reach the very top of *Reilig na Rí* on tattered pinions—which I much doubt—last I stood in the spire there was a distinct lack of windows. In fact, the space is remarkable for its paucity of view."

"So?"

"So, you're not thinking clearly. Or you're thinking of only one thing."

Water-Bearer shifted again. Its feathers tickled Richard's brow. Richard was growing used to the *sluagh*'s pungent perfume. His stomach no longer rolled when the tentacles in the monster's empty eye socket twitched. If Richard squinted past the obvious horror of Water-Bearer's mutations, the features behind the mottled flesh were sharp and fine, almost lovely.

It licked its lips, wormy tongue rolling, and then said: "Oh. Aye, of course. We seal the Stair."

Aine lifted her lantern and looked between the wright and the *sluagh*. "You said that magic was lost to you."

"Not lost," Water-Bearer said. "Only lesser. Weak and dying, as we are." It shifted and straightened, forcing Richard to sit more upright against its chest. The *draiochta* was working its magic, muffling his pain, so Richard didn't protest. It took an effort but he managed to open both eyes wide and watch as the *sluagh* set three talon-tipped fingers on Aine's step and whispered.

The surface of the step stretched upward when Water-Bearer lifted its hand, thick strings of dark taffy clinging to each finger. Then the *sluagh* hissed and grunted, and the strings stopped growing and turned brittle. At last they cracked away to dust.

"Useless." Water-Bearer snorted in disgust.

"Without blood," William corrected.

Aine set her lantern on the step and reached for her knife. "Use mine," she said. "It's what you've meant to do all along."

"To open the Gate." Water-Bearer's one eye blinked. Its wings shifted again. "Whatever my Prince believes, you're very small, and human, and the Mending magic is fading in your veins. Even with Richard beside me I'm afraid to use you up entire before the Gate is sprung."

William scoffed. "You've grown cowardly and cautious. And also forgetful, old man. My blood is as good as any for a small task such as this. Come. We're wasting time and I don't want to die on these steps." The smith dug again in his pack. He pulled forth one of the bowls he'd used to feed Aine and Richard stew. "Hold this, lass. Steady, now."

Water-Bearer moved, shuffling itself away from the wall and onto its feet, lifting Richard again into the cradle of its arms. In the shift and sway of wings Richard missed the slash of Aine's knife, but when Water-Bearer settled between risers and turned back to the wright, the shallow bowl was half-filled with dark blood and William was pressing a wadded rag against the inside of his forearm.

Richard giggled when he meant to curse.

"You should have saved mine," he said.

Aine looked horrified. Richard wondered if she thought he meant his arm. William only grunted. Water-Bearer clicked its tongue. "Your blood was dirtied, apostate. And may still be more dangerous than useful. Best keep that in mind if you live. " It awarded Aine its one-eyed stare. "Come, *siofra*. You'll hold the bowl. William's right. It's time for me to remember courage. I am *aes si*, member of the Dread Host, both revered and feared in *Tir na Nog*. This mountain is nothing to me."

Water-Bearer descended ten steps back into the darkness before gently setting Richard down on a stair cut wider than most of the others. Richard managed to sit up on his own, wriggling back against the wall. His stump screamed far away protest but he ignored it in favor of watching the *sluagh* prepare its magic.

Aine had left her lantern up the stair with William but the glow of the flame still managed to limn Water-Bearer in gold. When the ghoul straightened to its full height, ebony wings tucked back against its spine, it was taller than Richard had realized, shoulders broad beneath the thin tunic it seemed to prefer. The few hanks of dark hair still remaining on the monster's skull shone bright as feathers in the lamplight. It lifted its chin and inhaled loudly through its nose.

Sniffing the air, Richard thought. Tasting the tunnel.

"There," the *sluagh* decided. It hopped down three more steps in one bound, forcing Aine to hurry after, then reached up and set one palm on the low ceiling. "The earth is willing, here. Malleable. Hungry. Use your fingers, mix William's blood into the dirt. Here, and here." It indicated the step beneath its feet. "Quickly now, before I change my mind."

Aine did as she was told, dipping her fingers into the bowl and standing on her toes to paint red blood into the gray earth. As she worked the *sluagh* began to whisper and mutter. Water-Bearer spread its fingers wide in the air halfway between ceiling and step, beckoning, cajoling. Richard held his breath, trying to make sense of the *sluagh*'s murmured incantation, but the syllable and sounds were alien, unfamiliar and not at all like the fractured Gaelic Winter used, which Richard had been trying to teach himself.

An older language, Bobby whispered, startling Richard who had thought the voices in his head were temporarily muffled by the *draiochta*. *An older ritual. Pay attention, Rick. Could be important.*

But Richard was already fascinated and he didn't need his subconscious telling him to look sharp because he was hanging on Water-Bearer's every sound and gesture. The shine from the lantern was spreading, moving up and across the wall, around Aine's rapidly painting fingers, and back down the other side of the stair and beneath Water-Bearer's ruined feet. Richard glanced over his good shoulder back up the stair, but William and the flame hadn't moved. It was Water-Bearer's Cant warming the passage with stolen radiance. Water-Bearer's Cant and the added synergy of the blood in Aine's bowl.

Richard breathed out in stuttering surprise. "It's beautiful."

Water-Bearer hesitated, going briefly silent before rustling its folded wings and continuing on, weaving together sound and light and motion until the *sluagh* was little more than a golden glow and a string of blurred sound. Aine was a gray-cut silhouette in the painful incandescence. Richard's eyes stung and wept just as they had in the acrid *sluagh* atmosphere, but he didn't look away.

When the passage closed in on itself, it was less a collapse and more a stretching of floor and ceiling, a swelling of earth and a slotting together of puzzle pieces. Stalactites joined stalagmites, steaming as they fused. The stink of scorched blood made Richard look involuntarily at the stump of his arm, but the bandage was clean. It was William's blood, he realized, burning as it bolstered Water-Bearer's spell.

Then the floor and ceiling fused completely. Richard's ears popped. The unnatural light began to dim and retreat back up thirteen stairs to the lantern at William's side, thinning to nothing but the faint orange glow of a flickering flame as it went. Aine and the *sluagh* were no longer limned in gold. Aine's bowl was empty, turned upside down in her hands, the last few dribbles of red liquid falling harmlessly onto the stair.

Aine appeared calm. Water-Bearer was breathing hard, quivering from crown to claw. Its one eye gleamed green and wild and when it smiled it was with mad satisfaction.

"Too long," the *sluagh* purred, "it's been far too long since I attempted such a thing. No wonder we're dying. Why should one wish to live, without this?"

It flung out one hand, scratching five sharp claws over the perfectly smooth seal on the stair. The new wall reminded Richard of the bowl of a spoon, concave and seamless; even the stalactites and stalagmites vanished in the joining.

"I heard you," Water-Bearer told Richard. "Beautiful, you said. And, aye, so it is, but far more than that. This"—it tilted its pointed chin at the fade of magic released—"is what we were, what we were meant to be. We've gone so long without, I'd almost forgotten the taste of it, sweeter even than mortal gristle and bone." It fluffed its wings, ran dangerous fingers through inky feathers, and looked up the Long Stair at William as it promised, "We will have it back. No matter the cost, I swear it. Aye, *we will have it back.*"

16. Swordplay

The smoke trickled into the morning from a squat chimney atop a crooked hut. The smoke smelled sweet, like overripe apples. The chimney looked as if it had been pieced together in blocks of mud and brick and the hut wasn't much different, although Summer could see the curve of stacked logs behind the layer of dried mud. There were no visible windows. The front door had an actual handle and, Summer saw as they drew close, a real keyhole lock. The door was painted a cheerful red, bright against the mud walls.

They'd followed the water through blooming bromeliads and over the side of the cliff to the valley floor. Summer had been certain they'd have to ride the waterfall over the rocks, but just before Lolo threw himself eagerly into the rushing cataract, Brother Dan found a ladder of knotted rope secured to the cliff face by way of thick metal rings.

"It's not as far to the valley floor as we thought," the friar said. "Sixty feet, no more. The ladder looks solid. Someone's kept it in repair. Still, I'll go first." Before Summer could protest he twisted feet first over the edge of the cliff, gripping the rope in both hands. He toed the cliff side until his toes caught the knotted rung below. Spray from the waterfall immediately drenched the parts of him that hadn't already been dunked in the muddy stream. "Rope's wet but not slippery. Don't rush. One at a time, please."

And with that Dan was on his way, scaling the ladder one deliberate handhold at a time. Summer was impressed. For a man the size of a grizzly, he climbed with a monkey's confidence.

"Wow," Lolo said. He peered over the edge of the cliff at Dan's tonsured head. "Swimming the waterfall looks easier."

"You'd be crushed to death on the rocks at the bottom," Hannah argued. "However have you managed to survive so long? You've no sense at all."

"Bitch," Lolo retorted but without real heat. He scrambled over the side of the cliff before Hannah could respond and yelped when his feet dangled into thin air. But then, just like Dan, he found purchase with the toes of his shoes. His knuckles relaxed around the rope and he looked up, flashing Summer and Hannah a grin.

"Easy as pie," he promised, with just a tad too much enthusiasm. "But maybe don't look down." He laddered away into the spray, moving with much less speed than the friar.

"He's frightened," Hannah pronounced. She made it sound like a dirty little secret.

"Aren't you?" Summer asked. She really wanted to know if the other girl was as superior as she pretended. "You may be a fairy princess, but I don't see any wings. You slip you smash."

Hannah edged forward until they stood hip to hip on the edge of the cliff.

"I should push you over," the changeling said, looking not at Summer but at the top of Lolo's head already halfway down. "Stop you now."

Summer felt something like snakes twisting in her belly. She set her hand on *Buairt's* hilt but made herself stand without flinching. "You're won't."

Hannah blew a puff of annoyance through her front teeth. "No."

"Why?"

"You don't matter. *You're* nothing. I'd like to push you over, I'd enjoy it, watching you fall. But *he'd* just pick up the sword and take his vengeance, separate my head from my neck, I bet."

"Brother Dan?"

"Well, I'm certainly not afraid of the runt. He's as useless as you. The other—he stinks of God, just like Jeremiah. Jeremiah wanted me dead, too. But Jeremiah is a coward." The changeling shook her head without taking her eyes from the ground below. "Your Daniel has a warrior's stride and a prince's strength. What did he call us? Demons, he said." Hannah at last looked at Summer, dark eyes wide and worried. "He won't be satisfied with my mother's death, I think. Better watch yourself, maybe he'll decide to cut off your head, too."

"He won't." Summer's fingers gripped *Buairt* so tightly they throbbed in protest. "Even if he wanted to, I'd kill him first."

Hannah smiled, bright and dangerous. "That's the way, friend. Now you're thinking. This is our world, our realm. Those two below don't belong. They are nothing, and worse than nothing. Mortal man and boy, I know they'd rather see us murdered than bend the knee. Keep that in mind, *Samhradh*, when we come before my mother."

She dropped to the edge of the cliff, then twisted over the edge, grabbing the rope without hesitation. Hannah found the first foothold without looking. All the while, she kept grinning up at Summer.

"I'll go. So you don't have to worry I'll kick you off halfway down."

Summer stood alone on the edge of the cliff and tried not to hyperventilate. Hannah was only being a bully. Summer knew bullies, she'd met more than her share in the fancy private schools Papa had insisted she attend. At first Winter had been around to knock out a tooth or bloody a nose, but after he'd been sent away Summer learned to manage on her own. She'd bloodied a few noses herself before she'd mastered enough of a Glamour to make herself appear ordinary and unassuming.

But ordinary and unassuming wasn't going to cut it in fairyland. And she wasn't going to let Hannah bully her into second-guessing her friends, at least not Lolo. Maybe she'd have to keep one eye on Brother Dan. He'd spent time in prison, after all, and he'd both managed to outsmart Katherine Grey and outbluster Siobahn.

"Shoot," Summer sighed as Lolo shouted and waved from down below, motioning for her to hurry up. Brother Dan had turned away to study the forest. Hannah was almost at the bottom. "Shit." Because real swear words made her feel twenty times more brave. She wished she'd taken the time to learn Winter's collection of favorites in the Gaelic. As she made sure *Buairt* was secure and then scrambled over the side of the cliff onto the wobbly ladder, she just knew she was going to need them all.

"Hey, Summer," Lolo hissed as Summer studied the red door. "Skeps!"

Summer looked where he was pointing and saw three large woven baskets turned upside down on a log behind the mud hut. The log was wide and raised off the grass by way of a pile of stones at each end. The baskets were pointy at the top and wider on the bottom, like straw bells or funny grass hats.

"What's a skep?"

"Bee hives." Lolo explained eagerly. At Brother Dan's look, he shrugged. "I saw it on television," he explained. "Beekeeping the old fashioned way. You cut the skeps open to get the honey. Summer, do you think they're big bees like you said? Can we go see?"

"No," said Dan. "There's a dog guarding the back garden, there. Look at his face, he won't let us near the yard." Dan was right. There was a dog, a leggy black animal that reminded

Summer of a German Shepherd. It was watching them with sharp brown eyes. Its tail was up and on alert, its head lowered in polite but firm warning.

"We'll hello the house," Dan decided. "There must be someone home, I smell breakfast." He lifted two fingers to his lips and split the morning with a shrill whistle. The dog's ears swiveled front and back, but the animal didn't protest.

At first Summer thought they'd have to give up and walk on along the rutted road and into the forest. It had been all fields in the short walk between the cliff and the hut, the river rushing alongside, bromeliads left behind. But then the river sidestepped around the mud house, and the bees, and the garden and haystack behind, and slipped away into the trees.

From where they stood it seemed the forest stretched across the rest of the valley, from cliff to mountain range and back again. The trees on the edge were tight-packed and silver-trunked, heavy with wide waxy leaves. Summer could hear the pipe and rustle of birds in latticed branches. Ferns, some large and very green and others small and yellow, spread beneath the trees.

The red door banged open, startling everyone but Hannah. Lolo squeaked and even Brother Dan twitched. Summer's heart thumped in surprise but she managed to keep from jumping.

The *sidhe* woman in the doorway scowled. *"Dul amach!"* she said. Thanks to Papa's erratic language drills, Summer's brain managed to translate: "Go away!" She made to step back and slam the door, but Brother Dan was quicker.

"Mistress," he said hastily. "Pardon, mistress." He held his large hands up, palms out, the universal sign of surrender. "We're only lost and in need of some direction."

"Do you really suppose she speaks English?" Hannah asked, sour. Then: *"Sean mháthair, cabhrú linn le do thoil?"*

The woman had hair so gray as to be nearly white, worn in two long plaits down her back. Her skin was brown and weathered from too much time spent in the sun without proper SPF. There were distinct crinkles around her blue eyes and at the corners of her wide mouth; they flattened out when she frowned at Hannah.

"I am neither old nor thy mother," she said in flat, American English, a softer version of Dan's own accent. "Neither am I a babe, yet unskilled and unable to converse with Adam's children." She regarded Lolo and Brother Dan with raised white brows then looked directly at Summer. "You, though—you're very young to have brought two over across the Way, and through that particular Gate. Has no one taught you not to let them speak out of turn? *Síofraí* who can't hold their tongues don't last long at Court. Better to school your catch now than feed their bones to the Progress later."

Brother Dan shifted before Lolo could protest, clapping his hand firmly across the boy's mouth. Lolo squirmed but settled. Hannah smirked. The *sidhe* nodded. Summer thought she saw the woman's mouth flex in quickly suppressed regret.

"Better," she declared. "Mayhap you'll do. But not in those clothes." She shook her head. "Come inside and I'll see what I can find. *Fanacht!*" she said to the dog. "Stay, Collum." Then she turned and held open the red door in grudging welcome.

The one-room hut was clean and sparsely furnished. There were no windows, but a smear of Gathered starlight floating between the rafters and the peaked roof kept gloom at bay. Summer had never seen starlight spread outside the traditional globe. The sparkling cloud was beautiful, a miniature galaxy rotating overhead. She tried not to gape and resolved to learn how to conjure her own small star system as soon as possible.

"Sit," the *sidhe* bowed to Summer, hands folded at her waist. There was a single chair in the room, sturdy and made of log and twig, the seat cushioned by a bright patchwork pillow.

Summer

Because it seemed polite Summer sat, awkwardly twisting her belt so *Buairt* lay on her knees. Hannah crossed her arms over her chest, fists clenched. Summer could feel the changeling's sulk coming on. She hoped Hannah didn't do something stupid and get them all fed to the dog, who had followed them into the hut and arranged himself in front of the cold fireplace. Close up he was very big and not as friendly looking.

Brother Dan stood against the wall near the red door, his hand now wrapped around Lolo's shoulder. The friar was too large to make himself fade into the background, but Summer thought he was trying his best to appear harmless. For once Lolo didn't kick up a fuss. He stood quietly at Dan's side, studying the tips of his shoes like they were the most interesting thing he'd ever seen.

Besides the chair the room held a small trestle table, a low cot, a trunk painted to match the door, and a collection of patchwork pillows spread on the floor near the fireplace and across the cot. The black dog laid his head on one of the cushions as he looked between his mistress and her visitors.

"I'll have proper *brats*, of course. That'll do, I think, so long as you keep them well covered." The *sidhe* padded across the room and bent over the trunk, springing the lock with one hand. For the first time Summer noticed the woman was barefoot. Her slender toes were dirty, her heels cracked and calloused. "There are plenty in the forest eager to carry word of anything remarkable to Court."

"Yes, my mother's Court," Hannah said. Summer felt her heart sink and wanted to kick the other girl for her stupidity. "Where is it? Can you tell us how to find it?"

The *sidhe* didn't pause in pulling swathes of dull brown cloth from the bottom of her trunk. "Don't worry yourself, lass. It's not a difficult thing to find, *Chúirt Banríon ar*, the Fay Queen's Court." She gathered armfuls of the fabric against her front and carried it back across the room to Lolo and Brother Daniel. "Supposing it wants to be found."

"It will want to find *me,*" Hannah said. Summer did kick her then, twisting in the chair to strike the other girl's ankle with the heel of her shoe, a warning. Hannah hissed and bristled and her ponytail quivered in indignation. "I'm important. Do you know who I am? My mother—"

"Quiet!" the *sidhe* ordered. She dropped the folds of cloth and straightened, seeming to grow tall as the rafters, narrow and sharp, all pointed teeth and sunken cheekbones and fingers curved into claws. The starlight beneath the eaves flickered. "Hold your tongue! I've not let you across my threshold only to have you draw her attention *now.*"

Summer jumped to her feet, hand cupping *Buairt's* hilt. Brother Daniel shifted his bulk from the wall, swelling almost as tall as the angry *sidhe.* Lolo had Winter's Glock in his right hand and was pointing it at the dog who'd risen from its place by on the floor and was flashing gigantic, wet fangs at Hannah. It growled.

Hannah was the only person in the room who seemed to shrink. Her fingertips spat sluggish sparks, but they fizzled on the mud-packed floor. The changeling pulled her shoulders up against her ears and curled in on herself even as she edged behind the wooden chair.

"I'm important," she insisted, but she wouldn't look at the looming *sidhe* or the woman's quivering hound. "You'll see."

"I know what you are. You've her likeness. I see it now." The *sidhe's* mouth pulled in a snarl. "A lost sister or forgotten cousin. Beware." She set her hand on the black dog's head; he'd come to lean against her thigh, growing deep in his chest. Strings of froth dripped from his muzzle. "There's naught to say *she'll* be pleased to see your face. She'll kiss you for lost kin or kill you for jealousy. If I were you I'd hope for the second."

Summer

Summer liked dogs but the *sidhe's* hound was giving her goosebumps. The animal had grown along with its mistress and seemed large as a pony. There was a flash of red in its rolling eye and its tail flexed and curled like a cat's or a serpent. It watched Hannah with single-minded intensity, but when Lolo shifted nervously its growl deepened in clear warning.

"Sorry. We're sorry." Summer thought she should probably draw her sword but she also thought once she did she'd have to use it. "Hannah didn't mean anything. She's just naturally rude. Hannah, say you're sorry. Lolo"—she hissed out of the corner of her mouth when the dog flicked its tail—"put the gun away. I don't think he likes it."

Hannah muttered something that might have been an apology but the *sidhe* woman ignored her. Instead she bent over Summer, her blue eyes drawing stars from the tiny universe above their heads.

"Who are you?" she demanded. "Not what I first supposed, I think. Come back across the Way, aye, but with more than the usual commerce. Queen's kin when we believe her family dead and well waked. Wright-wrought scabbard, but the blade beneath aches like a rotten tooth. Mortal child with human technology in hand and the will to use it and no Glamour on his heart to keep us safe." The *sidhe* stretched her arms out and around like she wanted to pull Summer into an embrace only she kept reaching, thinning to mist, all but clawed hands and sharp teeth. "I don't like it. I don't like it at all."

"Run!" Brother Dan cried. "Get out!"

Hannah screamed and darted for the red door, running straight through the *sidhe's* cloudy form. She screamed again, this time in pain. Blood burst across her back. Strips of her sweater fell away, leaving behind great welts on her pale skin. Lolo howled and put himself between the changeling and the *sidhe's* talons, but the dog sprang at his throat, slavering jaws stretched wide.

Just like in those Matrix movies Winter loved, time seemed to slow to molasses. Summer saw the curve of the dog's spine as it braced itself for the killing strike. Using both hands, Lolo aimed the Glock, and squeezed the trigger.

But the gun was empty. Summer couldn't believe Lolo had forgotten. She wanted to yell at him for being stupid, but when she opened her mouth time sped up again, back to normal and then too fast. Lolo went down beneath the dog without a sound. Hannah crashed through the red door, knocking it open, and fell through. Sunlight pierced the windowless hut, catching ghostly wisps of *sidhe* where it coiled across the floor and around Brother Daniel's ankles.

Brother Dan started reciting something in Latin. The starlight in the rafters winked out. The *sidhe* woman hissed and started to grow solid again. The dog on the floor above Lolo whined and coughed.

"No," Summer said. She meant to shout but the word was hardly more than a croak past a tongue gone dry. She tried again, "No!" and yanked *Buairt* from her belt.

The sword shed its scabbard eagerly, coming at once to Summer's hand.

Summer didn't hesitate. She set her jaw and clenched both hands around the *Buairt's* hilt and plunged it down with all her strength into the black dog, parting flesh and cracking bone.

"Jesus Christ!" Lolo rolled sideways and out from under the convulsing hound. He was covered shoulder to thigh in blood and his face was the color of the Hudson on a foggy day. Winter's gun hung loose in his hand. *"María Madre de Dios*, it's already dead, okay! Be careful with that thing!"

Summer's mouth worked helplessly. She felt traitorous tears spill over onto her cheeks but couldn't wipe them away.

Buairt was stuck in the ground beneath the dog and no matter how desperately she tugged, she couldn't pull the sword free.

"Summer!" Lolo shrilled. "Look out!"

Summer turned her head in time to see the *sidhe* woman whirling, a tunnel cloud of burning blue eyes and fang and claw. Brother Dan, bleeding from his nose and chin, charged after in stubborn pursuit. Summer pulled desperately at *Buairt's* hilt, but still the sword stuck. She looked away from the howling *sidhe*, then set a foot hard on the dog's ribcage and strained.

Buairt popped free just as the *sidhe* swooped past Summer's right shoulder, so close Summer could feel cold breath on her neck. Summer stumbled backward, sat down hard on the floor, the sword lifted in both hands and dripping dark fluid from tip to hilt. It didn't look at all like blood.

And just like that it was over.

The *sidhe* turned from mist to solid and collapsed to the packed-mud floor. She fell to her knees and then to her hands. Slowly, as though pressed by an unbearable weight, she lay flat on her face in the dirt, chest rising as she drew air in panicked gasps.

"Kill me, then," she said through gritted teeth. "Strike me through as you did my loyal Collum and may this hag's curse be on thy head. *Siúl sa dorchadas i gcónaí.*"

"Donde haya oscuridad, que lleve la luz," Brother Dan retorted quietly. "'Where there is darkness, there will be light." Swiping blood from his upper lip, he squatted over the fallen woman. "Your curse has no power here."

"Kill me," the *sidhe* rasped. Her eyes were slits of blue hatred. "I welcomed you over my threshold and you've brought death into my home." Summer could almost see the life seeping from the woman's pores, sucked away by the hungry blade in her hand. As if sensing Summer's horror, the *sidhe* rolled her eyes, trying but unable to lift her head. "Who are you?" she wondered, hoarse. "That you can resist its pull? What are you?"

"No one." Still holding *Buairt* out, Summer backed carefully toward the open door. Lolo followed, but not before snatching up the bundle of brown robes.

"We need them," he explained when Summer scowled. "She was right. We need a disguise." He shrugged, unrepentant. "Also, you should probably kill her."

The jut of his chin made Summer think he was just trying to be brave and didn't really mean it, but she wasn't sure. She was afraid he was right.

"No," Brother Dan said. "Leave her. The sword's done its job; she'll be of no danger to anyone for quite some time, assuming she manages to rally at all. Mind your language, Lorenzo. Summer, come outside and clean your blade on the grass. The day's not getting longer and who can guess how far Hannah's run."

The friar stood. He stepped around the *sidhe* and over her dead hound and out the door, pulling Lolo after. Summer took a deep breath. The woman on the ground continued to stare, although her blue eyes were growing vacant. Summer thought she should probably apologize again.

Instead, she bit the inside of her cheek hard until she tasted salt. The pain made it easier to breathe, to turn her back on the woman and leave the windowless hut.

17. Spark Plug

There was a door at the top of the Long Stair, the first real door Richard had seen since they'd stepped foot in *Reilig na Rí.* The door was molded bronze all around, arched at the top and set into the rock wall with an almost seamless accuracy that Richard couldn't help but find impressive.

William had taken over the lamp. He held it as high as possible against the low ceiling, letting light warm the bronze. Time had given the door a rich patina, turning it more green than yellow. Richard saw that there were patterns in the aging whorls and swirls of color that reminded him vaguely of Van Gogh's *Starry Night.*

"My work," William said when he caught Richard staring. "I say mine. But in truth it took two of us to shape the metal and three more to work the hinges. The most difficult thing was convincing the Host to give up swords and shields for the melting. By then we'd run out of an honest source."

Richard reached past feathers and swept his remaining hand across the door's surface. The metal felt cold and greasy against his fingertips. He didn't see a lock or latch. Still, he thought it was very beautiful and well made.

Aine had more pressing concerns. "How is it unlocked? Have you a key?" She nudged the door with her foot. The bottom of her shoe left an imprint in the patina. Richard opened his mouth on a protest that she could so callously mar a work of art, but before he could speak the print faded away as if it had ever existed.

"Locked to you." Water-Bearer said, "Never to the denizens of this mountain." It shifted Richard in its arms then leaned one shoulder against bronze. The door swung inwards without so much as a scrape of protest.

William snorted and ushered Aine through after. Richard heard a puff of breath and the clank of metal on stone: the lantern, blown out and set aside because there was no longer need for candlelight. Richard was impressed a second time at the tightness of the door's seams, because while not a sliver of light had trickled through onto the Long Stair, the room beyond was ablaze.

The *draiochta* dulled his mind so that it took Richard longer than he liked before he understood what he was looking at.

"The Gate," he said. "It's the top of your Gate, the upper limit." Now that he recognized the portal he felt the heat of the room, the warmth radiating off walls and floor and ceiling. The room was hardly wider than the pulsing flame itself, no bigger than ten feet square, and the ceiling so low it barely skirted the Gate's pinnacle.

"Did you build the mountain all about it, then?" Aine wondered. Richard blinked. He hadn't realized such a thing was possible.

"To protect it from the poisons of this world," Water-Bearer agreed. It bent at the waist and set Richard down on the floor, then straightened again and stretched its wings as much as possible in the small space, groaning a little as it did so. "Our first and most imperative of magics, as the *doiteain domhain* began to tear it apart as soon as we fell through." Malice made the *sluagh's* alien face more dangerous than usual. "I imagine Gloriana had planned it thusly, that particular destruction. But we were too quick and too powerful. Even so, so many of us faltered in the doing."

"The bones in the walls," Richard guessed, dragging himself upright with his good arm. He sat on his knees, the floor warm beneath his thighs.

"So many dead," Aine said at the same time. She sounded more awestruck than sorry.

"We kept it from collapsing," Water-Bearer agreed. "It was a near thing, but we kept it alive." The *sluagh* regarded the wavering white radiance with his single eye. The fingerling tentacles in his other eye writhed and stretched, reaching toward the portal. "Aye, and I'd resigned myself to ending on this side of the cursed thing. But you were a pleasant riddle, apostate. The most distracting of surprises."

"You mean Aine." It hurt to sit upright so Richard lowered himself carefully prone on his back. The throb in the stump of his elbow seemed to echo the pulse of the Gate. Pain was creeping close again. He thought it might be time for another drink from William's flask.

"Nay," Water-Bearer purred. "I mean you, Richard. Trickster lad, you slip beneath the notice of this malignant world, you make the impossible possible."

"I'm a spark plug," Richard decided without enthusiasm.

The wright laughed. "If you like. I suspect it's the opposite. You've managed to diminish yourself so far beneath the gaze of the gods, those around you step out of time as well. Allowing strong magic where normally the *doiteain domhain* would interfere."

Beneath the gaze of the gods, Richard thought. He discovered he liked the lonely sound of it.

"Shall we proceed?" William suggested. "I fear even a blocked passage won't keep the Prince back forever. The Host will dig their way through by fang and claw once they realize exactly where you've taken their Mender, Miach."

As if on cue Water-Bearer stiffened, head cocked, and Richard realized the sound in the chamber had changed. Where before only the muted thrumming of the Gate echoed through the stone, now he thought he could hear the rasp of claw through the mountain wall and even, unbelievably, the sough of wings on the other side of stone.

"They're outside the spire," Aine gasped. "You were wrong, wright. They *can* still fly so high."

"Desperation," Water-Bearer agreed as Richard sat up again in alarm. "I think we'd best begin."

Richard saw his first blood sacrifice the day Winter turned fifteen and Lolo and Richard stole two bottles of Moet & Chandon from Capitol Wines in celebration. Up until that point life with Winter had been mostly snuffing *sluagh* and chasing after the occasional unusual criminal on the MPDC's dime.

They took the bottles and several bags of Thai takeout into the National Gallery after closing, because Richard wanted to touch Michelangelo's *David-Apollo* before it moved on. Winter liked the Gallery in general and said he supposed it was as fine a place to get drunk as any. Lolo said he didn't give a shit where they celebrated so long as he got to eat all the cashew peanut.

They slipped in just before the gallery doors were locked for the night and ate their dinner at the foot of the statue. The inside of the building was kept pleasantly cool for the sake of the exhibits and after an August day spent sweltering in the Metro tunnels, the change in temperature was pleasant enough to send Lolo into a doze, peanut sauce still sticky on his mouth and hands. Winter was working his way through the first bottle of brut and Richard, cradling its twin, had just about decided that the unfinished marble sculpture was more likely David than Apollo when Winter sat suddenly upright and hissed a warning.

Richard, who was confident enough in his knack to suppose they wouldn't be discovered even if one of the night guardsmen stepped smack in the middle of Winter's *pad thai*, mouthed a question. Lolo stopped snoring and opened his eyes.

"Someone's here," Winter whispered. He sat the bottle of Moet on the ground and climbed to his feet. Probably only Richard would have noticed that the *sidhe* was less than his usual, graceful self. He wasn't clumsy, never that, but he staggered a little over his own feet. Richard was secretly delighted to learn that fairy princes were not immune to good champagne.

"Not a guard," Winter said when Richard rolled his eyes. "Someone else. Something else. Something's...you know..."

"Up?" Lolo suggested. He'd refused to touch the alcohol and as a result was more alert than Winter and Richard combined. "Cool. Do you think it's an art heist? I hope it's an art heist!, like in that Thomas Crown movie."

Richard looked up at the blinking red eye in one corner of the ceiling. He knew from exploration that the visible cameras were more for show than practicality. There were other, more advanced, security measures throughout the building, including alarms both silent and ear-piercing.

"If it's a heist they've managed not to trip any sirens at all," Richard said doubtfully. "Pretty unlikely, don't you think?"

"Fantastic," Winter said, gray eyes gone wide with excitement. He plucked the champagne bottle from the floor and crooked it in his arm. "Come on, Richard. We'd better take a look."

"Why? It's not *sluagh*." But Richard climbed to his feet because it was Winter's birthday and they were all three busy pretending he didn't miss his life before the Metro, so Richard figured if Winter wanted to waste time sticking his nose into someone else's business as a distraction, he wouldn't kick up a fuss. "Probably some loaded pop star getting a private tour. Happens sometimes."

"Fantastic!" Lolo squealed, mimicking Winter. "Hope it's somebody ultra-famous. Hurry up, Richard. I want to *see.*"

"This way," Winter said, striding forward, following either his ears or his nose, Richard wasn't sure.

They walked through the Rotunda with its red walls and dark floors. Winter paused briefly to swig from his bottle, then screwed up his face in disgust.

"I can hear them," he said, tapping his head. The yellow gems in his ears winked, reminding Richard that his friend was, for all intents and purposes, deaf and yet open to the raw emotion behind every scarcely caught whispered word.

"Who?" Lolo bounced. The younger boy paid the priceless displays on the walls no attention; his excitement was all for the chase. "Where are they, Win?"

"Further down, West Court." Winter abandoned his Moet again, setting it this time on a glossy black visitor's chair. "Three—no, four. They don't know we're here. They've got one of the guards."

"Got one of the guards?" Richard reached for Winter but his friend was already past, ghosting down through the West Sculpture Hall between bronze statues, Lolo trotting eagerly behind. Richard hurried after.

"What do you mean, they've got one of the guards?" He snagged Winter by the back of the affected black trench his friend wore even on summer evenings. Winter stopped and looked around, but only half his attention was in the hall; it was obvious he was listening to whatever disembodied voices he heard in his skull, and now Richard could hear faint, rhythmic whispers as well. "Is that singing? Someone's singing?"

"Chanting!" Lolo bounced on his toes. "I think that's chanting. Is that chanting? Win, what're they doing? Oh, wait, I totally know! I read the signs! That room's the *Gods and Goddesses of Ancient Egypt!"*

"Blood ritual, sacrificial magic," Winter agreed, eyes narrowed to distant silver slits. "Happy Birthday to me. Some stupid human's read too much Crowley and fancies himself a warlock. Richard, better phone Healy. They've already sliced up one guard and they're not planning to stop until they let something nasty through." He tugged out of Richard's grasp. "I'll distract 'em. Lolo, once I do, see what you can do for the victim. He'll be the one bleeding out beneath the 2000-year-old bust of Horus."

Feeling nauseated, Richard dug in his trousers for his phone. Detective Healy wouldn't be surprised, but he wasn't going to be pleased, either. For all he used Winter as a consult, the detective was never at his best when it came to the supernatural. For that matter, neither was Richard.

"They can't really..." He swallowed and tried again. "I mean, with the blood ritual? It doesn't really work, does it? That sort of thing?"

"Of course it does," Winter tossed over his shoulder without inflection, "how do you think I managed to rip a Gate between worlds? It works a fucking treat if you've the stomach for it."

"It works a fucking treat if you've the stomach for it," Richard told Aine in a whisper, earning an angry roll of Water-Bearer's glittering green eye. Richard giggled at the *sluagh's* disgust because he'd had another dose of William's lovely curative and it was more fun to laugh than to weep.

"I've the stomach for it," Aine replied. She stood at his side. The sleeves of her shirt were mostly rags and tatters so she'd had no difficulty in tearing her left off, baring her arm to the buck knife she held in her right. "Or have you forgotten already?"

"Wait." Richard shook his head. "Last time, you nearly died." He scowled at Water-Bearer.

"Last time?" The *sluagh* had taken to pacing in front of the portal, wings twitching restlessly. Richard wondered if it was mentally rehearsing whatever magics it planned, a ghoulish Broadway diva before opening night, and had to suppress another giggle.

"Weren't you there?" Aine sounded indignant. "Didn't you see? I woke the Watchers, an entire set. Don't you remember? Richard's correct, I nearly died."

"I won't let you die," Water-Bearer said, pausing in its restless oscillation to consider Aine. "If only because I'll need you on hand to close the tear once we're safely through."

William stayed the changeling's hand before she could slice an artery in temper.

"Impressive, I'm sure," the wright soothed. "And lucky we are to have you. But Watchers are hungry things and Miach won't need so much from your veins as that, especially when he's tearing such a small hole, one no larger than the four of us need to pass through."

"Can you do it like that?" Richard wondered, fascinated. "Open it just a little bit? Is that doable?"

"It's a portal," Water-Bearer snapped. "Of course it's doable. Now be quiet and let me think how. Gates are difficult things. I'd rather not emerge fifty fathoms deep in the Bitter Sea."

Aine bit her lip. William rolled her knife on his palm, studying it with undisguised interest. Richard closed his eyes and lay on his back on warm stone and listened to the Dread Host scrape and moan and whisper on the other side of the wall.

"It can't be that difficult," he mused. "Winter was only eight when he managed to punch one through."

"Aye, and your friend didn't exactly hit *Tir na Nog* first try, did he?" the *sluagh* retorted. "Lucky for you and I, apostate,

225

this portal should recall from whence it originated. Come. Stand. On your feet. I need you upright."

Richard was beyond protest. He let William help him back to standing, swaying when the chamber waltzed around his head. The wright slipped an arm around his waist. Richard leaned into the other man's embrace, grateful for the support.

He met Water-Bearer's one-eyed stare without flinching. Water-Bearer looked back, blinking once and again. Then it nodded, obviously coming to some decision.

"Stand by me," it ordered. "The *siofra* between us."

William propelled Richard forward until he stood wedged against the *sluagh*. Water-Bearer was almost as warm as the mountain, its shoulder bony against Richard's own. The *sluagh* curved one wing around Richard. He couldn't help but lean into inky feathers.

Aine squeezed against Richard's hip, bowl and buck knife in hand. She looked straight ahead into the white radiance without faltering. She'd demonstrated once she was willing to risk mortal harm on a slim chance that she'd be returned home. He wondered if it was easier the second time around. He also wondered how much of the Mending magic she had left in her small form. The Mending hadn't seemed to help much in the Metro.

I should stop this, he thought, and it wasn't imaginary Winter behind that nervous realization, or even the part of Richard that sometimes sounded like Bobby. *This is probably a very bad plan.* He knew if he wasn't so muddled by *draiochta* he'd be able to come up with a better one, one that didn't involve putting their trust in the enemy.

Because Water-Bearer *was* the enemy. Richard had spent years killing ghouls and he'd liked it, felt just fine about it, because he knew what hungry *sluagh* would do to fill their stomachs. He'd heard all of Winter's grisly stories.

This is a very bad idea. He peeked sideways at Water-Bearer.

But the Dread Host was beating at the mountain and Richard knew they wouldn't be kept back forever. The Prince would break every last bone in Richard's body when it caught them and then feast on Richard's soft organs, and that might not be so bad in the end because Richard was tired and lurking pain was as much a monster as Water-Bearer, and what use was he without two good hands, even to Winter, especially to Winter…but the Prince would also do those same awful things to Aine once it was finished with her and Richard could tell Aine wanted to live, Aine wasn't ready to give up because Aine was brave like that and Aine had a home still waiting for her.

Richard had blown his home up trying to do the right thing, and look how that had turned out.

Besides which, Richard had made a promise. Which was really the crux of the thing, because Richard never broke a promise.

"I'm ready," he said, "do what you need to do. Just…make sure Aine survives this. I'll do my part. Close your eyes, and I'll make us all into nothing worth noticing."

Water-Bearer smiled, or at least Richard thought it did.

"Go raib maith agat," it said. "Thank you. Richard, son of Adam. Then, let us begin."

18. Cèilidh

"A *cèilidh*, m'lady?" Morris looked apoplectic. He coughed and stared down at his hands, clasped at his belt, white gloves properly spotless. "Are you sure? So soon after we've lost Himself?"

Siobahn stared back across her desk and wondered how Morris had ever survived Gloriana. If she hadn't herself seen the man funnel broken bodies into the Progress' hungering gut she'd never have believed him capable.

"My husband adored a good *cèilidh*," she replied evenly. "He'd not begrudge us celebration."

On the sofa by the crackling fire Barker uncrossed his legs and set both booted feet on the carpet with a thump.

"A celebration, my lady? Are we not premature?" His thumb tapped restlessly against damask. "I left Summer in Yorktown three days ago. Your optimism is admirable, but mayhap not tempt fate's fickle favor just yet."

"Alliteration, Barker?" Siobahn mocked. "You've been visiting our poet. Time runs differently across the Way. For all we know *Samhradh* may be sitting now upon my throne."

Barker propped his elbows on his thighs and his wrists on his knees. He didn't try to hide his disgust. "If the *geis* was broken you and I wouldn't be sitting here watching the snow fall on Central Park. And while your optimism *is* admirable, it's also foolish, and you, my lady, have never been that. What are you up to?"

Siobahn stretched in her chair, lazy as a cat, even as privately she seethed. Morris shifted from toe to heel and back again. Worried, she supposed, about Barker's blood on The Plaza's antique rugs. And for good reason.

"You've grown bold of late," she said, speaking to the inlaid ceiling instead of the red-headed *sidhe* sulking on her sofa. "I've given you a long leash, I admit. And I've been gentle. You loved Malachi as I did. You failed him and that shook you." Barker made an angry noise but Siobahn ignored him, preferring instead to enjoy the black and white filigree above her head. "I should have killed you then. Flayed you myself and used your skin for my rug." Barker tensed. She could smell new fear in the room. Morris reeked of it, metallic and pungent. Barker's dread tasted on her lips and on her tongue like numb acceptance. He wouldn't fight her, she realized, and that took some of the pleasure from her threat.

"You chased after my daughter with mine own interests foremost," she continued, and now she did look at him, studied his wide green eyes and furrowed brow. He really was beautiful. In another life she might have taken for one season the form of a handsome warrior and brought him willingly to bed. "And so I forgave you. Now you're angry and think to test your tether. Don't," she warned. "I count each exile precious but I'll not ignore insolence. Malachi was merciful; I am not."

"Nay," Barker agreed as Morris wrung his gloved hands. "Merciful you are not, my lady."

She met his unblinking gaze with her own. "You wish to die? You snap at my leniency like a rabid dog at his master's feet, hoping to be put down? You've finally had enough? You've tasted freedom, seen this rotten land past the boundaries of our island, and found it untenable?"

"Nay," Barker said again. Siobahn saw how his throat worked around the word even as his expression remained placid.

"Nightingale, then," she decided. Morris went still. Siobahn almost laughed. Did they suppose she didn't remember old tragedies, old gossip? She knew as well as anyone why Barker had aligned himself with Angus against Gloriana. Angus and his wrights may have shattered Alex Pope and knit him back together into something more than human and less than desirable, but it was Gloriana who'd ordered it done.

"I'd hoped—" Barker wet his lips. "I'd assumed it was—" He finished on a breath of despair. "Not here."

"Destroyed," Siobahn said because Barker couldn't. "I understand your shock. Move past it. You mourned his loss centuries ago; I recall the tales. Do you fall into recklessness grieving him yet again, *sidhe?* Because I haven't another oubliette to drop you in until you return to your senses. Angus was kind. My father knew what it was to suffer a broken heart."

"Aye," Barker whispered.

"M'lady," Morris interrupted. Siobahn knew he was thinking of her own broken heart. For that she almost forgave him his cowardice. "Your *cèilidh*. It takes some time to plan a party, especially in this town. Why, we started three months in advance for Summer's last birthday celebration, and that was barely enough time, and at Alice's Tea Cup, which is hardly The Campbell Apartment, likely a more appropriate venue for something such as this, but the private room has a waiting list longer than—"

"Enough." Siobahn clapped her palms. Morris clicked his teeth together, every inch the high-strung attendant but not before Siobahn caught the flicker of relief in his eyes. She tilted her head slightly in his direction, awarding him the point. She'd let Morris defuse the situation as he liked, let him nudge the conversation back on track, chatter while Barker remembered to look humble and Siobahn recalled that the red-headed *sidhe* was in general more useful than provoking.

"We'll have it tonight," she told Morris. "Barker's quite right. There's no better time than now to work strong magic for my daughter's benefit. Besides," she mused, "the temperature bottomed out days ago. The ponds will be frozen near-through. I fancy good music, strong drink, and dancing. Send word at once, Morris. We'll have it below Vaux's castle, in the darkest hours. Make it clear." She locked gaze with Barker. "The queen requires full attendance."

"Yes, m'lady." Morris turned to go, shaking his head. "Summoned twice in a handful of weeks. They'll not know what to make of it."

"Let them wonder," Siobahn replied, pleased. "Let them remember pomp and circumstance. They'll be better for it, when we return to Court. " But Morris was already gone, fled on his majesty's latest whim. Barker was stretched out on her sofa again, lost in his own head or pretending to ignore her rising excitement.

"You'll dance with me," she declared because she hated being ignored and Barker was one of the few of her exiles who could make her feel less than royal. "The very first *fada*, you and I. I've seen your jig. Only Malachi had a lighter step."

"Aye, of course, my lady," Barker replied absently. "As you wish."

Siobahn chose her dress carefully, costuming herself as Fay Queen instead of in the guise of Manhattan socialite she so often preferred for simplicity's sake. She spent an hour in front of her closet in the deepest night, waffling between couture and historical office. She spelled the floor to ceiling windows in her bedroom to quicksilver with a Cant so she could catch her reflection in Gathered light. She tore through one fantastic creation after another like a callow maid before her first *cèili* and it was true she wished more than once for Summer's opinion.

In the end she tossed aside Wang and Vauthier and Valli and even Dolce & Gabbana in favor of the ancient *léine* and *crois* she'd worn the day of her exile, the garb she'd chosen for the banishing ceremony, the tunic and belt that had come with her across the Way from *Tir na Nog* to sixteenth century New Angoulême. The *léine* was linen, dyed robin's egg blue and embroidered about the sleeves and hem with fine silver thread. The dye and the thread were the privileges of royalty, as were the fine chunks of turquoise and amber adorning the *crois*. The gem-studded belt had once belonged to Siobahn's mother. If she closed her eyes and brought a handful of the leather and stone to her nose she could smell the fleeting scent of childhood and affection.

Once there had been slippers to match the belt and a cloak for warmth. The slippers hadn't lasted those first sodden winter months without shelter. The cloak had saved a life, torn into strips and used as bandages the morning Malachi had snared his first island bear. Malachi had worn bear scars on his shoulder until his dying day but Siobahn still remembered the animal with absent fondness. The bear meat, smoked to hard jerky, had fed the exiles for weeks and the skin had become a rug in their nest of leaf and log and grass.

Siobahn tugged the tunic over her head, smoothing linen over her belly and arms. It fit as it had in her youth; snug across shoulders and breasts, loose over her hips. The wide *crois* sat low on her pelvis and when she arranged it just right it pulled the fabric of her tunic into flattering folds.

"Perfect," she told her admiring reflection and wished with a pang she could see the same admiration in Malachi's eyes.

She left her hair long and loose down her back and crowned her brow with a circlet of silver and fairy amber. She chose low-heeled black boots for her feet. On a sentimental lark she picked the old bear pelt from its place of honor now on her bedroom floor and draped it across her shoulders for warmth. Her reflection pirouetted on its own, eager for the dance. Siobahn dismissed the Cant with a flick of her fingers and went to meet her escort.

Summer

They waited for her in the hotel lobby: Barker and Morris and Nightingale and young Carran. Barker was Barker, all black leather and white silk and heavy boots. Nightingale, standing quietly to the side and watching late night arrivals flutter in and out through the lobby doors, had sculpted black miasma into a semblance of hood and gown. None of the busy mortals paid it any attention for the simple reason that human minds tended to ignore what they didn't want to see.

Morris and Carran had chosen disparate *céilidh* attire. Siobahn couldn't help but be amused by the younger *sidhe's* skin-tight denim and paisley button down. He'd ringed his neck and wrists with the glow-in-the-dark loops so popular in Manhattan clubs and pinned his dun locks up into odd little tufts and tails. He'd also painted the nails of his dirt-encrusted toes with starlight.

Carran bowed extravagantly and without a hint of mockery, welcoming his queen. Siobahn smiled her approval.

"Morris," she said gently, eyeing her man up and down. "How do you plan to dance a proper jig in that monkey suit?"

Morris' jaw twitched but he didn't quite return her smile. "I'm afraid I shan't be dancing, m'lady. Someone needs to see to it that security holds."

Siobahn, who knew as well as Morris that her exiles were the wolves out amongst the sheep of Manhattan, didn't bother to reply. Carran, thumbs busy on his mobile, jerked his chin toward the doors.

"Car's waiting outside," he said. "Plenty of room for us all. Good thing, too, because I didn't expect *it* along." The boy carefully didn't look at Nightingale.

Nightingale turned from its contemplation of the blissfully ignorant human behind the front desk and regarded Carran instead.

"Oh," it said, all baffled innocence even as its skeletal fingers flexed on black mist, gears and wires shifting. "Are there others still about who know how to sing the *rinnce fada?* As you'll not have a proper dance without the proper calling."

Carran blushed to his ears. "Not yet discovered the iPod, has it?" He shrugged. "No skin off my arse if you want it along. Might put a bit of a damper on the party. Literally." He shrugged again and strode toward the hotel exit. Nightingale watched Carran go, head tilted slightly to one side, blunt human tongue wetting pink lips.

"Have you changed so much?" it asked. Siobahn didn't think it expected an answer. She also thought the creature saw too much. Even Winter with his callous mistakes and stubborn pride would never, even as a child, have chosen the lure of mortal technology over the traditions of his people.

"As rain falls over stone," Barker agreed. And then, with dark amusement. "I'll drive, shall I, my lady? Morris seems distracted."

Belvedere Castle was beautiful in the hush before dawn and Siobahn, walking the path between bare trees, Barker's hand on her elbow, knew that she had chosen well. The wide pond at the castle's base was shelled in ice so thick it was more white than blue. Several *sidhe* were already making use of the slick surface, sliding about this way and that, arms linked in graceful chains or waltzing along in the light of long-stemmed torches burning on the shore and on Belvedere's ramparts.

Some enterprising exile had coaxed the army of lilacs at the base of the castle into early blooming. Pink and white and purple clusters wept nectar from skeletal branches, perfuming the night. The trees would suffer for the forced eruption, perhaps wither and die before spring, but Siobahn couldn't fault the beauty of the display.

"M'lady," Morris said into her ear. "The Glamour's set and anchored. No mortal will venture near this place till well after dawn. Even the birds and beasts are like to stay away."

Siobahn thought the last was excessive but didn't say so. Instead she stepped forward and hopped atop a bench on the edge of the frozen pond. She lifted a hand for silence and at once all sound of merriment ceased. As one the exiles bent knee and the response was so much better than the lackluster display in Malachi's Gold Street office that Siobahn laughed aloud in delight.

"Better," she said. Her merriment echoed off the castle ramparts. "So much better. At last we begin to wake from self-induced stupor. Exactly as we should. Wake, and dance, and taste anticipation. For soon enough the Way will be open and we'll be riding to war."

The handful of *sidhe* on the ice and the gathering group on the hill near the castle let out a ragged cheer. Someone, and Siobahn thought maybe it was Alice in her fishnet stockings, loosed a piercing whistle.

"Less than thirty." Nightingale climbed nimbly onto the bench at Siobahn's side. It was careful to keep its poisonous cloak from her flesh but small puffs of black fog fell from the ragged hem and spread like ink droplets on the concrete below. "You expect to take back the throne with this motley lot? Why, half of them are mad as Finvarra and the other slice undernourished."

"You will win back my throne," Siobahn said for Nightingale's ears alone. "The rest is but window dressing, easily swapped out."

Nightingale stared up and across at the *sidhe* cavorting again on the ice and undulating on the castle walls, made fantastic and unearthly by the light of the torches and the cloying scent of weeping lilacs. His face, human and wary and youthful, was as easy to read as a volume of his own poetry. Siobahn saw at once that he grieved her exiles even as they danced.

"You care so little for them," it wondered. "Even as they love you still."

"Those I loved are dead or gone," Siobahn retorted. She wrapped the bear pelt more tightly about her body. "All that matters now is my throne and *Tir na Nog*. In that, nothing has changed at all."

"You and the false queen," it mused, watching Barker as the red-headed *sidhe* scuffed across the ice on thick-soled boots and was immediately caught up in embrace after embrace, "bad as two wolf-bitches over the same fossilized bone."

"Aye," Siobahn agreed without rancor. "But 'twas Gloriana who ordered the Progress fed with the meat of her own people. Gloriana who used the syphoned blood of her subjects to magic up unnatural creations, Gloriana who stole away a passel of mortal wrights trained in human technologies." She gifted it her sweetest smile. "If not for Gloriana, Nightingale, you might be residing still as Court musician, unchanged and sweet and doted upon. If not for Gloriana, wordsmith, you might still be loved, and you might be able to touch him freely without fear of watching him fail to naught but ash and memory."

It stiffened and turned at last to look at her, obviously furious. She lifted a long finger to stall its vitriol.

"You're bound to me, by that same blood magic that made you loathsome," she said. "I'd hate to have you punished on a night such as this. Dawn's still hours away and the lilacs are blooming mid-winter. I wish to dance in celebration until my feet ache. Now: sing, sing us a dance. Call my *fada*."

Nightingale lowered its head in exaggerated obedience. It opened its mouth and sang.

"A thing of beauty is a joy for ever:

Summer

Its loveliness increases; it will never
Pass into nothingness; but still will keep
A bower quiet for us, and a sleep
Full of sweet dreams, and health, and quiet breathing.
Therefore, on every morrow, are we wreathing
A flowery band to bind us to the earth,
Spite of despondence, of the inhuman dearth
Of noble natures, of the gloomy days,
Of all the unhealthy and o'er-darkn'd ways
Made for our searching: yes, in spite of all,
Some shape of beauty moves away the pall
From our dark spirits. Such the sun, the moon,
Trees old and young, sprouting a shady boon
For simple sheep; and such are daffodils
With the green world they live in; and clear rills
That for themselves a cooling covert make
'Gainst the hot season; the mid-forest brake,
Rich with a sprinkling of fair musk-rose blooms:
And such too is the grandeur of the dooms
We have imagined for the mighty dead;
An endless fountain of immortal drink,
Pouring unto us from the heaven's brink."

Sunrise was but heartbeats away and Nightingale had lapsed into low verse, calling just above a whisper, its voice as beautiful an instrument as it was deadly. A few *sidhe* still danced but most had collapsed on the frozen lawn or lay sprawled on the ice. Several sat upon Belvedere's turrets, waiting for the pink sign of dawn. Siobahn's feet did indeed throb and her blood yet raced and she felt more alive than she had since Malachi had fallen beneath *Buairt's* poisonous tooth.

237

The heels of her boots were cracked from dancing. She'd lost the bear pelt somewhere in the night but she knew Morris would retrieve it for her and wasn't worried. Katherine Grey and her human lover were sitting together beneath a spitting torch, lost in quiet talk. Siobahn did not think they were speaking of treason, not from the way their fingers clasped and unclasped. She could so easily be jealous of those small, casual touches and of the frantic couplings she knew were occurring deeper in the park. *Sidhe* passions were rising to the spell of Nightingale's tongue and that was all the better for Siobahn.

She followed the sound of its voice across the flat ice and found Carran still dancing on the edge between pond and concrete path. He grinned at her, impudent in his youth. Suddenly she missed Winter so painfully she bent in two with the shock of it.

"Majesty!" Carran gripped her shoulders and kept her upright. "Majesty, are you ill?"

"Nay." She managed a grimace and forced herself upright. It wouldn't do to dwell on regret, especially where her son was concerned. "Nay, only tired. Here, boy, help me to the bench and I'll sit a while."

Carran did as she asked, all the while looking about for Morris. Morris, who was probably seeing to the breaking of the Glamour, because Siobahn recognized the trace of orange overhead. She sat heavily on the bench near Nightingale's left foot, careful as always not to brush the monster's miasma.

Nightingale didn't falter in calling, but it did glance down in acknowledgement.

"The queen is weary," Carran said. "She'll sit here while I find her man." The young *sidhe* wheeled and darted away into the new morning.

Siobahn folded her hands in her lap and wished she hadn't dropped her pelt. It was very cold now, so close to the frozen pond and with the sun not yet in the sky. Across the pond the lilac blossoms had stopped dripping sap and were laced with frost.

Nightingale stopped singing.

"You're weeping, Majesty," it said in a voice like silver bells, beautiful and terrible at the same time. "What sorrow takes you?"

"No sorrow," Siobahn retorted. She brushed at her cheeks in disbelief and found that they were indeed wet. "It's only reaction to the dance, Nightingale. Joy. Aye, certainly, joy."

Nightingale crouched, bending its bony knees until they were face to face.

"Joy is warm," it mused. "You're shivering."

It spoke true. Siobahn's flesh rose in goose pimples and her thighs and forearms quivered. She mentally cursed Morris for a laggard and wondered if she dared conjure warmth in front of her exiles. Would they see it for weakness, that she shook while they basked in the warmth of their own exertion?

To her horror more tears welled and ran over her lashes and down her cheeks, into her mouth, salty and chill.

"Majesty," Nightingale said sadly, even as its mouth curled into a faint smile. "Let me help."

Siobahn looked up in surprise, but not in time.

Nightingale reached out, flesh and black wire glistening, and brushed a single knuckle across her cheek. It soothed her tears with a gentle touch.

The Fay Queen suffered a burst of painful surprise and then there was nothing at all.

Summer

Winter

The *sluagh* were living in a mountain. I'm not sure why I was surprised; even away from the lake they wouldn't survive long out in the poisonous atmosphere. I think maybe I expected burrows in the ground or some sort of camp with sheltering walls built up of black stone. But, no, the Prince had commandeered a mountain the size of the Matterhorn and somehow made it its castle.

"Grown out of the ground," Gabby said. We stood smack dab center of a narrow suspension bridge, cataracts of clean smelling water roaring beneath us. The moon was far enough in the sky we had light again. As the horizon brightened so had the mountain appeared, a cracked tooth in the gray sky. "Very old *sidhe* magic, and powerful." She rolled her shoulders under her robes. In the new twilight I could see streaks of dirt on her hem and up her skirts from when she'd stumbled or fallen on our journey up the foothills.

I'd been led to believe conjuring a Gate was extraordinary. But the Dread Host had managed to conjure an entire mountain.

"They were very powerful once, the Royal Hunt," Gabby agreed. She looked away from the mountain, leaning over the side of the bridge instead. I followed her lead, breathing deeply. The spray from the river rose in great clouds, droplets beading on our faces and soothing our parched lips. I stuck out my tongue, tasting greedily.

"Looks like something off the Potomac," I said after a moment, meaning the bridge. "How's that even possible?"

"Wright-work," Gabby replied. I had no idea what she was talking about but she didn't seem inclined to explain so I let it be.

"If they've taken Richard and Aine into that," I said, frowning back up at the angry precipice, "we're going after. Look, see how the road widens? And that's the front door to Moria if I've ever seen one." Even from down below I could tell the dark gape in the mountain's face was big enough to spit out several *sluagh* at once.

"Best not enter by the front door, I think." Gabby leaned against thick bronze chains, turning her head, seeking this way and that. I couldn't guess what she was looking for. It made sense that there was more than one way in. Every good fortress has an emergency exit. I just wasn't sure how she planned to find it.

"It'll be the water," my mentor said. "Refuse flows downhill."

I licked sweet spray from my lips and let her see my doubt. She shook her head. Our hike and the wind off the river had pulled strands of white hair from her braids, turning the crown of her head into a puff. I thought she looked just a bit like a dandelion gone to seed.

She snuffed her starlight and pointed below, past the bridge and ahead to where the river bounced along the foot of the mountain.

"Follow the water backwards," she explained, "until we find the sewer tribute. Then trace that in, I think."

I thought she'd spent too much time as a mouse running in the Metro tunnels but I didn't dare say so out loud. She wagged a finger at me.

"Foolish child. This is the *óstach fiáin*, the host of hosts, born of the fay Court. They may be monsters, but they weren't always, and they'd never fain live in the filth. They raised a mountain. Certainly they also managed baths and latrines and the like?"

I laughed because Gabby sounded so certain. The situation was absurd. Cliché, the oldest trick in the book. Who needed a back door when you could sneak in through the sewers?

Then I tried to imagine the malformed, wretched *sluagh* Prince ordering up a stone urinal or soaking tub and laughed harder.

Gabby's cheeks crinkled in quiet amusement. "Come," she ordered. "You've young, sharp eyes. Help me find the way down."

It took some work and a lot of courage and even more precious time, but eventually we discovered a bit of cliff beneath the bridge where the stone was less a sheer drop and more an abrupt descent. I took off my Doc Martens, hung them around my neck, and we picked our way slowly down the rock face. Not for the first time I was glad of my *sidhe* heritage. Finger holds that would have baffled the human eye were clear to mine. My bare toes easily found crevices that would have made a monkey stretch. Lizard-like we scaled a good fifty-foot drop with ease.

I couldn't help thinking of that old movie, *Nosferatu*, one of Lolo's Halloween favorites, and then I remembered Brother Dan's thinly veiled references to demons. I thought about the church consecrated sword, *Buairt*, and how it turned *sidhe* to helpless lumps and then to corpses all because it had once been blessed by some guy in a miter who believed in good and evil, black and white.

Belief is a really powerful thing.

We reached the bottom of the cliff without falling to our deaths, which was no mean accomplishment, even for two fay. By the time we touched ground my fingers and toes were cramped. I was light-headed from forgetting to breathe. A narrow shore of black sand ran on either side of the busy river. The grit was cold and wet and my feet sank into the ground, but the water was clean and nothing burned.

There were plants growing in the shallows beneath the bridge, green mossy things with short, thin roots. Gabby pulled a handful from the water. Her mouth moved but I couldn't hear what she said. I put my hands to my ears, thinking maybe Siobahn's gems were reasserting themselves, but then I realized I couldn't hear her in my skull, either.

It was the roar of the river, of course, but it had been so long I didn't recognize white noise when it blew every other sound to nothing. Like the plume of spray, the barrage of water over rock brought a measure of odd peace, a surcease of sensation when I'd been so long with nothing but painful input.

Reluctantly, I tapped my ears again, this time making a point of catching Gabby's attention.

"Can't hear you!" I shouted. I felt the press of air in my lungs and the exhale of sound through my throat and the vibration of words in the bone bridge of my nose, but the river washed away the noise. It was lovely. I hated to have it spoiled.

"Oh, aye," Gabby said in my head, spoiling it. *"I keep forgetting—Never mind. It's threadwort, you see? Very valuable, even across the Way. Strange that it's taken root here."*

I shrugged my shoulders, making the boots around my neck bang against my chest. I opened my mouth on a question, then clicked it shut again. She wouldn't hear me, either, obviously. Not the natural way.

Pushing an internal dialogue into another person's head is like threading a needle while wearing dark glasses. It isn't impossible, but it also isn't easy. At least for me. I'd managed before once or twice, with Richard, who'd hated it, and Bran, who'd claimed a headache after, and once with Aine. But it isn't my particular strength. I just don't have that sort of finesse.

"Maybe the ghouls are gardeners as well as architects," I tried to infuse the thought with as much sarcasm as possible. By the twist of her mouth, I could see it worked. *"Down river?"* Past the bridge the river roared over a gentle incline then crooked sharply west to curve around the Matterhorn.

She nodded. We slipped under the darker shadow of the bridge and then back again beneath the white moon. Black sand squished pleasantly between my toes as we navigated the edge of the riverbed. I was glad we'd left pebbles and scree behind. The damp off the river seemed to ease those blisters on my hands and face that weren't already soothed by Gabby's blood salve. I knew it was probably my imagination. As far as I could tell the river water wasn't anything special. It was just clean.

Gabby gathered more threadwort as we walked. I wondered if she planned to carry a bouquet of the things through the mountain. Assuming we ever found our way inside. Secretly I thought we'd end up using the front door and hoping for the best.

I was wrong. The river grew deeper, quieter and slower as it hit the edge of the mountain, becoming a pale, peaceful watercourse beneath the white moon. Thin fingerlings ran off the foothills, trickling over rock and slope and into the greater torrent. Most of the feeder streams were hardly more than rivulets and not what Gabby was searching for.

When we stumbled across the *sluagh* sewer we almost didn't recognize it. I would have walked right past it if not for the sudden burst of stink. It wasn't so much run-off as a slick of mud and things much worse, painting the rock in a sluggish gray trickle.

"Oh, fuck me," I sighed, rolling an eye at Gabby. "Really?"

The river was slow enough now that she might have heard me, but if she did, she pretended ignorance. She only paused to tie her gown up around her legs and waist, baring long pale legs. She bundled gathered threadwort safely in the hem, then scrambled off the riverbed and onto the mountain, tracking up and along the slick of sewer.

I put on my boots and followed. The foothills were much less sheer at this level, and we were able to shuffle up and along without too much difficulty. In fact, I quickly realized that my mentor was, as usual, quite correct. The disgusting run-off wasn't naturally occurring. Some worker of miracles had managed to cut a shallow trough up and along the spine of the mountain. The trough was smooth as well-laid concrete, and if not for the stink and shock of *sluagh* garbage and shit, it might have been a pleasant climb.

"I hate this," I said when we were far enough above and away from the river. "Air's getting bad again, and I don't mean crap stink." My eyes were smarting with more than sewer fumes and I could feel the burn of bad air against my already damaged face. I'd barely had time to heal from the Cold Fire burns I'd earned in the pit beneath the Metro, and the new skin on my ear and eyebrows was sensitive.

"There," Gabby said calmly. She didn't so much point as incline her body. "Do you see? Just up ahead. There's the mouth of it."

I wiped my face with my wrist, blinked a few times, and finally picked out a darker shadow against black rock. The mouth of a small cave, not much wider than my shoulders, set into the side of the mountain just above our trough.

I paused. Craning my neck, I looked up. The mountain rose sharp and straight over our heads. If I leaned back and squinted I thought I could see the blot of the 'front door' a skyscraper's length still above us. I looked back down at the river. Even as we'd scaled the slope we were still not yet even with the bridge. We'd only lost elevation and the mountain looked very, very tall indeed.

When I squinted back up at the peak I thought I could see something pass between the white moon and the sheer summit. Then again, and again, until the garish orb was nearly blotted out by the clot of distant wings.

"*Sluagh*," I realized. From this distance they looked small and insubstantial as sparrows, but I knew better. I've spent half my life chasing the monsters; I'd recognize them from three worlds away. "They're outside the mountain."

And pissed off, I thought, but didn't bother saying out loud. It was obvious from the agitated swoop and roil of the distant ghouls that something was up.

"Now what?" I wondered. Whatever was going on up there, it had to do with Richard and Aine, I just knew it. A good part of me wanted to kick up a fuss and diversion, catch their attention, draw them away from the peak.

"And then?" Gabby demanded. "Throw stones whilst they smash us against the river bed? Use your head, child. We're no good to anyone as we are, clinging to the side of a mountain." She stood on her toes and peered into the mouth of the sewer. "It's not so bad," she said. "Drier in than out. Boost me up, please."

She sounded suspiciously eager. Too much time as a mouse, I figured. Preferring tight spaces to open air. Exposed on the side of a mountain, the *sluagh* army flocking overhead, I realized I couldn't blame her. She was right. We'd do no one any good perched as we were without weapon or defense.

I tried not to think of Richard and Aine as I turned away from the blotted sun and grasped Gabby with both hands around her waist.

"On three," I warned. "One. Two. Three." *Sidhe* are bird-bone light. A little heave and then she was in, reaching down to pull me after.

It was a simple tunnel, remarkable only for the smooth, curved walls and ceiling, a perfectly proportioned half pipe. The bottom was trenched but mostly dry. It made me wonder if maybe there were a lot fewer ghouls using the system than when the mountain was first raised.

The ceiling brushed the top of my head, which made it low. Gabby had to bend her knees. We shuffled forward maybe twenty feet before the roof and walls opened up. We stumbled out of the tunnel and stopped.

The space around us felt cavernous but it was difficult to tell because the only light came from a handful of sickly blue orbs struggling to chase away darkness. I stood very still, straining past the pounding of my heart in my ears. I could hear the drip of sewer behind us, and Gabby's nervous panting, and a faint humming that reminded me of the vibrations I picked up along the Metro line.

"No Wards," Gabby said after a moment. "What have they to guard against but themselves?"

"Oh, I don't know." I wanted to ask her for a light, but felt stupid, a little kid afraid of the dark. "Nasty place like this, they're probably rats the size of elephants. No offense. What's that new smell, anyway?"

I couldn't place it at first because I'd been expecting more shit stink and damp. But the space around us was ripe with garden scents, leaves and roots and something spicy like Indian takeout gone old.

"Kitchen." Gabby said. "Kitchen midden?"

"Ugh," I said, thinking again of mutant rats. I relented. "Light?"

It might have been my imagination but Gabby's starlight seemed less bright than usual even as she sent it circling overhead and back and forth. I looked quickly at her face before I took in our surroundings. The corners of her mouth were pulling in a worried frown and she'd wrinkled up her nose again.

"No more blood," I warned, knowing she was thinking of it. "I don't care if this place is doing a number on us. You may be *aes si* but you're no Mender. I'll not lose you too."

She stared at me without speaking. I thought maybe she was tallying up all the people I had recently lost against the risk in opening her veins again. I tried my best to look firm, glaring until she nodded.

"Aye, as you wish."

I missed being able to read her mind. It made me feel off balance, not knowing what she was feeling. I'd hated it for so long, the barrage of multitudes against my brain, but now that I was the only one in my head I...didn't miss it, not that, but I recognized the advantages.

"Ah, I was correct," she continued, distracting me. "Kitchen heap. That would explain the threadwort in the river, wouldn't it? Discarded leaf and seed washed out of the mountain and transplanted below. Oh, and see. Journey-root. That tuber grows only in the *Gairdin Mhuire*. They came prepared, then. They must have had some warning, as we did." Her frown grew deeper.

I'd been right about the feel of the space. We stood alone in a large chamber, a large square chamber, less perfectly formed than the sewer tunnel but the right angles were pretty impressive. Shallow trenches ran perpendicular and parallel to the walls, entering the room through multiple basketball-sized holes spaced throughout. Each smaller trench joined a larger trough that ran straight center through the floor, gently downhill, and out the tunnel we'd used to breach the mountain.

"Well done," I said. "If you like fourth century Roman engineering."

Summer

Most of the aqueduct was long dry. A shallow stream ran through the main trench, dammed in places with fallen rock and rotting vegetation and bits of what I thought was bone. The kitchen midden was mostly mold. I had no idea how Gabby recognized any sort of actual plant matter in the small gray pile.

I walked forward, side-stepping trenches, turning this way and that, trying to keep under the glow of Gabby's starlight so I didn't trip and fall onto something disgusting. The pockets of sickly light in the ceiling interested me; some sort of Cant, I thought, but grown stale and old. There were many more dead black patches where the magic had gone out than there were remaining blue lamps.

Gabby's drifting globe found the way out before I did: a narrow stone stair, five steps up along the side of the west wall to a door. I leaped up the stairs, one hand on the wall for balance. The wall was unusually tepid against my palm, the door made of tarnished bronze. There was no obvious latch but it swung open easily enough when I kicked it, outwards and away. A swirl of warmer air washed past my cheeks, making me shudder in surprise.

I stuck my head cautiously through the opening and glimpsed more thin blue light.

"Right," I said. Gabby had climbed the steps behind me and was trying to get a look past my arm. "Shall we?"

There were *sluagh* skeletons in the walls. I didn't notice them at first, because as we walked farther into the mountain the old lighting spells died completely. Gabby's Gathered starlight kept us from stumbling into walls or turning in circles in our haste, but I did almost as well with my eyes closed and my hand on the wall. The *sluagh* had gone very zen with their mountain. It wasn't at all what I expected. I knew from my father's stories that the original fay tended toward excess and dramatics in everything they did; even after centuries living among mortals the exiles were still more burlesque than Buddha. Summer has a bit of that in her. I like to think I've bypassed the gene, myself.

It appeared the Wild Host had a different set of aesthetics, at least when it came to mountain raising. As far as I could tell they'd just cut a wide curving path from bottom to upper levels, the opened rooms in regimented rows on either side. The room thing was a guess, because we didn't bother opening any of the bronze doors off our path, but I can tell you the doors, at least, were laid out in impressive mathematical precision, marching mirror images of each other all along the incline.

"Do you suppose it's like this the entire way up?" I whispered. It was deadly quiet all around, and the scuff of my feet and the hiss of Gabby's breathing seemed very loud. I was pretty sure we were the only ones for at least a mile in any direction, and that was really creepy. I'm a city kid. I like bustle.

Gabby didn't answer. She was busy working her starlight back and forth along the path. I let my fingers trail along the wall, thinking that once these halls must have been full of feathers and ichor and tentacles. The realization made me shiver, and that's when my hand brushed the skeleton in the dirt. At first the texture of bone in the wall didn't compute, so I stopped and looked. In the flicker of Gabby's light I got the impression of a bone, pinions and a yellowing clavicle, and, just a little above, a grinning, sharp-toothed skull.

I'll admit I jumped and cursed. Gabby whirled, took a closer look, and then sent starlight up and down the wall.

It was a graveyard. There were skeletons everywhere. Many were fully formed, as if they'd been laid to rest vertically in the stone, while many more appeared to be bits and extra pieces, lonely segments sealed away. At first I tried counting skulls but once I hit fifty-seven I decided I just didn't want to know.

I couldn't help it; the bones in the wall made me think of Aine that first morning, literally trapped in the Metro tunnel. Surely it couldn't be a coincidence.

"What happened to them?"

"Sacrifice," Gabby replied. She'd wrapped her arms about herself in a tight embrace. "Or accident. I'm not certain. Mayhap it's a tomb of some sort."

"They're *everywhere.*"

"Aye," said Gabby sadly. "They are."

After that we walked quickly and quietly, our eyes on the ground. I think neither of us knew what to do with the horror of the bone *sluagh*. In my experience the creatures always went up in flame and ash and goo when they died. I'd assumed they were just ichor and hatred packaged in tooth and claw. The skeletons in the wall made me revise everything I thought I knew. I don't like being wrong.

The air grew warmer. We were moving at a good clip. We didn't say it out loud but we were both afraid of what we might find at the top of the mountain. And neither of us were going to be able to jog uphill in the dark indefinitely.

The same guys who sang about prophets and subway walls also wrote a ditty about God's sense of humor. It goes: blessed are the sat upon, spat upon, ratted upon. I used to wish I could listen to it again, after Siobahn took my ears. Most of the time I don't believe in God, but if I did I think He'd have a wicked sense of mischief.

Because just as Gabby and I were running on our last reserves, and pretty much ready to fall on the floor and weep in frustration, we heard voices. Angry voices, shouts and growls. *Sluagh* voices, raised in disagreement, up ahead and not far off from the sound of the echoes.

Gabby snuffed out her small light and we froze, barely daring to breathe, thinking we were done for. But the shouting only grew more heated and it occurred to me slowly that maybe we'd somehow snuck under the radar. Whatever was going on up the corridor it was enough of a distraction that our muffled tread and our patch of Gathered starlight had gone unnoticed.

"Now what?" I pushed the thought into Gabby's head. And then, *"I'm not turning around."*

"Nay," she agreed. *"Walk on. Carefully. I hear two, I think. I smell three. Come, child. Quietly."*

I don't know how she could pick out three separate bodies from a cloud of *sluagh* stink, but she was *aes si* so I didn't argue. We snuck forward, pressed hard against one wall, eyes wide to catch any light or movement. I'll admit I might have said a prayer or six to the God I don't believe in.

As my eyes adjusted I realized it wasn't quite as pitch black ahead as I'd assumed. Blue light flickered sadly, just enough to make out a blockage in the path. The *sluagh* were howling now, shouting in the Gaelic, and mostly I picked out filthy curse words and imprecations. Also, the thump of flesh upon flesh and then screams of pain.

"They're fighting," I told Gabby, fascinated. *"I think they're fighting."* We crept close, quiet as two mice, and I saw that I was right. They were battling; great hulking *sluagh* princes, the third already dead on the path, throat torn open, wings spread, a distorted fallen angel.

The two still standing were at it tooth and claw, tangled in each other's limbs and wings, struggling over a single gleaming prize pressed between them. Their eyes were wild, their breath coming in great, furious gasps, and already both were bleeding ichor and missing chunks of flesh.

"Póg mo thóin," I said, and I said it out loud, not quietly. "Is that the Horn?"

"Aye," my mentor replied, rapt. She didn't bother with silence, either. The *sluagh* were too wrapped up in their contest to pay us the slightest attention.

"Danu take us and shake us, you're right, they've got Finvarra's Horn."

Gabby widened her eyes at me and tugged on my sleeve, encouraging me to step back away along the wall, out of sight. I shook her gently off. The *sluagh* were snapping and snarling, completely oblivious. For the moment we were safe. And besides, I wanted a better look at the legendary Horn.

I don't know what I'd imagined. Maybe something like a silver trumpet or a small French horn. I expected it to look as beautiful as it sounded, bright and shining, something worth coveting.

The Horn wasn't that at all. It hung between the two remaining *sluagh* on a leather cord, caught in the middle of a vicious tug-of-war. It was narrow tube, like a flute, but long as my arm and curved just south of a U-shape. And Finvarra's Horn certainly wasn't shining silver; it was badly tarnished, blackened by time or use.

It looked innocuous but I remembered its clarion call in my skull, a Summoning I couldn't have ignored to save my life. I knew all the stories by heart. Finvarra's Horn was meant to lead armies.

That the *sluagh* had the Horn here in their prison was impossible. But there it was. And, really, it was too powerful a prize to pass up. With Finvarra's Horn in my hand I'd have a fantastic advantage over the *sluagh* and even Gloriana, if we ever managed find our way to *Tir na Nog*. Two birds with one stone. Siobahn would have to sing my praises.

"Nay, Winter," Gabby hissed. I'd been edging forward without realizing it. She grabbed at my sleeve again. "Foolish idea. We haven't got a weapon between us."

"Screw that," I hissed back. "There's no way I'm letting Finvarra's *fucking* Horn slip through our fingers."

Gabby winced. The *sluagh* paused mid-snarl and swiveled as one in our direction. The hair on the back of my neck immediately stood at horrified attention.

Up until we crossed through my Gate into *sluagh*-world I'd lived my life as hearing impaired. Diction, tone, and volume were as much a mystery to me as blood magic is to your average mortal. Gabby and I had been walking beneath the white moon for a relatively short period of time, certainly not enough time for me to relearn sound. The small scratch of gravel beneath my boots had jangled my nerves while the roar of the river had been the equivalent of an auditory valium.

My head and my ears were all mixed up, my wires crossed. It was an honest mistake and hardly my fault that the words I'd meant to whisper bounced down the passage as an ill-timed and overly enthusiastic shout.

The two *sluagh* stared, the Horn spread on its taut leather cord between them. Gabby made a sound like a squeak. I held my breath, hands curling defensively at my side. We'd never escape at a run. *Sluagh* are deadly fast and anyway all one of them had to do was blow a little melody on that tarnished Horn and I'd be a willing slave. Gabby probably wouldn't resist its call much longer than I, not with her magics fading.

We were doomed. We were going to die and the bastards would probably make us dance like puppets on a string before they grew bored and snacked on our bones.

And that's exactly what would have happened if the *sluagh* Prince hadn't chosen that moment to rear out of the darkness in a flutter of feathers and fury. The Prince was screaming in incomprehensible, mangled Gaelic when it fell upon the first of the Horn-wielding *sluagh* and tore the poor monster limb from limb. Ichor fountained when the murdered *sluagh* fell.

The Prince roared again. It wheeled on the remaining ghoul and that *sluagh* dropped Finvarra's Horn as it scuttled sideways down the tunnel.

The *sluagh* Prince paused. It was obviously caught between the pull of the Horn and a desire to finish the mayhem it had started.

I'm small and I'm quick. Quick-witted with quick reflexes and an extraordinarily quick grasp of any situation. I lunged, and ducked, and rolled, and sprang up with the coveted Horn in both hands. As easy at that, the prize was mine.

Needless to say, that's when all hell broke loose.

Summer

The Manhattan Exiles

- Volume Three -

Fall

March, 2016

www.sarahremy.com

www.ingramcontent.com/pod-product-compliance
Lightning Source LLC
Chambersburg PA
CBHW071135170626
46809CB00002B/623